# SEVEN TO ONE . . .
# WITH A TORPEDO RUNNING!

He could see the enemy torpedo, racing toward *Truculent* at a speed that would intercept the British sub in another four minutes.

"White Star, White Star, this is White Star Three!" Wilder called. "*Truculent* is under attack!" He keyed in the computer command that would transmit the tactical data he was receiving now to the other fighter subs, now some four miles astern.

Without waiting for orders, Wilder goosed the Barracuda's engine, hurtling past *Truculent* a few meters off her starboard side. Her massive hull and his ULTRA-C lasers painted the oncoming Japanese submarines until they shone like fluorescent beacons.

With odds of seven fighter subs to one and a torpedo already running, Wilder hesitated, wondering what to do next.

By the same author

*Sharuq*

# STINGRAY

## *Bill Keith*

**HarperPaperbacks**
*A Division of HarperCollinsPublishers*

This is a work of fiction. The characters, incidents, and
dialogues are products of the author's imagination and are
not to be construed as real. Any resemblance to actual events
or persons, living or dead, is entirely coincidental.

HarperPaperbacks   *A Division of* HarperCollins*Publishers*
195 Broadway, New York, NY, 10007

Cover illustration by John Berkey

First printing: January 1994

Printed in the United States of America

HarperPaperbacks and colophon are trademarks of
HarperCollins*Publishers*

❖ 10 9 8 7 6 5 4 3 2

# CHAPTER
# 1

Officers' Housing
Kings Bay, Georgia
April 16, 2120 hours

"**S**o what do you think it's going to be, Bill?" Commander Thomas Morgan Gray asked, setting his mug on the coffee table before him. "War?"

On the sofa opposite, Commander William Parker, thin and balding, reached thumb and forefinger up beneath his glasses and pinched the bridge of his nose. He'd been putting in long hours on the repair of *Leviathan*, and he looked tired.

"God knows, Morgan," Parker said. "From the sound of things, the UIR's spoiling for a fight. I guess the real question is whether or not the pols in Washington are going to let themselves get backed into a corner."

"Hell, they already have," Gray said. Leaning back in his chair, he ran his fingers across his scalp, an unconscious gesture. His hair, shaved to bare skin a few weeks before, was still brushcut short. Across the room, the television was tuned to CNN. On the screen, an earnest-looking anchor in Atlanta was

1

describing the latest wave of anti-American rioting in the United Islamic Republic.

"Okay. The question is how far the REMFs get backed into that corner then, and how long it is before they decide to do something about it." The TV's image had changed, showing now a sea of dark, angry faces in a plaza in Cairo. Signs and banners in crudely lettered English proclaimed DEATH TO AMERIKA and DOWN WITH USA. Parker shook his head. "Damfino, Morgan. My crystal ball's gunked up worse than *Leviathan*'s portside strainers. I'd've thought Cairo would've backed off after Cienfuegos. They were testing us, after all, seeing how far they could push us. And we showed 'em we wouldn't stand for piracy in our own waters."

Morgan Gray sighed and looked away. It was mildly unsettling to be sitting here in such *normal* surroundings, talking about the inevitability of war. An hour ago, Heather and John had hugged him good night, and now they were asleep in the next room. From the kitchen behind him came the clatter of pots and pans, sharp above the sounds of the TV and the voices of Cecily Parker and Gray's wife, Wendy, as they prepared dessert. A tableau of perfect, peaceful domesticity.

The Grays' house still had the bare, painted-concrete walls and unfinished look of most Navy tract housing. Wendy and the kids had been here less than a month, and there were still cardboard boxes in the corners, waiting to be unpacked after their move from Connecticut. The Parkers had become their best friends here at their new duty station, but this was the first time they'd been able to invite them over for an evening of dinner, conversation, and a round of Trivial Pursuit.

But then he'd been dumb enough to turn on the news, and the conversation had swiftly centered on politics and the war scare, not exactly ideal topics for a relaxed evening with friends. Every day since the submarine battle that the press had begun calling the *Sharuq* Incident, the calls for holy war in the Islamic Republic had grown louder, more insistent, more strident. Bill Parker was right. The Islamics did want war, and it did not look like a war that the United States would be capable of winning.

Not when the Japanese were all but openly siding with the UIR.

In the opening years of the twenty-first century, the United States stood almost isolated in a world fast growing hungrier, more crowded, and more hostile. Across Eastern Europe, the flames of war and revolution continued to gutter and snap among the fragmented patchwork of republics stretching from the Adriatic to the Kara Sea, while the ragtag remnants of the Commonwealth of Independent States squabbled amid the bones of the old Soviet empire. South, a new world power stretched from Morocco to the Horn of Africa, from the Nile to Kazakhstan. Founded in the blood and fury of the *Qaumat*, the pan-Arabic fundamentalist uprising of the late 1990s, the United Islamic Republic ruled an estimated one billion Muslims and claimed to speak for the hungry, the dispossessed, and the poor worldwide. Most of Europe, still dependent on Mideast oil, stayed neutral or actively supported UIR policy.

In the Far East, Japan had emerged as the technological giant of the new millennium; Tokyo's spy satellites and orbital railguns, dubbed "Starwarsaki" by the Western press but capable of targeting anything from individual tanks to boosting ICBMs, had overnight rendered the West's strategic forces virtually obsolete. Japan, like Europe, had fallen in behind the UIR behemoth. They, too, still needed Mideast oil to support their continuing industrial growth. Increasingly, as act followed act on the world stage, the United States found itself confronting the UIR, with a hostile Japan behind the scenes providing the Islamics with the high-tech props they needed to pursue their avowed aim of world liberation.

The United States now got most of its oil from the North Slope and from South America. No one in Washington wanted to think of the rearrangement of global power once those reserves ran dry at last.

The *Sharuq* Incident had brought the U.S. and the UIR to the very brink of war. An old Soviet submarine, an Oscar SSGN purchased from Russia by the UIR in the late 1990s and renamed *Sharuq*, had been dispatched to the naval base of Cienfuegos, Cuba, which Cairo had secured for its own use through a secret treaty. From there, the Islamic sub had begun raiding the supertankers plying the sea-lanes between South America and the United States, sending two to the bottom before an American task force built around the SSCVN-1 *Leviathan* had run her down and sunk her.

Commander Parker was the Executive Officer of the *Leviathan*, once the pride of the Soviet Navy, now half of a revolutionary experiment in modern naval tactics, a submarine carrier. Ten years before, *Leviathan* had been the *Slavnyy Revolutsiya*, the *Glorious Revolution*, one of eight Typhoon submarines, the largest undersea vessels in the world. After the collapse of the Soviet Union, though, her masters had needed hard currency more than nuclear deterrence. Her ICBMs had been removed, and the *Glorious*

*Revolution* and one of her sister Typhoons had been put up for sale. The U.S., eager to keep the struggling CIS government afloat, had snapped them up for the bargain price of two for three billion dollars.

Gray was skipper of the second part of this experiment in naval tactics, a squadron of high-speed, SFV-4 Barracuda minisubs that played the role of fighters to *Leviathan*'s aircraft carrier. In fact, Gray had been the commanding officer of a real fighter squadron, flying F-22s off the U.S.S. *Roosevelt* until the "accidental" sinking of another nuclear carrier by one of Japan's orbital defense facilities. The *Lincoln* disaster had conclusively and bloodily demonstrated that the age of the great supercarrier had gone the way of the dreadnought, the ironclad, and the three-masted ship-of-the-line. Gray, with a number of other former naval aviators, had volunteered for Project Orca, which had begun with classes at the Navy's submarine warfare school at New London, Connecticut. After graduation—and an intense round of training in simulators and aboard the real thing in Long Island Sound—Gray had been assigned to *Leviathan* as commander of her Barracuda squadron. He'd come aboard while she was en route to her first operational patrol, the circuit of Cuba that had ended with the bloody fighting south of Cienfuegos.

Gray let his eyes focus on the TV screen. The anchor was talking now about a formal protest from His Majesty the Emperor to the U.S. ambassador in Tokyo, but he wasn't listening to her words. For a moment he lived again that black terror as he followed the UIR sub into the lightless depths. Gray's torpedo, fired from his SFV-4 at almost point-blank range, had locked the *Sharuq* into her final dive, sending her plunging into the cold, deep waters of the

Cayman Trench. In one sense, then, the uproar in the world press over the *Sharuq* Incident was his fault . . . though he'd been operating under orders, and other subs, American as well as Islamic, had been sunk that day besides the ex-Soviet Oscar.

Would the UIR really go to war over the *Sharuq*?

Wendy, tall and long-legged, came in from the kitchen with a tray, followed by Cecily, a petite blonde. "You two heroes want some brownies?" she demanded. "Or are you going to sit out here jawing politics all night?"

*Heroes,* Gray thought, almost bitterly. *Right.*

He'd been scared to death through most of the action against the *Sharuq* . . . when he hadn't been battling with the admiral in charge of the task force over the proper disposition of the Barracudas. He'd damn near died in that final confrontation, but for the three weeks since they'd limped back into Kings Bay, life had been an almost blissful routine of working 0800 to 1630. Wendy and the kids had made it to Kings Bay early, and he was able to drive to work each morning almost like a normal husband and father.

For the past week he hadn't even been working in his cubbyhole of an office aboard *Leviathan*. The big American Typhoon had been pulled from the water and was now in "the Barn," the base's huge, new dry-dock facility above Pier Three. While *Leviathan* was laid up, while shipfitters and construction workers swarmed over her torpedo-torn aft-starboard hull, the members of her Barracuda squadron were using a Quonset hut nearby as ready room and training center. An SFV-4 simulator flown down from New London had been set up there, and the men of the minisub squadron had been using it to go over the action off Cienfuegos again and again, identifying mistakes and weaknesses, smoothing out the rough spots in their tactics. If nothing else, Cienfuegos had proven that the fast and nimble Barracuda minisubs could indeed be used in undersea combat the way fighters were used in the sky, on patrol, for interdiction, for high-speed strikes against enemy submarines.

Now it was up to Gray to put together a formal tactical doctrine for the SFV-4s, and he was enjoying the work. The nature of undersea warfare was changing before his eyes, and each new design modification or computer simulation study seemed to accelerate the pace of that change. It was exciting and demanding work . . . and worthwhile, he thought. If the *Lincoln* disaster had made aircraft carriers and the other monsters of the surface, "skimmer" navy obsolete, it had also opened the door to this entire new revolution in submarines.

No, Gray was convinced that he was no hero. He'd been too damned scared to even think during the battle, and these past few weeks he'd been all too content to enjoy a normal job, with normal hours.

"You know, Bill," he said as he helped himself to a couple of the proffered brownies. "I don't think Matar's going to let it go that far." Saadeddin Matar, the so-called Mahdi, was Speaker for the people of the UIR, absolute dictator, under Allah, of those one billion Muslims. "I don't think he wants a war any more than we do."

Even as he said it, Gray knew the words were little more than wishful thinking. The UIR was a vast empire of diverse peoples, cultures, and interpretations of the holy Quran, incorporating both predominantly Shi'ite nations like Iran, and Sunni nations like Saudi Arabia, Egypt, and Morocco. The only thing that kept such an artificial union together was the age-old threat of an outside enemy. For the UIR, that was the West . . . and the United States in particular. The threat of war, of *world* war, hung over America and her few remaining allies like a storm cloud.

Parker waited until both women were out of earshot. "It's going to be war," he said softly. "Matar can't let the knuckle rapping we gave him at Cienfuegos go unchallenged. If he does, that ramshackle empire of his is going to fragment. If he pushes us into a war, he'll be able to ride it out to the end. Remember Saddam Hussein?"

Gray did. Crushed by the Western coalition in the Gulf War of '91, Iraq's leader had continued to manufacture crises with the UN and the United States, inviting further air strikes for no other reason than to distract his own hungry people from the brutality of their own government. The situation in the UIR was similar.

Much later, after the Parkers had gone, Morgan and Wendy clung to each other in bed, adrift in the comfortable afterglow of sex. There'd been an almost frantic urgency in Wendy's lovemaking, tonight, almost as if . . .

"You're going to be getting new orders soon, Morg."

. . . as if she'd been storing up the touch and warmth and taste of him against the day when he'd have to leave again. Gray pulled back from her far enough to focus on her face. The hard, blue-white glow of a streetlight filtered through their bedroom curtains, casting light enough for him to make out her closed eyes, her parted lips, the curve of throat and shoulder and breast. How Navy wives—especially how *submariners'* wives—knew when their men were leaving or coming home was one of the last great, unsolved mysteries of science. As far as he knew, he was staying with the *Leviathan*; and with the battle damage she'd suffered during her clash with *Sharuq*, she wasn't going anywhere for several weeks at least.

"What makes you say that, Wen?" he asked. "The Big Vi's going to be stuck in drydock for quite a spell."

"I don't know. Just a hunch. And I've been hearing talk. Cecily said tonight that something's up. Something pretty big."

"Maybe they're getting transferred." Though since Bill had just taken the number-two slot aboard *Leviathan*, under Captain Ramsay, it wasn't likely they'd send him anywhere else soon. "There's lots of scuttlebutt, of course, with all the war talk."

"Is there going to be a war?"

"Maybe." He couldn't lie to her. "I don't really know. But as long as the Vi's stuck here, so am I. Right?"

"Maybe." But she didn't sound as though she believed it, and Gray found that he didn't quite believe it either. She pulled him close and held him for a long time. Then they made love again.

His orders to Washington came through the next day.

# CHAPTER
## 2

**White House Situation Room**
**April 18, 0930 hours**

It is one of the ironies of history that the famous
White House Situation Room, beloved of spy nov-
els and technothrillers, bears little resemblance
to the high-tech communications center usually
depicted in fiction. Located in the White House West
Wing basement, one floor below the Oval Office, it is
actually a cramped and austere suite of rooms—a
spartan conference room with an adjoining communications center. There are no banks of television
sets, humming computer consoles, or wall-sized projection screens. Unlike the big Crisis Management
Center in Room 208, in the Executive Office Building
next door to the White House, the Sit Room is decid-
edly low-tech, a concrete and wood-paneled cell that
Henry Kissinger once described as "uncomfortable,
unaesthetic, and essentially oppressive," a room so
small that only a handful of National Security
Council advisers and their aides can squeeze inside at
once.

This morning, every place at the long conference
table had been taken, and Morgan Gray fidgeted with

increasing nervousness. A small, folding projection screen had been unrolled at one end of the room just to one side of a wooden podium, and a slide projector set up on a wheeled cart at the other. He didn't know what was in the projector's carousel, though, since his presentation did not rely on visual aids. That, he decided, must be some other part of this circus.

It was Tuesday, just two days after Gray had been relaxing with family and friends in his new house down in Kings Bay. His orders had been faxed into headquarters Monday morning, directing him to report to the office of the Chief of Naval Operations, Admiral Christopher Shapley. By Monday afternoon, Gray had been in the CNO's office in the Pentagon's E-ring. Shapley himself had not been there, but Gray had been interviewed at length by one of the CNO's senior aides, and he'd been told then that he was already scheduled to deliver a briefing in the White House Situation Room the next morning.

And now, after threading his way past several Secret Service checkpoints, visitor logs, and metal detectors, here he was, with a laminated ID card clipped to the lapel of his dress whites. His heartbeat quickened a bit at the realization that the Oval Office was located somewhere just over his head.

How, he wondered, had Wendy known about the new orders? Her seeming foreknowledge of his leaving Kings Bay was eerie . . . but at least he'd been able to promise her that he would be back by the end of the week, though she hadn't seemed to believe him. His orders, signed by Shapley himself, called for him to brief the National Security Adviser and his staff on the potential of the SFV-4 in modern submarine combat. Nervously, he opened his laptop computer on the tabletop before him and called up the notes he'd typed out for himself last night in his motel room. He was a very junior naval officer at a table of admirals, captains, and powerful civilians, and he felt very much out of place. The others in the room, including the CNO's aide who'd briefed him the day before, ignored the naval commander completely, busying themselves with their own notes, papers, and portable computers.

Despite his preparatory brief, Gray was worried. He wanted to make a good impression, but he'd never been very good at public speaking, and the tightly packed gathering of brass and civilians suggested that there was more to this meeting than his evaluation of his personal experiences with SFV-4 combat. The close atmosphere of the Sit Room was charged with tension.

"Commander Gray?"

He turned, rising. An admiral, the shoulder boards of his dress whites heavy with gold, stood behind him. Gray had never met the man personally, but he'd seen his photograph often enough, in wardrooms and passageways aboard every ship and shore station he'd known in the last three years. "Admiral Shapley. Good morning, sir."

The CNO's dark brown eyes and silver hair added to his hard, no-nonsense look. "Don't get up, son. I just wanted to say I read your after-action on the Cienfuegos affair. Damned thing read like a Grier thriller."

"Uh . . . yes, sir." Raymond Grier was a popular novelist whose naval technothrillers were on the *Times* best-seller list more often than not. Had the admiral meant that as compliment or criticism?

Before he could resolve the question, a civilian staffer walked into the conference room. "Gentlemen, the Assistant to the President for National Security Affairs."

Neil McIntyre strode in and took his place at the head of the table, opposite the projection screen. He was a short, brisk man with thick-rimmed glasses, a three-piece suit, and an almost visible awareness of his own importance. It was an awareness that was certainly justified, for the National Security Adviser, with direct access to the President, was without question one of the most powerful men in Washington.

"Gentlemen," he said, nodding. "This will be a quick one. I'm scheduled to meet with the President in forty-five minutes, and I've got to know what to tell him. John? Suppose you start the ball rolling."

According to the ID card pinned to his lapel, "John" was John Orsini, an analyst with the NPIC. Anyone from Washington's National Photographic Interpretation Center would be CIA, though NPIC was run as a "service of common concern" for the entire U.S. intelligence community.

Removing a telescoping pointer from his jacket pocket, Orsini walked around the table and took his place at the podium at the front of the room. His casual manner suggested that he was used to assemblies such as this one. "Thank you, sir," he said. "Lights, please."

The room's lights faded, and the slide projector whirred to life. A submarine appeared on the projection screen, a very large submarine, judging from the scale shown by the figures just visible in the open cockpit atop the long, low sail. A line of numbers and code characters across the bottom of the shot gave NPIC classification data and a date and time three days earlier. The slide evidently had been reproduced from data transmitted from a KH-12 satellite.

"Gentlemen," Orsini began without other preamble. "This shot was taken last Saturday, the fifteenth. The

submarine you are looking at is the *Teigei*, the first in
a brand-new class of Japanese submarine. One of our
satellites caught her in Yokosuka Harbor as she was
putting out to sea. Next."

The view changed, this one at a lower angle, looking from the stern forward toward the bow. Unlike
*Leviathan*, a converted Typhoon-class boomer with
missile tubes arrayed forward of the sail, *Teigei*'s conning tower was mounted far forward and was dwarfed
by the sheer bulk of the rest of the vessel. To Gray's
experienced eye, she looked something like an
American ballistic-missile submarine, except that the
conning tower was long and low and rose smoothly
from the deck like the sail on an ex-Soviet Alfa.

"Her name in Japanese means 'Great Whale,'"
Orsini continued. "Like their recent Tyogei, the, uh,
'Long Whale' class, she is nuclear-powered, probably
with two pressurized, water-cooled reactors. She rep-
resents an astonishing leap in Japanese submarine
technology. Next."

This time two submarines were visible, in an
oblique shot that reduced both vessels to black slivers
trailing long, white wakes. The second submarine was
half the length of the first.

"The big one is the *Teigei*," Orsini explained.
"She's traveling with an escort, one of their Tyogei-
class boats. The Tyos were the very first Japanese
atomic-powered subs and are probably similar in
range, size, and operational capabilities to our Los
Angeles attack boats. They became operational in
1999 . . . possibly in ninety-eight.

"Apparently, they took what they learned with the
Long Whales and put it to use with the Great Whales.
The Tyogeis are three hundred sixty feet long and
displace something like six thousand tons sub-

merged. *Teigei*, however, is a monster, five hundred fifty feet long, with a beam of forty-eight feet and an estimated submerged displacement of eighteen thousand tons. That puts her in the same general class as our own Ohio-class boomers—a hair shorter and a bit broader in the beam."

Gray pursed his lips, wondering where all of the numbers had come from. Modern-day Japan was notoriously isolationist, largely closed to *gaijin*, or non-Japanese foreigners. Possibly they were estimates based on satellite measurements, but there would be considerable room for error in such data.

One of the civilians at the conference table stirred uneasily. "Mr. Orsini, are you saying that the Japs are fielding a ballistic-missile sub?"

"No, sir. Japanese public and foreign policy is anchored on the principle of a nuclear-free world. No ICBMs. Remember their Sky Shield deployment?"

"Starwarsaki," someone at the table said with a derisive snort, and several others chuckled. The humor was forced, however. It was less than four years since the American supercarrier *Lincoln* had been sunk in the Persian Gulf—supposedly by accident—by a Japanese railgun satellite. A two-kilo length of metal, a "crowbar" magnetically fired with a computer's pinpoint accuracy and slamming into the flight deck of an aircraft carrier at better than seven miles per second, had spelled the end of the effectiveness of America's nuclear arsenal. It had also, as an incidental side effect, ended once and for all the strategic usefulness of her lumbering surface battle fleets and carrier groups. Technology and the startling shifts in global politics were joining to force modern naval warfare into the secret, hidden sanctuary of the darkness beneath the waves.

"Let's have the next slide, please," Orsini said. This time the screen showed a close-up of the *Teigei*. The colors were unusually vivid, the contrasts sharpened to show minute detail. Gray could clearly make out the flush-deck fittings of two of the strangely elongated hatches on the deck just aft of the sail.

"Though she's built on the same lines as an Ohio," Orsini continued, "the *Teigei* is definitely not a boomer. We believe her to be a sub carrier, an SCVN equivalent of our own *Leviathan*."

Murmurs and low-voiced comments rose from around the table, interrupting Orsini's monologue. Gray sat back in his chair, stunned. A Japanese carrier sub? He'd thought the United States had the only two, *Leviathan* and her sister giant out at Bangor, Washington, the *Behemoth*. And those two had been converted from Soviet ICBM subs. Orsini was saying that the *Teigei* had been *designed* as an SCVN from the beginning.

"Gentlemen!" McIntyre said sharply. "Please, you can argue your opinions later. Proceed, John."

"Thank you, sir." Orsini used his pointer to trace several elongated hatches on the monster sub's afterdeck. "While we cannot see inside, *Teigei* was obviously constructed along the general lines of a ballistic-missile sub. We expect that instead of the usual missile tubes, however, she has an enclosed hangar deck storing from eight to ten miniature subs, one- or two-man submersibles similar to our SFV-4s, together with the gear for launching and recovering them. Apparently, judging from the positioning and shape of the deck hatches, launch and recovery are effected horizontally, rather than vertically. This almost certainly sharply reduces the number of minisubs *Teigei* can carry."

It would indeed, Gray thought. *Leviathan*, until her purchase from Moscow by the United States during the mid-1990s, had mounted twenty missile tubes forward of her sail, seven-foot-wide cylinders originally designed to hold and launch SS-N-20 nuclear missiles. Those tubes had been converted during *Leviathan*'s refit to airlock cradles for twenty minisubs of various designs.

The single disadvantage of the arrangement was imposed by the missile-tube configuration. SFV pilots had to launch straight up, like a missile, and recovery depended on "trapping" in a steel mesh net extended from the tube on telescoping supports, then being drawn tail-first back into the empty tube. Though efficient, the recovery system was complex and prone to breakdown, while the pilot was forced to launch and recover in a head-down attitude that was uncomfortable and potentially disorienting. The Japanese system must avoid that problem, but a near-horizontal launch meant that both launch and recovery would take longer, and the mother sub would not be able to carry as many fighters as the redesigned American Typhoons.

"*Teigei* submerged shortly after leaving Yokosuka Harbor," Orsini continued. "We can only speculate about her destination, but intelligence reports suggest that Tokyo intends to support her Islamic allies now in the wake of the disaster at Cienfuegos."

"What do you mean?" McIntyre interrupted. "That she's headed for Alexandria now? Or Cuba?"

"We really have no reliable information on that, sir," Orsini replied. "It does seem unlikely at this juncture, however, that Tokyo is planning on becoming actively involved in the UIR's anti-American jihad. They have too much to lose if they get involved in open war with us now, and everything to gain by staying out of it. They're more likely to continue providing their Islamic friends with matériel, training, and behind-the-scenes moral support, rather than risk an open break with Washington." He rapped the screen twice with his pointer. "Actually, since Tokyo knows the schedules of our satellites almost as well as we do, we should keep in mind the possibility that they *allowed* us to see *Teigei* leaving port. A warning, possibly, that they intend to support Cairo, as they supported them in the Gulf Crisis of oh-two. Or they could be telling us that they could become directly involved, given sufficient provocation."

"It's also possible that they simply don't care whether we see them or not," a civilian seated beside McIntyre pointed out. Gray wasn't close enough to read his ID badge, but he had the look of someone in intelligence and he was old enough to be fairly senior in whatever position he held. "We are not, after all, at war with them. At least not yet."

"Granted, Mr. Cabot," McIntyre said. "And what the President will want to know this morning is whether this means we're going to be at war with them this evening. Tokyo's been playing this one pretty close to their vest."

Cabot? Gray knew the name. That must be Richard Cabot, the current Director of Central Intelligence.

"We can't make a guess at their intentions until we know where *Teigei* is going," Cabot pointed out. "If they head for the UIR's big port at Alexandria, then they're offering technical support, training, and a boost for morale. If she shows up at Cienfuegos, I'd say we have a problem on our hands. A submarine as large as *Teigei*, presumably with *Leviathan*'s capabilities and based at the UIR's port in Cuba, well, that would not be a good situation, Mr. McIntyre. We saw last month what one obsolete, ex-Soviet Oscar SSGN could do to threaten our sea-lanes to South America. *Teigei* is brand new, with unknown capabilities."

The survival of the U.S. as an industrial power depended on the oil tankers from Guyana and Venezuela which, together with the Mexican reserves, now amounted to better than ninety percent of America's oil imports. The UIR's *Sharuq* had come close to shutting the Caribbean pipeline down entirely.

"Which leaves us with the question of how effective *Teigei* could be," McIntyre said thoughtfully. "Admiral Shapley? I understand we have an expert with us here this morning."

"Yes, sir. Commander T. Morgan Gray was in command of the SFV-4 squadron that sank the *Sharuq* three weeks ago." The CNO looked at Gray. "Commander?"

"Thank you, Admiral." Self-conscious, feeling every eye in the room on him, Gray stood and took Orsini's place behind the podium. He resisted the urge to take his laptop portable with him, determined to look at his audience instead of the computer's screen.

"Gentlemen," he said. "I was invited here by the office of the Chief of Naval Operations to tell you what I know about the SFV-4 Barracuda. Perhaps I should start by explaining that I didn't start off as a submariner. I'm a fighter jock, and I suspect that's why they tapped me for Project Orca."

In fact, Gray had been Assistant CAG— "Commander Air Group," though the Navy no longer called them "groups"—aboard the U.S.S. *Theodore Roosevelt*, flying the Navy's hot new F-22 fighter. Later, as the Navy began redirecting its efforts in the wake of the *Lincoln* disaster, he'd been given a choice: fly a desk at Oceana Naval Air Station, or volunteer for

Project Orca. With no clear idea of what he was getting into, Gray had chosen the latter.

Project Orca represented a massive leap forward in submarine technology. The brainchild of McDonnell Douglas, an aircraft company, no less, the SFV-4 was a revolutionary design that literally flew through the water. Traditional submarines submerged or surfaced by changing their buoyancy, filling or emptying their ballast tanks. The SFV-4 Barracuda was a negative buoyancy submersible; it climbed in the water precisely the same way a jet climbed into the sky, on lift generated by its stubby wings. And like a jet, it was jet-propelled; water gulped down through intakes was expelled astern at high speed by powerful MHD pumps.

The differences in design between an old-fashioned submarine and a Barracuda were precisely those between a lighter-than-air dirigible and an F-22 fighter. An SFV-4 fighter sub could attain over twice the speed of the fastest prop-driven sub, and it could dive deeper, surface faster, and maneuver better than any other submarine in the world.

Or at least that had been the case until the appearance of the *Teigei* off Yokosuka. If the Japanese "Great Whale" was indeed a carrier sub, it must be designed to carry something like the SFV-4. Given the current superiority of Japanese technology, it was a fair bet that their fighter subs incorporated some new twists that even McDonnell Douglas couldn't match yet. The pace of advancing technology during these past few years had been nothing less than astounding. As he continued to describe the SFV-4 Barracuda to his silently attentive audience, Gray wondered just what a Japanese fighter sub might be capable of in combat.

After describing the Barracuda, Gray went on to talk about the fight off Cienfuegos, where America's fighter subs had seen combat for the first time. He had just finished describing how he had sent a torpedo into the huge UIR submarine *Sharuq* at point-blank range, ending the battle.

"Commander," Cabot said, interrupting him. "You say it was your minisub that sank the *Sharuq.* Now, *Sharuq* was a . . . what?"

"An Oscar-class guided missile submarine, sir. An SSGN. She carried twenty-four SS-N-19 antiship missiles in launch tubes between her double hulls."

"And how big is an Oscar?"

"Five hundred fourteen feet long, sir. With a submerged displacement of sixteen thousand tons."

"Sounds like a motorboat taking on a battleship."

"Torpedoes make great equalizers, sir."

That raised a ripple of laughter from the others. Cabot smiled. "So it would seem. Would your SFV-4s be as effective against surface vessels?"

"Yes, sir. Better, in fact, since skimmers—ah, surface ships, I mean—don't have double hulls." *Sharuq* had already taken a hit in her flank when Gray found her. He had guided his torp through the gaping crater in her side to pierce her inner pressure hull and send her to the bottom.

"What kind of range do you have, Commander?" McIntyre wanted to know. "What's the SFV's fuel capacity?"

"Since the Barracuda uses water as reaction mass, it doesn't have to carry fuel. Its range is limited by its power supply—advanced fuel cells and superconductor batteries. Normal endurance is three to four hours, with a top speed of about one hundred knots. The endurance is reduced quite a bit if we have to fight on the way."

"And you consider this to be an effective weapon?"

"Yes, sir, I most certainly do."

McIntyre leaned across the conference table and began speaking in low, urgent whispers with Cabot and Shapley. The three men were joined in their hushed conversation by several aides, leaving Gray feeling like he'd been forgotten.

"Damn it, Mr. McIntyre," Shapley said after a moment, his voice loud enough to carry above the murmur. "We don't have any alternative. If the bastards decide to escort the Islamics through the Strait, our SSNs won't stand a chance."

McIntyre leaned back in his chair, one arm across his chest and the other bracing his jaw with thumb and forefinger. "I am forced to agree, Admiral. Go ahead and have your staff work up the operational orders. I'll tell the President that that's the way we should go." He seemed to see Gray, still standing behind the podium, for the first time. "Ah, thank you, Commander. That will be all."

The meeting was breaking up. Confused, Gray retrieved his laptop and switched it off.

Shapley came up behind him. "A good briefing, Commander."

"Thank you, Admiral. Uh . . . what just happened?"

"Our nonwar with the UIR has just escalated, Commander. And I'm afraid you're going to be in the middle of it."

Gray said nothing, but his eyebrows asked the question.

"We're sending you to Spain. I want you and your entire squadron in Rota ASAP."

Which meant he wasn't going home to Kings Bay.

Damn. How the hell had Wendy known?

# CHAPTER
## 3

**R**ota, Spain, located on the northern shore of
the Bahia de Cadiz, had originally been a
Spanish naval base until it was leased to the
United States in 1953. Since that time, the six-thou-
sand-acre facility had been an important logistical
base for American naval forces in the Med, providing
the U.S. Sixth Fleet with fuel, ammunition, and spare
parts.

Gray had arrived at Rota early that morning, after
a grueling, all-night flight aboard a military transport
out of Andrews Air Force Base. After checking in with
the Rota personnel office and handing his orders to
an aide to Captain Derek Maxwell, he'd found his
way to the bachelor officers' quarters, been assigned a
spartan room with a window overlooking the white-
capped Bay of Cadiz, and crashed for four hours. His
body was still on eastern seaboard time, six hours
behind continental Europe, and it was going to take
him a day or two to get it back on track.

It was surprisingly cool for southern Spain, even
for early spring, and an intermittent drizzle had been

23

misting the air since Gray had groggily arisen. A low, gray overcast blocked the base's view of the mountains in the interior, and a sea-hugging haze obscured the towers and church steeples of Cadiz across the bay. Since the eastern U.S. was experiencing a streak of sultry heat and humidity, he'd not packed his jacket or sweaters for his trip to Washington, and his first business that afternoon had been a quick trip to the base exchange for a lightweight windbreaker and an olive-drab "boonie hat" he could wear with his civilian clothes. He'd brought one set of khakis and one set of tropical white longs with him to Spain, and he was going to have to be careful of them until Wendy could ship him some spare uniforms.

He'd also found the phone exchange and called home. It had still been morning there and Heather and John were in school, but he'd had ten precious minutes with Wendy, with the promise to talk longer that evening.

The whirlwind speed of his transfer to Spain had left him stunned worse than the jet lag from his ten-hour flight. Back when he'd been a naval aviator, he'd been able to count on his upcoming rotations ashore or to sea, at least as much as any Navy man could count on anything. A typical carrier deployment was six or seven months long, and though a tour of sea duty might be extended by a military crisis, the rotations were generally regular enough that he'd usually known what to expect, at least to within a month or two.

This, however, had come like a bolt from the blue, a scant month after his transfer from New London to Kings Bay. It left him feeling vulnerable, somehow, reminding him that others controlled his life and career. It was a fact of military service that officers and enlisted men both went where they were told to go, when they were told to go; it was a fact of life that those orders were never written for the convenience of those who had to obey them. "If the Navy had wanted you to have a wife," ran the old enlisted man's saw, "they would have issued you one with your seabag." Every military family lived with the daily uncertainty of where they would be posted next year . . . or next month. Gray had heard that it was especially bad for submariners' families; the nature of their work, and the attendant secrecy, made even letters home infrequent and unsatisfyingly concise.

Not for the first time, Gray wondered about life on the outside, as a civilian. The traditional goal of Navy fliers—a pilot's slot with one of the big airlines—was closed to him. When the Navy had started scaling back its aviation program, most of its fliers had opted for civilian life, and the airlines had been flooded with applications. That had been one reason that Gray had opted to volunteer for Orca.

Had he made a mistake?

It was almost time for evening chow, but Gray didn't feel like eating. Instead, he found his way to Rota's piers, walking through the chill, gray drizzle, water dripping from his boonie hat. Since the *Qaumat,* the Islamic fundamentalist insurrection that had toppled governments from Morocco to Kazakhstan and united them under the Mahdi's UIR, the Mediterranean had ceased to be an American lake. The Sixth Fleet still operated out of Naples, but Italy had steadily been drawing closer to Cairo's orbit lately. Under a new agreement between Washington and Rome, the U.S. Navy would be scaling back its presence in the Med over the next few months.

In all the Mediterranean, the United States could

only count on Spain as an ally. As the UIR brought diplomatic and economic pressure to bear on Europe, America's relationships with her other traditional allies in the region, France and Greece, were growing strained. Spain, alone of Mediterranean Europe, received more oil from Great Britain and the North Sea than from the Mideast and was able to stay in the Western camp.

Besides, Spain maintained two ancient, slender toeholds in Islamic North Africa, at Ceuta just across the Strait from Gibraltar, and at Melilla 150 miles to the east. Cairo had demanded that these two centuries-old colonies, as well as the Canary Islands just off the Moroccan Atlantic coast, be turned over to the United Islamic Republic. War between Spain and the UIR seemed imminent, and Madrid was counting on her alliance with the United States for her very survival.

The piers at Rota, therefore, were crowded with U.S. Navy ships, Sixth Fleet vessels deploying out of the Med, others providing a show of American support for Spain. Several guided missile destroyers, a number of frigates, and a guided missile cruiser, the *Leyte Gulf*, were tied up at the quays. An amphibious warfare ship, the *Nassau*, was riding at anchor in the bay, along with the helicopter carrier *Inchon* and an LPD, the *Trenton*. *Nassau* and her large, gray consorts were the heart of a Marine Expeditionary Unit, or MEU, recently deployed to Spain as a show of force to Cairo.

Not, Gray reflected, that any of those skimmers riding at anchor in the bay or tied up alongside Rota's pier would help much if Tokyo decided to throw in publicly with her Islamic clients. The *Lincoln* disaster still weighed heavily on Gray, as it did on most of America's military command. Three quick strikes from space, and the three thousand Marines of the

MEU would be dead or swimming for their lives. The entire nature of modern combat had been trans-formed, seemingly overnight, and the United States was still struggling to adjust to this new and high-tech way of waging war.

Morgan Gray and his minisubs were America's first real effort at adjusting. As he stood on the pier in the gray drizzle, water dripping from his boonie hat, he wasn't entirely sure he wanted the honor. Not if it meant being torn away from Wendy and the kids like this.

He'd all but memorized his orders.

1. UPON RECEIPT OF THESE ORDERS, YOU WILL REPORT TO CAPT. DEREK N. MAXWELL, USN, U.S. NAVAL STATION, ROTA, SPAIN, NO LATER THAN 22/4/06 AND AWAIT FURTHER INSTRUCTIONS.

2. SEPARATE ARRANGEMENTS HAVE BEEN MADE FOR TRANSPORT OF SFV-4 FIGHTER SUBS AND PERSONNEL, HENCEFORTH DESIGNATED SUBMARINE FIGHTER 1 (SSF-1), KINGS BAY TO USNS, ROTA.

3. WHILE SUBSEQUENT SFV OPERATIONS WILL BE UNDER DIRECTION USNAVEUR/COMSIXTHFLT, EXPECT PATROL/TRACK OPS, GIBRALTAR AREA DESIGNATED ARGENT SPEAR.

"Expect patrol/track operations, Gibraltar Area." No matter how Gray read them, his orders seemed to point to heightened confrontations with the UIR. A steady stream of Islamic ships—surface vessels and submarines—had been crossing from the big UIR naval base at Alexandria to Cienfuegos, Cuba, and they'd all been transiting the narrow straits at Gibraltar. If a shooting war started, "the Gib" was clearly where the action would begin.

Perhaps what had surprised Gray most was the fact that his operational orders called for him to deploy his squadron directly from a naval shore station rather than from a mother ship. The arrangement was no different, in effect, than basing an air squadron ashore at a naval air station, but the stubby little Barracudas, with their folding wings and stabilizer, had been designed to deploy from the seven-foot lumen of a Typhoon's missile tubes. It was strange to walk down to a broad, concrete launching ramp by the piers and see his twelve Barracudas there, beached like so many dead whales. Each was resting on a cradle and swaddled in a tarpaulin, as much to mask its shape from prying Japanese spy satellites orbiting overhead as to protect it from the elements. The SFV-4s had been crated up and shipped from Kings Bay aboard an Air Force C-17 heavy-lift transport, arriving at Rota last night, hours ahead of Gray's flight out of Andrews.

A heavy set, black machinist's mate chief had pulled back the tarp and was going over one of the minisubs, attended by a coterie of wet, dungaree-clad enlisted men with flashlights and clipboards. MMC Raymond Huxley was the squadron's enlisted crew chief, the man responsible for keeping the high-tech boats operational.

"Evening, Chief," Gray said.

The junior ratings turned and saluted, but Huxley, lying flat on his back as he probed the depths of a circuitry access hatch, merely looked out from under the tarp, smiled, and nodded. "Hey, Skipper. Welcome to sunny Spain."

"Right. When'd you guys get in?"

"Aw, they flew us over with my babies, here. I'm just checking to see they didn't scratch the paint."

"Yeah? How do they look?"

"No problems, Commander." His head vanished under the tarp again for a moment. "Buckley! We need a goddamn C-40 circuit board on number five. Mark it!"

"Aye, aye, Chief."

Huxley's head reappeared. "Nothin' we can't handle, anyway, with a little cooperation outta the U.S. Nav-Europe supply munchkins. When you need 'em, they'll be ready."

"Fine, Chief. I'm counting on it."

Gray had already gained an appreciation for just how important maintenance was for these vessels. They were ultra-high-tech from snub bows to aft trim tabs, from their laser ULTRA-C navigation to their micro-Cray onboard computers, fast, smart, and deadly. If something went wrong with the technology, *when* it went wrong, it would be underwater, possibly deep underwater where sunlight never penetrated and the pressure was measured in tons per square foot. Under those conditions, a malfunction, any malfunction, was deadly, and Huxley and his crew took their duties very seriously indeed.

He wondered again about the name he'd seen on his orders, Captain Derek Maxwell. Gray had heard about the man, former skipper of a Los Angeles attack boat, the U.S.S. *Baton Rouge*. He had the reputation of being a real fire-eater, as hard on his men as he was on himself.

And now Maxwell was in overall command of SSF-1. If he was half the hard taskmaster the scuttlebutt claimed, he would have some hard questions tomorrow about the Barracudas and their readiness for action. Gray decided that he'd be smart getting the answers to some of those questions tonight.

Besides, Gray felt he had a reputation to live up to
. . . or in this case, to recreate. Once, while he was stationed aboard the *Theodore Roosevelt* but before he'd
been bumped up to Assistant CAG, he'd stayed up all
night working with his crew chief and a Hughes con-
tractor, tearing apart the APG-65 multimode radar in
another squadron's F/A-18, trying to find an elusive
fault in the circuitry. "Cold Steel" Gray had had a rep
as an ice-cold aviator who flew by the book with a
machine's precision.

He'd also had the reputation of being an officer
who didn't mind getting his hands dirty with his men.

"Hey, Commander! Commander Gray!"

He turned at the familiar voice. Lieutenant Joseph
Young, call sign "Monk," was coming up the board-
walk with five other SSF-1 pilots. Lieutenant Mike
Seegar—inevitably nicknamed "Cigar"—was with
him, and Hernandez, Dominico, Wilder, and Oz
Franklin. All wore khaki uniforms, with aviator's jackets to keep out the drizzle. Because he'd gotten in so
late and slept all day, Gray hadn't seen them since
he'd left Kings Bay.

"Oh, God!" Gray exclaimed. "The Eagles are here!
Spain's never going to be the same!"

SSF-1's official squadron name, derived from their
call sign during the Cienfuegos op, was the Blue
Hunters. Unofficially, however, aboard *Leviathan* and
among themselves, they were still the Bald Eagle
Squadron. During their first deployment aboard the
nuclear-powered *Leviathan*, some of their new shipmates had contrived to mix hair remover with their
shampoo, after which they'd been regaled with tales
of reactor leaks and radiation poisoning aboard aging
Russian submarines. Gray had won acceptance for
himself and for his men by going along with the gag;

they'd shaved their scalps bare and called themselves the Bald Eagle Squadron . . . or, occasionally, the Mutant Menace.

The names had stuck, even after their hair started to grow back in.

"We're missing someone," Gray said. "Where's Bob this time?" Lieutenant Robert Koch was the last of the Blue Hunters' original complement, a steady, taciturn man who still received a lot of ribbing because he'd unavoidably missed the submarine battle off Cienfuegos.

"He's not with me this time," Hernandez said, grinning. The dark-haired Hispanic had been with Koch during the Cienfuegos scrape. Both men, Gray knew, felt like they'd not been fully blooded with the rest of the squadron.

"Aw, he's with the longhairs," Franklin said. The "longhairs" were the three new men in the unit, Douglas, Blackwell, and Mackey. They'd joined the Blue Hunters just a week before, after Cienfuegos. "Gettin' 'em settled in."

"There's one conscientious soul," Gray observed. "What about the rest of you?"

"We have the evening free, Skipper," Lieutenant j.g. Frank Wilder said, grinning. "We thought we'd go into town and check the place out. Maybe sample the local sherry and look over the local talent. You want to come along?"

"'The local talent?'"

"I got a buddy with the Seabees here, Commander," Seegar said. "He says there's this place in Jerez where the girls—"

Gray held up a hand. "Cigar, I don't want to hear about it."

He felt a nagging worry about these men leaving

the base, not so much because of any actual danger as because they were *all* new here, not just Douglas, Mackey, and Blackwell. Every one of them, himself included, was a new submariner, warden of a new technology, in a strange country on an ill-defined mission.

Still, he had neither the grounds nor the authority to keep them on base. His gravest concern was what their host country, Spain, would think about this gang of former aviators descending on one of their peaceful towns.

"Morning muster's at oh-seven-hundred hours tomorrow, gentlemen," Gray said sternly. "Be here, or your ass is grass. If I find I have to come bail you people out of some Spanish jail . . ."

"Hey, Mom!" Seegar protested. "We'll be good!"

"That's right, Skipper," Wilder added. "We're *always* good! You oughta come along."

"Negative, Wildman," Gray said. "I've got things to do. Thanks anyway."

"Anytime, Commander," Franklin said, grinning. "You should get out more, y'know?"

Lieutenant Gary Franklin had done it the hard way—a black kid from Kansas City who'd made his way up the ladder in a profession still dominated by whites. He'd been a naval aviator flying Hornets until Project Orca had come along, when he'd decided he'd rather fly *anything*, even a submarine, than a desk.

Laughing, the six trooped off together back up the hill toward the BOQ.

Gray sighed. Aviators lived hard and played hard, always pushing the outside of the envelope, trying to prove themselves both to their buddies and to themselves. The change in venue, from air to undersea, had not tempered the spirits of these aviators at all.

They were good men, every one of them, but Gray was already sure that he was going to have his hands full keeping them in line.

He turned back to the rows of beached SFVs. The tarp was off one of them, and he was struck again at how ugly the stubby little craft were with their gaping intakes and the seafoil wings tightly folded and twisted back against the vessel's flanks. The nose looked a bit like that of an A-6 Intruder, blunt and rounded, but the canopy was opaque and the whole craft was half the size of the old Navy attack plane. Gray knew from experience that there was barely room inside for the pilot.

"Okay, Chief," he said. "What can I do to help?"

Together, they began inspecting the rest of the fighter subs.

## Jerez de la Frontera
## April 21, 2020 hours

The place was called Enrique's, according to the big neon sign outside, and if it was located in a seedy part of the town, at least the girls were friendly and the drinks were cold going in and warm going down. Jerez de la Frontera was the nearest fair-sized town worthy of the name, twelve miles inland from Rota as the crow flies, but more like eighteen in a rickety gray bus winding inland through the hills above the sea. Seegar and the others had elected to bypass Rota itself with its dark city walls and medieval air, as well as the tiny, seacoast village of Puerto de Santa Maria, in search of some hot local nightlife. They'd found it, or a good facsimile, at Enrique's.

They'd changed to their civvies before they'd left

the base, but it was obvious enough to anyone who cared that they were Americans. The three bargirls who'd joined them had taken one look at their close-cropped haircuts and assumed they were Marines.

"Hell no!" Wildman exploded, nearly dropping the miniskirted *señorita* perched in his lap. "Goddamned jarheads? Us? You gotta be kidding!"

The group had started their evening at Enrique's sampling the excellent sherry from the vineyards above Jerez de la Frontera, but they'd proceeded on full afterburners to cheaper, harder stuff that Seegar called JP-5, high-octane jet fuel. All of them were flying high now, as their companions sipped glasses of something that was undoubtedly cold, expensive tea.

"We're aviators, *chica*," Hernandez said. "*Comprende?*" He mimicked a plane taking off with his hand. "*Los aviadores!*"

The woman sitting between Oz and Dominico looked across the table at Hernandez, her eyes wide. "Oh, pilots. *Sí.* Off the big carrier in the bay." All three girls spoke passable English. If there was a language barrier at the table, it was with Hernandez's Tex-Mex Spanish.

"She must mean the *Nassau*," Dominico said. "Nah, honey. We're Navy. An' you never call a Navy aviator a *pilot*. It's insulting!"

"Yeah, we're better'n any goddamned pilots," Seegar growled.

"Hell, Hector," Young told Hernandez. "We ain't aviators anymore. We're submariners now, remember? No more clean, open sky and a good trap on the deck for us!"

"Shit, Monk, I was tryin' to forget." He ignored his empty glass and took a pull at one of the bottles on the table.

Franklin frowned. "Hey, maybe we shouldn't be talking about this stuff in public, you think?" He glanced meaningfully at the three women with them.

"There, that proves we ain't submariners," Hernandez told Young. "Damned submariners never say jack shit about nothin'."

"Don't sweat it, Oz," Wildman said easily. "Our orders ain't classified and nobody cares if we're here. Not even the damned Mahdi."

One of the women smiled. Her eyes and face were so heavily made up she looked like a porcelain doll. "Ah, but you Americans are here to fight the Mahdi, no? He makes much trouble for us, over Ceuta."

"If all the Americans are as brave as these six," the woman with Seegar said, giggling, "then the Mahdi doesn't, how you say, have the chance!"

"You said it, baby," Seegar said, hugging her close and nuzzling the cleavage exposed by her frilly, low-cut red dress.

"Hey, hey," Wilder said. "I thought you were married, Cigar."

"Mind your own damned business, Wildman. You ain't even lost your cherry yet!"

"I have too! Where do you think I got the handle 'Wildman'?"

"Oh, the man's got a rep," Young said.

"Hey, what's this 'Ceuta,' anyway?" Oz wanted to know.

"Spanish colony on the south side of the Straits," Dominico replied.

"Military base," Hernandez added. "A presidio."

"Yeah. It's belonged to Spain since sixteen-something, and to Portugal before that. Ever since Morocco went and joined the Mahdi's pan-Islamic revolution, Cairo's been agitating to get the place back."

"La Ceuta is for centuries more Spanish than Moorish," one of the women said. "Is a matter of national honor, no? And you Americans will help us defend our honor. I know this, *en absoluto*."

"Abso-damn-lutely," Seegar said with a grand flourish of the bottle. "Maybe we ain't aviators now, but by God we're the best damned submariners in the whole damned fleet, and we are here to kick Mahdi ass!"

"Yeah!" Wilder chimed in. "Kick ass and take names!"

"Bottle's empty," Hernandez said. "Bartender! *Cantinero!* More of the same . . . and for the girls too!"

It promised to be a rewarding evening.

It had already been a rewarding evening for the dark-skinned, hawk-faced man sitting alone at a table near the roisterous Americans and their Spanish whores. Though he was known at Enrique's as Carlos, his real name was Sidi ben-Hassan and he was a Moor, a descendant of the militant Islamic tide that had swept across the Strait of Gibraltar into Europe in the eighth century. The Moors had remained a part of the character of southern Spain even after Ferdinand and Isabella had crushed the last remnants of the Moorish kingdom in 1492; more recently, in the years before the *Qaumat*, they'd been the beachhead for a new Islamic invasion as North African Muslims poured across the strait in search of jobs.

Among those immigrants had been thousands of militant Islamics, members of the Party of God, the Muslim Brotherhood, and other, even more extremist factions. For them, service to the cause of Islam was service to Allah, and they'd proven themselves useful as eyes and ears of the Mahdi when Cairo had once again, after centuries of slumber, become the center of the world.

No one in Enrique's guessed that "Carlos" spoke English as well as Spanish, Arabic, and French. He'd spotted the Americans as soon as they'd entered the bar, and he'd been able to move to a closer table and unobtrusively listen in on their boasting and bravado. He drank strong coffee—alcohol was forbidden to a loyal follower of the Prophet—and dissected each phrase, each word he heard.

Pilots turned submariners? It seemed an unusual combination, and one that his controllers would be interested in, especially with all of the Americans' talk about helping their Spanish allies. Ben-Hassan continued to eavesdrop until one of the whores reminded the Americans that there were rooms available in the back. There was some noisy and half-drunken discussion after that; some of the Americans wanted to go somewhere else, while others wanted to stay at Enrique's. Eventually, three of them got up, paid their tabs, and left, leaving the others to conduct their business transaction with the women.

Ben-Hassan's pulse quickened. Three were staying! Excellent!

As the Americans left with the women, he hurried to the back of the bar to place a long-distance call.

He was already fairly sure he knew what his orders would be.

# CHAPTER
## 4

Lieutenant Michael P. Seegar lay naked on the mattress as Maria gently stroked his chest with expert fingers. "That was nice, Mike," she whispered in his ear. In the wan night glow of the town filtering through a small and filthy window, he could just make out the pale sleekness of her body lying next to his. "We go again? Only twenty dollars more."

He'd already paid her fifty, and it had been worth it, even if the bed was nothing but a mattress and one dirty sheet on the floor. The letter from his wife, delivered to him two days ago back at Kings Bay, still burned in his mind, and his liaison tonight with Maria had been as much for revenge as sexual release.

So Kathleen wanted a divorce, did she? Well, let her have it and to hell with her. He was twenty-five years old, and good-looking enough in a rugged kind of way that he didn't need the services of women like Maria, though in a strange port like this one they were certainly a convenience.

Hell, he didn't need Kathleen, or any one woman,

38

for that matter, not when there were skilled professionals like Maria. The dark-haired beauty's passion as she'd ridden him had met his anger and frustration and submerged it, leaving him pleasantly sated and after-sex drowsy, almost asleep.

Well, perhaps not sated. He still felt that damned undercurrent of restless emptiness that had brought him here tonight. Was there time for another round?

Raising his left arm, he peered at the luminous dial of his wristwatch. Twelve-ten . . . and the last bus to the base was leaving the Plaza San Dionisio at the center of town in less than an hour. "Shit," he said gruffly. "Afraid not, honey. I got me a bus to catch. I best get dressed and head on back."

Rolling off the bed, he retrieved his boxer shorts from the floor, pulled them on, then got up and padded across to the wall that separated his tiny room from Dominico's. He slammed the plaster hard three times with his fist. "Hey, Dom! Reveille! Time to pull out!" He heard a muffled and inarticulate answer through the thin wall. Turning to face Maria, he grinned at her as she sat up in the bed. "Sounds like your friend plumb wore my buddy out."

"You be back, Mike?"

"Hell yeah, sweetheart." Impulsively, he picked up his slacks and fished his wallet from the hip pocket. Extracting another twenty, he placed it on the dresser top where he'd put two twenties and a ten a couple of hours earlier. "That's a tip, babe, just 'cause I like you so—"

The door to the room banged open explosively, slamming against the dresser hard enough to send a water glass on top crashing to the floor. Two men, muffled in cloaks and their faces masked, crowded through the opening. Seegar caught the oily glint of

light reflected from the barrels of two automatic pistols.
"What the hell—"

A pistol barrel whipped through the air and
caught Seegar in the face, smashing him back against
the wall. Maria screamed and started to scramble to
her feet, but a harsh *snap!* hammered at Seegar's ears
and chopped the scream off short. Dazed, Seegar saw
a round, red, thumbnail-sized hole appear as if by
magic between the young woman's breasts, tumbling
her back in a sprawl of legs and blood-soaked sheet,
half on the mattress and half off.

"You bastard—"

The pistol barrel connected with his face again
and Seegar dropped to his hands and knees. His first
thought—that the intruders had come to roll him for
his money—evaporated in a sudden, adrenaline-
charged clarity born of blood and pain. The shot that
had killed Maria had been *silenced*. Ordinary john
rollers wouldn't bother with sound-suppressed
weapons.

Then someone hit him again and the clarity vanished with the shock of a head-on collision, catapult-
ing him into darkness.

**Jerez de la Frontera**
**April 22, 0015 hours**

Frank Wilder was already out of bed and buttoning
up his shirt, looking around the room with sour distaste. He still wasn't sure why he'd let Cigar talk him
into this. Anna had been enthusiastic fun, certainly,
but now, with the light on, the claustrophobic room
was oppressive. With no furniture save bed and
cheap, upright dresser, with nothing on the cracked

plaster walls save a large and, he thought, inappropriate crucifix, the room was still so crowded there was almost no room to walk.

He went to the single, small window, threw the latch, and opened it, leaning into the night air and letting its damp chill clean out his lungs and chase away the cobwebs. He was on the second floor in the back of Enrique's, looking out toward the center of town. He could see the imposing bulk of the Alcázar, an ancient, Moorish castle, and the cupola and bell tower of a nearby cathedral.

Pulling his head and shoulders back inside, he realized the tiny room stank of booze, sweat, and the ripe odor of Anna's body. Hell, he stank too, and he felt sick at his stomach. Worse, with all the VD lectures he'd heard during his three years in the Navy, he couldn't help worrying about disease. AIDS was spreading through prostitute communities all over the world, and though he'd used a condom, the fun just wasn't worth the danger.

He felt bad too because it was like he was betraying Debbie, somehow. He wasn't married yet, like Seegar or Dominico or Hernandez, but he was going to be soon, and his liaison with this . . . *stranger* had left him feeling dirty.

This was awful. Young and Franklin and Hernandez had been right. He should have headed back to Rota early with them.

"I like you a lot, Lieutenant," Anna said. "You come back to Anna soon, *sí?*" She was stretched out on the rumpled sheet in what she probably thought was a seductive pose. In the naked glare from the room's single light, she looked less than appealing, dumpy and sweat-matted, her thick makeup smeared like an Impressionist painting. Come back again?

Never! Never in a million years! Yeah, the Wildman might have a rep to maintain, but he'd had enough of the fleshpots of Spain.

He was trying to formulate a polite answer when he heard a muffled crash from a nearby room . . . Dominico's or Seegar's, he couldn't tell which. "What the hell's going on over there?" he wondered aloud, and then the door to the tiny room crashed open and a man with a sound-suppressed pistol burst in.

Despite the alcohol still buzzing in his brain, Wilder reacted with a fighter jock's reflexes, leaping onto the low bed astride the screaming girl, snatching the heavy crucifix from the wall like a club and swinging it in a flat, whistling arc that collided with the gunman's weapon.

The weapon fired, shattering brittle plaster at Wilder's back, but the intruder screamed with the pain as the crucifix broke something in his wrist. The gun clattered across the floor and Wilder swung again. The crucifix was heavy, gilt-painted terra-cotta, and it shattered with a satisfying *whack* against the gunman's skull. The man went down in a limp sprawl at his feet.

He heard shouting outside, and the first thing he thought was that this must be some kind of terrorist attack. "Dom!" he bellowed. "Cigar!" A woman was screaming, but it took a moment to register that it was Anna.

Scooping up the pistol, he leaped for the door. The hallway outside was narrow and poorly lit, but he had an instant's nightmare glimpse of men with masked faces and guns, of Dominico's naked body crumpling as a thug hammered the back of his head with a pistol butt, of a nude woman screaming and running toward him, arms outstretched, black hair flying, as one of the invaders opened fire with a *crack-crack-crack* of suppressed pistol rounds and slammed her, wide-eyed, mouth gaping, into a wall.

Anna knocked him aside from behind in the same instant as she bolted into the passageway, bare legs scissoring in the half-light. Wilder, acting on raw instinct, twisted away, leaping for the open window as another round splintered the doorframe. He crashed onto the tile-covered roof over the porch behind Enrique's kitchen as two more gunmen burst into the room behind him. A green-painted garbage Dumpster was to his right in the alley below. Two flying steps and he was hurtling through the air, then thumping onto the top of the Dumpster with a metallic boom. Someone shouted at him from above. Two sound-suppressed shots snapped from the window, the slugs ringing like gongs as they punched through the Dumpster's side.

Wilder hit the cobblestone pavement barefoot, the pistol still clenched in his hand but forgotten as he raced for the safety of the alley's entrance. Damn, those guys were *shooting* at him! The sheer shock of it propelled him unthinking around the corner and into the street.

Other patrons of Enrique's were spilling from the building's front entrance now, bar patrons and employees and a scattering of the joint's girls and johns in various stages of undress, all in a milling panic of confusion. Wilder heard something heavy hit the Dumpster in the alley and kept running, his bare feet slapping painfully on hard, wet pavement.

He wasn't sure where to go, remembered that the town's cathedral was close to the Plaza San Dionisio, where he was supposed to meet the bus back to Rota.

He'd seen the cathedral towers from the window, so the plaza was that way.

Ignoring the screams and shouts behind him, he kept running.

**Jerez de la Frontera**
**April 22, 0730 hours**

"You are the man's commanding officer?"

"Yes, sir," Gray replied. "There should be two others as well. A Lieutenant Seegar and a Lieutenant j.g. Dominico."

Captain Suarez, the *guarda civil* officer who'd phoned the base early that morning, looked up from the papers on his desk. Behind him, on the wall, a portrait of the Spanish king frowned down on the proceedings as though viewing them with some mild disapproval. "No, señor. We found only the one. But he is in trouble enough for three men, I assure you." Reaching into a top drawer in his desk, Suarez produced a handgun sealed inside a transparent plastic bag. "He was carrying this when my men picked him up near the Plaza San Dionisio."

"Now, where in hell did he get that?" the man with Gray wondered.

Donald Larabee was a special agent with the Criminal Investigation Division, or CID, attached to the naval station at Rota. Wearing a dark suit and a conservative tie, he looked the part of a government agent. When he'd been told that one of his men was being held at the Jerez city jail, Gray had hoped to sort things out without involving criminal authorities, but the *guarda civil* office had already notified Rota's shore patrol section, and the report had been filed from there.

"Not exactly standard issue," Gray said as he examined the pistol. It was, he saw, a Beretta Model 1951, but with the snubbed muzzle threaded to accept a screw-on sound suppressor. The suppressor was in another plastic bag, a heavy black cylinder nearly as long as the Beretta's slide.

"We have had a serious problem in this region with drugs smuggled across the strait from Africa," Suarez said. He glanced at the CID man. "It is why we notified your office. Drug smugglers are often armed with such weapons."

"I'm not about to believe that Lieutenant Wilder was smuggling drugs," Gray said, handing the pistol back. "Just what makes you think he was?"

"There was some . . . excitement at a place in town last night. A bar, restaurant, and brothel. There was a gun battle there when armed thugs broke in, apparently intent on attacking some of the, ah, patrons. Two women are dead. This"—he held up the pistol—"may have killed one of them, though we are awaiting tests from the lab to be sure. It was definitely fired at least once, one bullet is missing from its magazine, and one of the women was shot once through the chest with a 9mm round, the same caliber as this weapon." He replaced gun and silencer in the drawer.

"And what does that have to do with my man?"

Captain Suarez leaned back in his seat, a half smile on his sharp features. "We may not have all of the latest gadgetry in high-tech criminology, señor, but we do know what we are doing. We have had our eye on Enrique's for a long time. Prostitution. Drugs. We are called to the scene when there is a gun battle, and two deaths. Witnesses say several of your men were there, and minutes later we pick up your man, carrying a silenced pistol. I believe your expression is, we put one and one together, yes?"

"I'd like to see my man, if I may."

"Of course."

They had Wilder in a windowless room in the back. It was bare except for a table and two folding chairs. "Skipper!" he said as Gray and Larabee entered.

"Hello, Wildman. This is Special Agent Larabee, CID. What the hell did you get yourself into?"

"I swear, Commander, I didn't do nothing wrong. We were attacked. And they got Dom and I think they must've got Cigar too. I saw them hit Dom over the head."

"Who," Larabee said, pulling a notebook from his suit pocket, "is 'they'?"

"Damned if I know, sir. There were a bunch of them, though. At least four, and I think more. They . . . they shot a girl, right in front of me. Put three bullets into her back."

"Good God," Gray said. "Why?"

"Damned if I know, Skipper. I think they were after us."

Gray exchanged a glance with Larabee. "Terrorists?"

The CID man shrugged. "Could be. Tell me, Lieutenant. You're sure you hadn't seen these men before?"

"I'm sure, sir. And—and the gun. They said it was mine. It wasn't. I took that off the guy that broke in on me and . . . and the person I was with. I guess I sorta forgot I had it until the cops stopped me in the street. I was trying to find someone—a cop, a shore patrolman, someone, y'know? Next thing I know I'm under arrest."

Gray nodded. "You tell them about Dominico and Seegar?"

"Yes, sir. But I don't think they believed me. At least, they didn't seem to take it too serious."

"Okay, Lieutenant. Larabee and I will handle this. You just try to stay frosty, right?"

Wilder smiled weakly. "I'll try, sir. But it'll be tough. They don't have air-conditioning in my cell."

In the grimy passageway outside, Gray looked at Larabee. "You think it could be terrorists?"

"Could be," the CID man said. "But it doesn't feel like that, you know?"

"What do you mean?"

"Oh, there are anti-American groups around. With the UIR to give 'em legitimacy now, a lot of Muslim extremist groups have been hitting Americans in Europe. Kidnappings for ransom, sometimes. Bombings to call attention to some damned holy cause or other. But they tend to be big, splashy things that everyone can see. A hundred people slaughtered in a coffeehouse or an international airport, something like that. Not middle-of-the-night shoot-outs in the back of a whorehouse. I doubt that this'll even make the local papers."

"That's what I was thinking," Gray said. "It sounds to me more like someone was trying to kidnap our people."

"Could be. Why?"

"Intelligence, Mr. Larabee. Someone is interested in what my squadron is doing here, and they're finding out by picking up some of my people for questioning. It's the only thing that makes sense."

"I dunno. . . ."

"Hell, it makes more sense than the idea that a twenty-four-year-old naval officer was involved in a drug deal his second night ashore in a strange country, doesn't it? How'd he make contacts so fast? Hell, how'd he make *enemies* so fast? Besides, I know Wilder, Dominico, and Seegar. They're all fast, smart, and like action, but they're basically straight arrows. They love excitement, hot planes, and fast women, but none of them are daredevils, and they don't do crazy things for kicks. They wouldn't have been fighter pilots if they did."

"What were they doing in a whorehouse, then?"

Gray made a face. "Do you really have to ask that?"

"Okay, okay," Larabee said, holding up his hands. "You could be right. And I'll see if we can have the case transferred back to the base, get him back into our custody. Those Spanish jails can be rough."

"I'd appreciate that. I think he's telling the truth, Mr. Larabee. I'm sure of it, in fact."

"We'd better bring the Intel guys in on this. If you're right, then someone's being damned inquisitive about what you people are doing here."

"Exactly," Gray said, "what I was thinking."

The anger in him was a hot, hard knot, the tension that of a crossbow string drawn tight. A touch, and he would let fly. Some bastard had grabbed his men, *his* men, for interrogation, possibly for torture. If they hadn't hesitated to kill those women at Enrique's, then they wouldn't hesitate to dispose of Dom and Cigar when they were through—probably at the bottom of the Bay of Cadiz.

For Morgan Gray, the assault on his men was almost worse than a direct, personal attack. He wondered if Dominico and Seegar were still alive, and if they were, where they were right now.

# CHAPTER
## 5

U.S. Naval Station, Rota
April 22, 1115 hours

"**G**oddamn it, Commander," Captain Maxwell said. He was an imposing man, six-two and powerfully built, with eyes as pale blue as the polar ice he'd once traversed aboard the U.S.S. *Baton Rouge*, and red-brown hair graying at the temples. "I don't like this one little bit. This doesn't sound like a simple assault in some liberty port's back alleys."

Gray took a deep breath. He was sitting in Maxwell's office, in the "B-Block" complex of offices above Rota's harbor area. The busy sounds of clattering typewriters and humming office printers floated through the closed door from the offices outside. Behind Maxwell's desk, a window looked out over the harbor, and beyond the steel-gray expanse of the Bay of Cadiz. The drizzle had lifted at last this morning, and the church towers and office buildings of Cadiz were clearly visible seven miles across the bay to the south.

"I have to agree, sir," Gray replied. "After we visited Wildman at the jail, I went with the guy from CID to see the barkeeper at Enrique's. According to him, the assailants got the room numbers of the three Americans from one of the B-girls. He said he thinks there was a van parked outside, and that the bad guys tossed a couple of man-sized bundles into the back before they drove off, but there was so much confusion that no one knows for sure what happened. I gather the police are having a hard time finding witnesses."

"Hell, the locals're probably too scared to say even if they know," Maxwell observed. "Besides, what are three Americans, more or less?"

Gray shook his head. "A lot of the businesses hereabouts depend on Navy customers, Captain. And they hate *los Moros* with a passion. You know, I think they have memories going back twelve hundred years, to the last time the Moors invaded Spain. They don't want to see that happen again, and they know the Americans are on their side. I think they'll help us if they can."

Maxwell grunted. "Maybe. It's out of our hands now, anyway. I've informed Washington, and they have people on it. From here on out, it's in the hands of Navy Intelligence and the SEALs."

Navy Intelligence was treating the disappearance of Dominico and Seegar as an espionage case, which meant the full array of America's intelligence assets, spy satellites, agents, and high-tech eavesdroppers would be bent to the task of locating the two men and their captors. The SEALs were the Navy's Sea-Air-Land combat teams, trained, among other things, for counterterrorist and hostage rescue work.

"In the meantime," Maxwell continued, "Operation Argent Spear is go. I'm going to want you and your men to get started on that this afternoon."

"Yes, sir. Do we have a specific objective?" Argent Spear was the code name for patrol-and-intercept operations in the Strait of Gibraltar. So far, though, Gray hadn't heard what they might be patrolling for.

Maxwell nodded. "Since your dance with the Islamics at Cienfuegos, Commander, the UIR has been funneling supplies through the strait to their base in Cuba. Submarines too, possibly. Our people have been trying to track them, but we can't tell for sure how much is going through. Argent Spear is designed to gather intelligence on what Cairo is sending to Cienfuegos. Washington figures you people with your ULTRA-C minisubs can do a better job than traditional subs, and from what I've seen, I'm inclined to agree. What's your current operational capability?"

"Twelve SFV-4s were shipped across from Kings Bay," Gray said. "Of those, three were downgrudged by my maintenance chief and are waiting for parts from the States. With Dominico and Seegar missing, I've got ten pilots, counting myself. One's on the sick list as of this morning."

"Anything serious?"

"Sprained ankle, sir. He was taking advantage of Rota's stables and fell off his horse."

Maxwell smiled. "Doesn't sound too bad."

"No, sir."

"How soon are you ready to begin patrolling?"

"We're ready now, sir."

He nodded. "Okay. I'll want you to go over a patrol scheme with my chief of staff. Set up rendezvous points, patrol sectors, call sign conventions, and all of that. I'll want to know where to come looking for you if you get into trouble."

"Yes, sir."

"I've also set up a meeting with a Commander Adams from Washington. He has some new toys he's going to want you to check out with the SFVs."

"Toys?"

"I'll let him explain it all to you. If everything checks out, you'll make your first patrol run tomorrow at 0900 hours."

"Very good, sir. I'll take the first flight out myself."

Maxwell cocked his head and looked at Gray curiously. "'Pilots'? 'Flights'? You sure you people are in the right place?"

Gray shrugged. "All of us are aviators, Captain. *Were* aviators, anyway. Some of the guys are still touchy about being called pilots, but it seems a pretty fair compromise since they're 'flying' boats, now. As for 'flights,' well, we're having to make up a lot of the terminology as we go along, though. This is all pretty new. The SFV-4 is a hell of a lot more like a high-performance aircraft than a submarine!"

Maxwell seemed amused, his mouth creasing back in a hard half smile. "Hmm. I saw in your report from Cienfuegos that you were using terms like 'BARCAP.' I never knew submarines could carry out barrier combat air patrols."

"I guess 'CAP' is easier to pronounce than the acronym of 'combat submarine patrol' would be, Captain."

"I suppose so." Leaning forward, Maxwell reached out and flicked a forefinger at the gold device pinned to Gray's dress white shirt just above his ribbons. His nail struck the pin with a tiny click. The gesture was so sudden Gray was caught off guard. "*That* says you're a submariner now, Commander. I have my doubts."

Gray's mouth hardened at the unexpected turn in the interview. "Sir?"

"It usually takes a year for a man to win his dolphins. You picked yours up on your first patrol."

"That's correct, sir. Captain Ramsay felt we proved ourselves at Cienfuegos. If you—"

"Hell, I'm not trying to second-guess Ramsay. If he says you earned your dolphins, then you did. All I'm saying is that being a submariner is more than that piece of tin we're so proud of. It's a state of mind. I wonder if you and your people are thinking like submariners now, or like aviators."

Inwardly, Gray sighed, hearing behind Maxwell's words the old intraservice rivalry he'd heard many times before.

"We do know our jobs, Captain."

"I hope so, Commander. Just don't let your aviator background screw you up. You're submariners now, at least in the eyes of the Navy Department. That means you keep a low profile, at sea, and ashore. I'm canceling all liberties off the base, as of now."

"I expected that, sir. In view of what happened in town, it's probably a good idea."

"Pass it on to your men. As for you, I'll want you back here to see my chief of staff at . . ." He consulted a desktop calendar. "Make it 1530 hours."

"Aye aye, sir."

"Dismissed."

**Tangier, Morocco**
**April 22, 1810 hours**

Mike Seegar sat alone in his cell, trying to make sense of where he was. The walls were of gray stone blocks, rough-hewn and damp with condensation in the humid air. The chamber was four feet wide and per-

haps ten long. The only amenities were a pile of
straw, a wooden bucket, and the narrow slit of a window high up in one four-foot wall. At the other was
the door, massive, wooden, and bound by black iron.
His watch was missing, so he didn't know how long
he'd been here, but he could see a dazzlingly blue
patch of sky through the window, and the breeze
through the open slit was hot and dry.

Gently, he probed the tender spot on the back of
his head where someone had clobbered him. He was
wearing his boxer shorts and nothing else. He
remembered being in the back room at Enrique's,
remembered the gunmen breaking in and killing the
girl.

After that . . . well, he remembered coming to
somewhere at sea. He'd known at the time he was in a
small boat because he could feel the *slap-slap-thump* as
it sped through the waves at high speed, could hear
the throaty roar of twin diesel engines and smell the
telltale odor of diesel fuel. He'd been blindfolded,
and his wrists were handcuffed behind his back. It
had felt as though he was lying on the deck atop a
pile of rough, burlap bags that stank of raw fish. A
warm mass pressing against his back turned out to be
Dominico, also just regaining consciousness, also
blindfolded and handcuffed.

Though Seegar had no doubt that someone was
keeping an eye on them, he'd started questioning
Dom, asking if Wildman was there, and then a blow
out of the darkness had rocked him back to uncon-
sciousness.

He'd awoken . . . here.

But where was here?

His first thought, muddled by the rough handling,
had been that he was in a Spanish jail. Prostitution

was illegal in Spain, still a Catholic and quite conservative nation. But that idea didn't explain the boat, nor did it explain gunfire in the night and a murdered woman. Those midnight intruders had not been cops.

Terrorists, then. That had to be the answer. He and Dominico had been kidnapped by terrorists, possibly for ransom, possibly to make some sort of anti-American statement. Now, if only . . .

*"Allahu akbar!"*

The words, sung more than spoken, a wailing ululation, floated into his cell through the open window. They brought with them a stab of raw fear, confirmation of what he'd not quite let himself think about. Mike Seegar did not understand Arabic, but he'd heard that eerie chant often enough, in movies and documentaries about the Middle East, in news broadcasts from Cairo and other cities of the UIR.

It was the cry of the muezzins from the city's minarets, calling the faithful to prayer.

Were there Muslims in Spain? Seegar didn't know. He did know that he'd not heard that cry since he'd arrived at Rota. Put that together with the boat ride. . . .

He was no longer in Spain. He was in North Africa—Morocco, most likely, possibly in Tangier, the big port directly across the strait on the Atlantic side. He'd studied charts of the Strait of Gibraltar often enough back at the base. The strait was seventeen miles wide at this point and perhaps seventy miles south from Rota. A fast boat could have gotten him here in three or four hours.

He was in Morocco, then, the westernmost flank of the United Islamic Republic.

Sitting on the straw in one corner of his cell, Mike Seegar drew his bare knees up tight against his chest and shivered. Moments later, he heard the clash of keys in the lock of his cell and knew they were coming for him.

Outside, the wail of the muezzin quavered hauntingly in the sparkling, sun-drenched air.

**U.S. Naval Station, Rota**
**April 22, 2230 hours**

Gray spent all that afternoon catching up on administrative work at Rota's small airfield, and after a hurried supper at the nearby officer's mess, he was back and at it again. One load of spare parts and electronics had arrived that afternoon, and he was working with Huxley on the seemingly endless rounds of paperwork that attended every request and receipt in the Navy's vast and complex logistical system.

As he worked, pecking away at a computer terminal set up just inside the open door of a hangar as Huxley and the others offloaded and logged in the supplies, Gray thought about Maxwell's sharp-edged injunction. Was the man on their side, or not?

The question was not rhetorical, and it was important that Gray learn the truth. Navy politics could be vicious; the careers of high-ranking men had been ruined when they came down on the wrong side of a question involving navy budgets, programs, and operational philosophies.

Ever since World War II, the U.S. Navy had been effectively divided into three services: the surface Navy, naval aviation, and submarines. In wartime, the three worked smoothly together as one; the U.S. Navy was unique within the American military establishment for being the one service that fought effectively in or on all three combat mediums—ships and subs controlling sea; carriers projecting their force through the skies; and the "Navy's infantry," the U.S. Marines, operating ashore.

In peacetime, however, these various arms of the Navy competed with one another for the lion's share of defense budget appropriations. The battle between the surface, aviation, and submarine contingents had grown especially cutthroat during the years immediately after the fall of the old Soviet empire, when budget deficits and the lack of any serious external threat teamed to cut American defense expenditures to the bone. As always happened in peacetime, there was a growing movement in Congress to combine the aviation elements of all services—Air Force, Army, Marine, and Navy—into a single air arm. Other armchair military theorists pointed out that there was no longer any need for the Marines as a separate ground combat service, that their mission could be handled more efficiently and more cheaply by the Army.

Both suggested alterations would steal considerable clout, as measured by appropriations dollars, away from the Navy, which fought back with every political weapon in its arsenal. Within the Navy community, the battle between the surface, undersea, and aviation factions took on all the viciousness of outright bureaucratic war, as each group maneuvered against the possibility that sweeping changes in the Navy's force structure would be mandated by Congress.

Things had become even more frenzied during the mid-1990s, when Congress had tightened its oversight of military spending programs while ordering certain expenditures out of a shrinking budget—including the controversial purchase of two ex-Soviet Typhoon ballistic-missile submarines from Russia.

That purchase had caused a near mutiny within the upper ranks of the Navy brass. Political in nature—ordered by Congress as an excuse to support the tottering Russian government—it had been unpopular with the aviation and surface branches of the Navy because it gave the submariners a huge technical and operational windfall from the Russian collapse; it had been unpopular with the submariner faction because that three billion had come from the Navy's budgetary appropriations, money that *had* been earmarked for American-made submarines.

About the only people happy with the Typhoon purchase had been the Navy's research-and-development people, who'd seen them as test beds for the new SFV technology, and *they* were busy fighting threatened congressional cuts in the R&D budgets.

Ultimately, the submarine service had emerged as the big winners in the current round of budget wars, mostly because the *Lincoln* disaster had, for once, set Washington moving. As Pearl Harbor had all but ended the Navy's reliance on big battleships in favor of aircraft carriers and naval aviation in World War II, the sinking of the CVN *Abraham Lincoln* had ended their reliance on carriers, conferring the crown of strategic superiority instead on the submarine navy.

All in all, Gray decided, it was nothing short of miraculous that anything got done within the Navy bureaucracy, or the vaster bureaucracies of Pentagon and Congress that surrounded it. Fallout from the ongoing budget wars had contaminated every aspect of Navy politics. Aviators still looked down on submariners, and vice versa.

Which meant that Gray and the others in his squadron, aviators transferred to submarine service, were quite literally caught in between, not fully

accepted, or even trusted, by either side. Captain
Maxwell was a case in point. A veteran submariner, he
still did not trust aviators—possibly with good cause,
Gray realized. Aviators had the rep of being free-
wheeling, brash, and loudly convinced that they were
the Navy's elite, the best, inherently superior to everyone else in the fleet. Submariners on the other hand,
members of the "silent service," had the reputation
for being closemouthed and taciturn, with a suspicion of outsiders that bordered on paranoia; and they
too considered themselves to be the Navy's elite.

There were bound to be sparks when the two services were forced to mingle, as had been the case
when SSF-1 was created.

The offloading and paperwork was complete . . . or
as complete as it could be that day. Transports had
been flying in all evening, most of them with gear for
the MEU docked at Rota, but at least one more ship-
ment for the sub group was still due in from
Stateside—Mark 62 torpedoes, with a current ETA of
sometime after midnight. He'd just checked his
watch, seen that it was well after 2200, and decided
that it was definitely time to knock off for the day
when the drone of a large aircraft on the runway
caught his attention.

He walked to the hangar door and watched the aircraft, a huge C-17 taxiing toward the hangar area,
rumbling slowly into a pool of light cast by banks of
floodlights near the hangars. Thinking that the
squadron's Mark 62s might be aboard, the flight a
couple of hours early, he leaned against the hangar
door and watched.

The transport's cargo was from Stateside, all right,
but it wasn't torpedoes. From his vantage point Gray
could see a line of big, tough-looking men filing

down the C-17's ramp. They wore civilian clothes, but each had a large, military-looking seabag slung over one shoulder, and the hard look on their faces carried the force of a blow even at this range. He watched as they formed up in a line on the tarmac close by the transport. They stood there, motionless, as one of their number ran down a muster list, then silently filed off the runway and into the night, heading toward one of the other hangars.

SEALs, without a doubt. If anyone could find American hostages held in the area, it was those grim-looking warriors flown in from the Navy's Special Warfare base at Little Creek, Virginia.

It was good to know the SEALs were on the job.

But Gray still wondered if there was a chance in hell of finding his men.

# CHAPTER
## 6

**Strait of Gibraltar**
**April 23, 0915 hours**

R ota and the Bay of Cadiz are just thirty-eight miles north of Cape Trafalgar, of Nelson fame. Southeast along the coast from there it's another thirty miles to the southernmost tip of Spain at Tarifa, where a lighthouse keeps vigil over the Strait of Gibraltar from Punta Marroqui. The coastline twists to the northeast there, and seventeen miles farther up the coast is Algeciras Bay, beneath the brooding cliffs of Gibraltar. At that point, where the warm and salty waters of the Med mingle with the Atlantic, the strait is only ten miles wide, and Mount Hacho, the southern Pillar of Hercules, is visible as a gray-purple swelling against the rugged line of the Moroccan coast. There, the Spanish colony of Ceuta lies in Hacho's morning shadow, astride the narrow isthmus connecting Hacho with the mainland.

Gray could see none of this, however, neither the familiar monolith of Gibraltar nor the lesser-known landmarks to the south, for he was leading Blue Hunter Squadron through the strait at a depth of 150 feet.

"Blue Flight, this is Blue One," Gray called as his stub-winged, snub-nosed Barracuda gave a hard shudder. "The current's picking up, boys. Hang on and enjoy the ride!"

"Yeah!" Lieutenant Joseph Young said. "Surf's up!"

They were riding the strong surface current flowing from the Atlantic Ocean into the Mediterranean. The Med, shallow compared with the Atlantic and tightly landlocked, lost water rapidly to evaporation, and the current rushing east past the Pillars of Hercules to replace it was a strong one. Below 260 feet, a deep countercurrent flowed the other way, as Mediterranean seawater made dense by salt forced its way west into the Atlantic.

During World War II, German U-boats had first made use of this two-way undersea avenue, coasting silently past the British antisubmarine defenses at Gibraltar by riding the current—shallow heading east, deep heading west.

Gray's ULTRA-C painted the water around him in blended tones of blue and green. ULTRA-C—the acronym stood for Underwater Laser Tracking/Communications—was the technological breakthrough that had opened a whole new era in submarine warfare. Using a laser frequency that could penetrate seawater for considerable distances, ULTRA-C subs could communicate with one another where radio transmissions were impossible, and their computers could analyze reflected laser light as well as sound to build up remarkably detailed images of the sub's surroundings through a system called SUBVIEW, for SUBmarine Virtual Imaging Electronic Window.

With SUBVIEW, Gray could look to left and right in his cramped SFV-4 cockpit and see the other three

Barracudas of Blue Flight, "flying" in tight fighters' formation. The Barracudas, with much smaller computers than those on *Leviathan*, could not process as much raw data as quickly as the big subs, so the images were smoother, more brightly colored, and cleaner than they would be in real life, obviously the products of computer animation.

Still he could see the hull numbers painted on the blunt snouts of the other fighter subs—Oz in 108, Monk in 102, and Lieutenant j.g. David Douglas in 104.

Gray shook his head at the panorama. It was still hard to believe it was real, that he was actually locked away in a fighter-sized carbon-fiber-and-ceramic bottle 150 feet beneath the surface of the sea.

As it had been explained to him during his training at New London, it was the one high-tech toy that might give American forces a solid advantage over the Japanese, if the current battle of words and economies escalated into outright war.

As far as anyone in Washington knew, the Japanese had nothing like ULTRA-C. They'd led the West in computers for some years now, but their laser technology, especially laser imaging, was still lagging well behind the best in American research, and most military authorities didn't expect them to have a system comparable to ULTRA-C for at least five more years.

Besides, everyone knew that the Japanese didn't innovate as much as imitate. At least, so said the official line in Washington.

Gray didn't agree with that. While Tokyo had obviously borrowed the concept of the Strategic Defense Initiative—"Star Wars"—from the West, their Sky Shield SDI program had been almost entirely home-grown, and there was no question that "Starwarsaki" had given the Japanese the military high ground of space. It was a high ground that would not easily be taken back.

If they could accomplish wonders like Sky Shield, what else might they have been working on in secret over the past few years?

"I'm reading one-zero-nine-zero feet to the bottom," Oz Franklin reported, interrupting Gray's morose thoughts. "Looks like we're moving into the middle of the strait."

"Roger that, Oz," Douglas replied. "We're in the groove."

*In the groove.* The bottom profile of the Strait of Gibraltar was a steep-sided, east-west slash averaging 1,200 feet deep.

The bottom was lost in the blue haze below. A deep chugging sound, like mounting thunder, slowly rumbled out of the distance ahead.

"Blue One, Blue Three," Franklin called over the ULTRA-C link. "Hey, Skipper? I'm reading damned heavy screws at zero-nine-five, surface contact on the approach. Don't know what it is, but it's a big mother."

Gray checked the sound profiles with his computer war book, watching as jagged traces of sound from the approaching ship matched with those stored in his computer. In seconds, he had a match. "I make it a tanker, Oz," Gray said. "It's big, all right. Over two hundred kay, dwt."

"I'm trying to get a reading, Skipper, but I can't. Looks like interference from another pattern."

"You're probably picking up another ship," Young suggested. "Boost your filters to isolate the target."

"Okay," Oz said. "Got it. Damn, it's like rush hour up there."

The Strait of Gibraltar was one of the busiest sea-lane choke points in the world, with a large ship passing on the average of once every six minutes. Even with the threat of war between the Islamic empire and the rest of the world, traffic past the Gib was heavy. Oz Franklin's computer had been unable to identify the tanker's sonic profile because there was so much background noise from other ships in the immediate area. The "filters" he'd engaged were in fact software, a program running on his computer that filtered out incidental sound from his sonar pickups.

"Set your recorders running," Gray ordered, pressing a switch on his console. The recordings they were making would be analyzed in detail and added to Rota's sound library. Eventually, any ship passing through the strait could be tagged and identified just by the sound it made.

"There she is," Young said. "Zero-nine-five, range two thousand. What's her make, do you think, Skipper?"

Gray looked up and saw the shadow, like a long, dark, slow-moving cloud drifting toward him across the emerald roof.

"I don't know," Gray replied. "Could be Greek or Italian. She could also be UIR, out of Syria or coming up the Suez Canal."

"Aw, she's just a skimmer, man," Douglas said, the scorn evident in his voice. "I'd rather be hunting subs."

"Patience, Blue Four," Gray said. "I'm sure you'll get your chance."

Like thunder, the tanker rumbled slowly overhead, over twice as long from bow to stern as the fighter subs' depth beneath her keel. Gray listened to it fade into the distance astern as he continued to watch his console display.

Nothing . . . nothing. The surface sea-lanes were crowded, but the four fighter subs had the strait to themselves.

The patrol continued, the monotony growing.

Seegar, Gray thought suddenly, bitterly. Where are you, guy? Where's Dominico? Where did they take you? Can those SEALs get you out?

The thought that two of his men were prisoners somewhere while he cruised silently, *uselessly* through the depths was almost intolerable.

**Tangier**
**April 23, 0930 hours**

Abd el-Sikkin was a CIA spy.

At least, that was how he fancied himself in his private moments as he conjured bloody images of vengeance. He also thought of himself as a freedom fighter and a revolutionary, and those titles, perhaps, were more in line with the truth. El-Sikkin was a Berber, and that by itself was enough to set him against the latest of Morocco's conquerors.

The Berbers were originally a Caucasian people who had lived in the mountains and hinterlands of northwest Africa since long before the Phoenicians and Romans fought for mastery of their land. Though the lands that would one day be called Morocco, Algeria, and Libya were overrun by invaders time and time again, the Berber lust for independence blunted the impact of each conquest. When the Arabs burst upon the world in the seventh century, sweeping across North Africa with the torch

STINGRAY **67**

of Islam, the Berbers accepted the new religion, yet managed to express their independence by adopting a schismatic and puritanical Shi'ite variant rejected as heretical by the rest of Islam. Not until Hassan II became King of Morocco in 1961 did the country's central government manage to claim control over the countless Berber clans and villages in their ancient strongholds within the Rif and the Atlas mountains.

During the great fundamentalist insurrection, the *Qaumat* of the late 1990s, the Berbers initially took part in the riots that rocked cities from Casablanca to far Dushanbe and Tashkent. With the appearance of the Mahdi, however, and the creation of a single, Islamic fundamentalist state stretching from the Atlantic to the Himalayas, the old Berber refusal to submit to a central authority, any central authority, had reasserted itself. Berber chieftains in the Rif south of Tangier had declared the Cairo government infidels, despite the fact that they were Muslim, and had taken up the sixth pillar of Islam, jihad.

Abd el-Sikkin did not share the pale blue eyes and light hair of some of his more Caucasian-looking brothers. He looked Arab, with swarthy skin and jet-black eyes and hair. His family had lived for over a century in the shadow of Tangier's Kasbah, but they still shared the fierce love of freedom of the Berber clans in the mountains. Not long after Morocco signed the Treaty of Cairo, joining the United Islamic Republic, el-Sikkin had become a "walk-in" at the American consulate, approaching a U.S. Marine and blandly asking in broken English to talk to someone with the CIA.

Ultimately, he'd talked to an assistant chargé d'affaires named Smith who, while never claiming to represent American intelligence, never denied it either. For two years, el-Sikkin had periodically met with Smith or other American consulate officers, passing on information about UIR rallies, religious or anti-American demonstrations, and propaganda, information for which he was paid pleasant if not princely sums. Eventually, with covert help from his American friends, el-Sikkin had even found a job with the headquarters staff of Morocco's parachute brigade stationed at the capital at Rabat.

As a civilian clerical worker, el-Sikkin had come up with occasional tidbits for his American controllers on troop deployments, or advance news of new weapons purchases from Japan. When the battalion was redeployed to his hometown of Tangier, el-Sikkin had reported the fact to his control and had gone along to the new headquarters building in a restored Italian castle overlooking the ocean ten miles outside of town, not far from the airport.

Then the *Lincoln* had been sunk in the Persian Gulf, and the United States had broken off diplomatic relations with the UIR. Consulates and embassies in all of the UIR's member countries had been closed, and el-Sikkin had found himself without employers.

He'd kept his job at the brigade headquarters, however, and dreamed of the day when he could score some major intelligence coup. He hated the UIR masters of his country, most of whom were Saudis, Iraqis, or Egyptians—foreigners, in other words—whose rule of the freedom-loving Berbers was rapidly becoming intolerable. For four years, Abd el-Sikkin had continued to bide his time, collecting information that he kept, somewhat carelessly, in a journal hidden beneath his mattress at home, and waiting for the day when he could again make contact again with *al-amireekàan.*

"You!" an Arab lieutenant barked at el-Sikkin as he sat hunched over his gray steel desk. "Hurry with that form! Bring it to Room 401 when you are done!"

"*Ya sidi!*" he cried back. "Sir!"

The form, inserted now in the ancient manual Remington typewriter before him, was a prisoner transfer form. Two prisoners, recently arrived at Brigade HQ, were being turned over from Force 777 to UIR intelligence, and the form, with duplicate copies written in French, Spanish, and filled out by hand in Arabic, was their receipt.

Force 777 was a commando team, once an Egyptian counterterrorist unit, but now used by the UIR in reconnaissance, intelligence gathering, and covert operations. Though not part of the Tangier paratroop brigade, they'd been assigned to the same headquarters and security unit, and el-Sikkin had already done quite a bit of paperwork for their staff. UIR intelligence, of course, was UIR intelligence . . . the dark men from Cairo and Baghdad who wore power and ruthless efficiency like shadowy cloaks. Every military base in Morocco had at least a few of these men; there was a small army of them in Tangier, preoccupied with covert intelligence missions across the strait in Europe.

The two prisoners, el-Sikkin decided, must be foreigners captured by Force 777. Completing the final entry on the Spanish form, he pulled the paper from the typewriter, gathered up the other copies, then bundled them all into a manila envelope, which he carried out of the office and down the stone-lined passageway.

Room 401 was up the stairs and down a long, red-carpeted passageway in a room that had once been the office of a Spanish governor. Two soldiers stood by the door, waving him through when he said he had papers to be signed. Inside, a swarthy-skinned, mustached man in a civilian suit sat at a desk near a window open on a veranda, overlooking the sea. Several soldiers were there as well, along with armed men in civilian clothes who looked like Force 777 to el-Sikkin.

In one far, dark corner, a naked man stood swaying, his face to the wall, his wrists handcuffed at his back. A soldier stood to either side, helping him stand upright.

"What do you want?" the civilian seated at the desk snapped as el-Sikkin entered.

"Prisoner transfer forms, sir," el-Sikkin said. "As were requested."

The man held out his hand. "Here."

El-Sikkin stood before the desk as the man leafed through the forms, then began signing each copy. A sharp crackle of sound erupted from the dark corner, followed by a moan, then a vicious laugh. El-Sikkin turned his head, staring.

"Stay awake, American," one of the soldiers with the naked man said, speaking English. He held a slender, black rod in his hand, and as the prisoner swayed he rammed the end against the man's buttocks. There was a blue spark, a crackle, a stink of burning. The prisoner gasped and nearly fell, but the other soldier caught him, forcing him to stand upright.

"Do not look at the prisoner," the civilian at the desk snapped in Arabic, and el-Sikkin whipped his head back around as though he'd been stung. For the rest of the time he kept his eyes on the window, staring at the blue-meeting-blue of the horizon, on the white wheelings of gulls above the rocks.

But he could not erase from his mind what he'd

already seen: the prisoner's back and thighs striped with welts and bruises, his feet grotesquely swollen and bloody; the bastards had whipped him, then applied the bastinado. And now he could hear the man's interrogators as they talked to him gently, almost lovingly.

"How long can you go without sleep, American? It's been a long time already, yes? You should tell us what kind of submarines you have brought to Spain, and how you intend to use them. Then you could sleep, in a real bed. Ah-ah! No nodding!" Then came the crackle of the electric prod, a tormented groan from the prisoner.

"Name . . . Seegar, Michael. Rank, lieutenant. Service number five-five-four, one-three, two—"

Another snap of an electrical discharge, louder and longer this time. The victim screamed. . . .

And then the papers were signed and el-Sikkin was hurrying from that hellish room as though propelled from behind, his shirt soaked with sweat, his heart pounding in his chest.

Americans! The prisoners were Americans . . . and if he'd understood aright, they'd been captured across the strait in Spain!

As far as he knew, no one in the headquarters knew that el-Sikkin spoke English, a fact he'd been careful to keep secret ever since he'd started passing secrets to the Americans. They wouldn't guess that he'd heard and understood as much as he had.

Back in his office again, el-Sikkin wondered what to do with this new-won information. He was sure that American military authorities would be interested in the fact that two of their men were here, being tortured for information. But how to contact them? It was no longer possible to walk into an American consulate, not with the UIR masters of the African coast from the western Sahara to Sinai. He had no radio, no covert signaling equipment. Now, as he examined the possibilities, el-Sikkin forced himself to face the hard reality that he was not a CIA spy, not any longer.

He was simply a man who hated what the foreigners were doing to his country, to his people.

And while the fact of torture itself did not bother him much—the ruling powers in this land had used such methods against his people for thousands of years, and their employment came as no surprise now—the knowledge that they were torturing the two Americans for information filled el-Sikkin with a surging, furious resolve.

He would strike back at the foreigners, now, and the American prisoners would help him do it.

# CHAPTER
## 7

**Strait of Gibraltar
April 23, 1045 hours**

"**M**y God, my God," Franklin called softly. "Will you look at that cliff up ahead?"

"Roger that," Young said. "Kind of makes you feel insignificant, huh?"

"Okay, people," Gray called over the laser com circuit. "Let's can the chatter. Keep your ears perked for targets."

The four Barracudas of Blue Flight had encountered no Islamic submarines on this, their first patrol into the Strait of Gibraltar. Every few minutes, another ship passed majestically overhead, filling the water with slow thunder which they dutifully recorded, but there was no sign of the UIR subs that were supposed to be spilling from the Med in veritable convoys on their way to Cuba and the Caribbean.

They'd been at sea for over two hours now. Their power levels were down by better than fifty percent, and it was time to be heading back. Turning west once more, Gray had led them deeper into the abyss separating Europe from Africa, dropping to a depth of six hundred feet. Below the 250-foot level, "devils

**73**

two-point-five," they'd encountered the lower layer of cooler, denser, saltier water flowing in a reverse current out of the Med and into the Atlantic. They were riding that current now, as German submariners had done over sixty years before.

The cliff that Oz had commented on stretched below and ahead of their formation, a near-vertical wall of rock painted on the SFV-4s' heads-up displays in shades of gray, green, and blue. In this part of the strait, between Algeciras and Punta Leona on the Moroccan coast, the Atlantic sea bottom rose gently to a V-shaped prominence eight hundred feet beneath the surface, then plunged, *plunged* one thousand feet into darkness on the Mediterranean side. Five and a half million years before, the Mediterranean had been an arid, sunken desert lying well below sea level, the slowly sinking stress fault a result of the rebound of Africa from Europe in the ongoing drift of the continents. For millennia, the gray waters of the Atlantic had been held at bay by a natural dam of upthrust granite, buttressed north and south by mountains that one day would be named Gibraltar and Hacho. Then, as the valley floor dropped farther, the granite wall began to crumble.

And the Atlantic had come pouring in.

Today, almost nothing visible remained of that torrent that had equaled in sheer, roaring volume a thousand Niagaras. The headlands at Gibraltar and Hacho remained, as did the cliff, sunken and invisible beneath eight hundred feet of water and long forgotten. The Gibraltar falls must have filled half the Mediterranean valley with thunder for century upon century as the sea filled up, but that had been long before there were humans around to wonder at it.

Young was right, though. The cliff, a tiny remnant of that long-vanished waterfall, was still vast enough to make a man feel very small.

The quartet of fighter subs passed west high above the cliff in loose formation, their ULTRA-C lasers revealing only the upper ramparts of that granite wall. The base of the cliff was lost in darkness, perhaps a thousand feet farther down. Gray wondered what it must have been like to stand on the peak of Gibraltar to the north and stare south across that awesome cataract.

Noisy, he decided.

Thunder approached from behind, but the slow, throbbing thunder of a large ship rather than the deafening crash of the long-vanished Gibraltar falls.

"Heads up, people," he called. "Here comes another one. Start your recording."

**Tangier**
**April 23, 1130 hours**

Two hours after he'd seen the American prisoner at headquarters, Abd el-Sikkin was at the Tangier waterfront. Telling his supervisor he was sick, he'd left the base, climbed into his battered '95 Toyota, and driven the dusty roads, first to his apartment off the Avenue Hassan II, where he picked up money and a Beretta handgun, then to Tangier's dockyard.

Despite the reassuring pressure of the Beretta tucked into the waistband of his slacks and hidden by the shirttail deliberately left untucked, he did not feel at all like what he imagined a spy should feel like. He'd seen every James Bond movie made—not easy in a conservative Islamic country—and somehow he simply could not muster the requisite air of self-assurance and savoir faire that he knew to be necessary for the part. More than once he talked himself into giving up this scheme, but the sight of UIR soldiers on the waterfront hardened his resolve. He would tell the Americans . . . somehow he would tell them.

The only difficulty would be in reaching them.

Tangier's port area was sheltered behind two long moles almost completely enclosing the harbor. Walking with a nonchalance he could not feel over the pounding of his heart and the sweat turning his palms slippery, he made his way toward the ferry terminal and hydrofoil dock.

Since the UIR had come to power, there was little activity here. Cruise ships from Europe no longer called at the docks, the docks were no longer mobbed with merchants and touts hawking their souvenirs, hotel rooms, transport, jewelry, drugs, rugs, food, or sexual companionship. Ferry service to Algeciras and Gibraltar had been suspended for years, and the big passenger hydrofoil that had once whisked passengers across the strait had been replaced by rows of sleek, deadly-looking UIR patrol craft.

Trying not to stare at the soldiers patrolling the waterfront with their Egyptian-made AKM assault rifles, el-Sikkin walked along the pier until he came to a twelve-meter cabin cruiser tied to the wharf. It was an old vessel, one that had seen better days and those long before. Once it might have been a wealthy man's pleasure craft. The name across its transom in Western letters, ominously perhaps, read *Bazzaka*—Arabic for "snail."

A man was working on the cruiser's afterdeck. "God give you a happy morning!" el-Sikkin called, in traditional Arabic greeting. "Is your boat for hire?"

"Eh?"

"Your boat. Is it for hire?"

El-Sikkin watched greed wrestle with caution in the man's dark face. Many of these people had made their livings chartering boats in the years before the UIR had come; now they ran water taxi services across the harbor or along the coast, or fished, or offered short, marine excursions for UIR officials and their families or mistresses. But the police and military both maintained a keen lookout for smugglers—an ancient and honorable profession in Tangier—and a lone man such as el-Sikkin looking for water transport was suspicious.

"Perhaps," the man said carefully. "Where do you wish to go?"

"Ksar-es-Seghir," el-Sikkin replied, naming a tiny coastal village to the east, halfway up the coast to Ceuta.

They bargained for several minutes more, settling at last on a price of one hundred guinay, UIR. The boat owner became even more reluctant when he learned that his prospective passenger wished to leave now, at once, and that he had no luggage with him. Surely, this was a criminal fleeing the local authorities!

Another ten minutes of haggling and an extra thirty guinay convinced him. In minutes, *Bazzaka*'s engines had coughed and sputtered to uncertain life, the owner's assistant had cast off the fore and aft lines, and the boat was lumbering into the harbor.

Out past the moles, north past Cape Malabata with its lonely lighthouse, then east along the coast, *Bazzaka* chugged at a slow but steady pace. El-Sikkin stood for a time on the cruiser's afterdeck, watching the shoreline. After a time, however, he walked forward into the covered pilothouse, where the owner, a snaggletoothed, leather-skinned man in his fifties named Mohammed Kerim, stood at the wheel.

"Just how fast can this old tub run?" he asked.

"Oh, she's fast enough, Allah willing," Kerim replied with a shrug. "Why? Are you in a hurry?"

El-Sikkin glanced around at the horizon. They were well clear of the Tangier moles now; the Malabata light was a tiny, erect finger against the gray shore astern.

Now was the time.

Smoothly drawing the Beretta, he showed it to Kerim, then aimed it at Kerim's assistant. "Yes," he said. "As a matter of fact I am. Alter course for Gibraltar."

The owner's eyes widened. "But . . . that is *forbidden!*"

El-Sikkin gestured with the gun in what he hoped was a frightening manner. He was growing less sure of himself with every passing minute, and he was terrified of losing control completely. "You will obey! Now! Take this scow to Gibraltar as fast as it will go!"

Kerim seemed to consider, then gave another shrug, almost Gallic in its expressiveness. "As Allah wills." He pushed the boat's throttle forward, and the chug of the engines thundered into a stinking, fume-spitting roar. He had to raise his voice to be heard above the noise. "But do not expect to outrun navy gunboats! If they see us on their radar, they could chase us down."

"I will worry about the gunboats!" el-Sikkin replied, forcing his chest out with pride and, he hoped, a believable touch of swagger. "You get us to Gibraltar, and all will be well!"

Five minutes later, el-Sikkin was indeed worried about the gunboats . . . two of them in particular that had appeared astern in the direction of Tangier and were chasing after the *Bazzaka* at full speed, white foam spreading from their knife-edged bows like mustaches. A flicker of light winked once on the prow of one of them, and el-Sikkin wondered if the craft was signaling. Seconds later, a waterspout geysered into the sky a dozen meters to starboard, drenching the cabin cruiser with spray and sending a shudder rumbling through her wooden deck.

"By Allah!" he screamed above the roar. "Can you go faster?"

For answer, Kerim shook his head sharply, his shoulders hunched against the spray, his hands clenched to the cruiser's wheel. A second explosion thundered in the water astern. "We are going all out now," he yelled back. "There is nothing to be done now but surrender!" He reached for the throttle.

"No!" el-Sikkin screamed, desperation clawing at his throat. They were less than halfway across the strait; the Rock of Gibraltar was still a gray, pyramidal blur in the haze ahead. "No! We go on!"

The patrol boats were visibly drawing closer.

**Strait of Gibraltar**
**April 23, 1235 hours**

The cliff of the Gibraltar falls was well behind them now as they rounded Point Marroqui and began angling northwest, toward Cape Trafalgar. With the force of the Gibraltar current lessening, Gray had given the order to return to devils two—two hundred feet—for the final leg of their return to Rota.

"Blue Two to Blue One," Young called over the tactical channel. "Hey, Skipper. What do you make of the sonar trace? On a bearing of, call it one-seven-oh."

Gray studied his main console display screen, which had been set to give a visual readout of all sounds picked up by the fighter sub's sonar. After studying the murky array of V-shaped lines for a moment and listening to the accompanying, churring roar, he shook his head.

"Blue Flight, Blue One. I think we're picking up at least three vessels here. Designate target one as Alfa. I make it a small vessel, possibly a pleasure craft, twin screws at high speed. I've got two more targets, designated Bravo and Charlie. They're farther off. My war book is suggesting Spanish Lazaga class."

"Roger that," Young said. "I confirm. It sounds like the Lazagas are overhauling Alfa."

A sudden, deep-throated boom echoed through the water.

"What was that?" Douglas cried.

"Gunfire," Young answered. "That was a shell exploding in the water."

"A shot across the bow, maybe?" Oz wondered.

"What the hell are Spanish patrol boats doing this far into the strait?" Douglas asked. "It looks to me like they're well into Moroccan waters."

Gray called up additional data from his war book, rapidly scanning the three-view schematics and columns of data appearing on his main display. Lazaga-class patrol boats were about 190 feet long and massed 303 tons each. They could hit twenty-nine knots on twin diesels, and each carried a crew of forty-one. Armament included four Exocet antiship missiles, antiaircraft weapons, and a 76mm OTO Melara cannon mounted in a turret on the forward deck.

"The Spanish sold four Lazagas to Morocco back in the early eighties," Gray pointed out, reading the war book entry. "These two are probably Moroccan boats. They could be chasing smugglers."

Another dull boom sounded through the water, and then another.

"Hey, Skipper. Can you plot Alfa's route yet?"

Gray was already doing just that, having his SFV-4's computer draw in the location and projected course of the smaller vessel on a map of the strait.

"Gibraltar," he said. "Looks like they're making a break for Algeciras Bay."

Gray's mind was racing. His patrol orders gave him considerable latitude but basically boiled down to sneak-and-peek: patrol the area, keep eyes and ears open, but don't give yourself away. Those two oncoming patrol boats had downright primitive sonar gear, if they had any sonar at all, and posed no threat at all to Gray's tiny command. In any case, they were after the smuggler, not Blue Flight.

And yet . . .

He decided that he very much wanted a better look at what was going on up there. If the small boat they were tracking was indeed a smuggler, their best move would have been to put in at one of the small coves or fishing villages along the Moroccan coast, probably at Ksar-es-Seghir, which was closest. It sounded like they weren't pushing more than eighteen, maybe twenty knots, which meant sooner or later the bigger patrol boats would run them down, or at least get close enough to smash them to toothpicks with naval gunfire. Why the hell were they running for the European side of the strait?

Besides, the inactivity, the long and boring hours of silent cruising, recording tankers and freighters without even a trace of UIR submarines, was wearing at him. This incident, at least, offered a chance for some excitement.

"Blue Two, Blue Four," he called. "Stay at depth. Blue Three, you're with me."

"Roger, Blue One," Oz called back. "Where we heading, Skipper?"

"Up to the roof," Gray said. "I want to have a look around."

Pulling back on his control joystick with one hand, he brought the SFV's nose up, while with the other hand he increased the thrust of the fighter sub's MHD jets.

Flying through the water, the two stub-winged vessels rose swiftly through the emerald sea.

### UIR Patrol Boat *Commandant Azouggarh*
### April 23, 1241 hours

The *Commandant Azouggarh*, hull number 307, surged ahead through the choppy waters of the strait at top speed, sending spray slashing across the foredeck and splattering across the bridge windows like a heavy rain. Her commanding officer, *Qayid* Ali Fahim, ordered the windscreen wipers switched on so he could see. Peering past the back-and-forth sweep of the wiper blades, he raised his binoculars to his eyes and tried to make out the distant cabin cruiser. It wavered in his vision, sometimes vanishing as it slid into the trough of a wave.

"Range to target!" he snapped. "Bearing and speed!"

"Range fifteen kilometers!" the bridge radar operator replied. "Bearing zero-four-five, speed eighteen knots."

"A stern chase is a long chase" held an adage as ancient as war at sea. Given the relative speed of the two patrol boats and the fugitive cabin cruiser out of Tangier, it would take the better part of an hour to close that range of nine miles, and by that time the target could be well inside Spanish waters. They'd already changed course, he saw, coming left off of a straight heading for Gibraltar and angling to the north, toward the nearest point of the Spanish coast. That, Fahim saw, would put them ashore somewhere in the vicinity of Tarifa.

Fortunately, he didn't need to close the gap—only stop them. *Commandant Azouggarh*'s Italian-made OTO Melara cannon, widely respected as one of the finest naval cannons made, had a sixteen-kilometer range. Each 6.5-kilogram shell had a warhead of 630 grams of cast Compound Three explosive, plus over four thousand .2-gram tungsten spheres. A hit anywhere near that cabin cruiser would shred its thin hull and leave it a leaking, riddled hulk.

And Fahim's orders had been explicit, relayed from Tangier Naval Command with a Priority Red flash seconds after he'd sighted the small craft on radar and reported it: stop the defectors at all cost.

"Continue firing, *Mlazim*," he said, addressing *Azouggarh*'s weapons officer. "Continue firing until the target is destroyed."

A flat crack from starboard caught his attention. *Azouggarh*'s consort, the *Commandant Al Khattabi*, had just joined the action. The other patrol boat was plowing through the strait, her sharply raked prow like the tip of a thrusting sword. It was a contest now to see which of the Islamic warships scored the kill.

*Crack-crack-crack!* Empty brass cartridges danced and sparkled on the forward deck as *Azouggarh*'s turret began slamming rounds toward the distant target at a rate of better than one per second. Gouts of water were rising now around the fleeing target.

The action would not last more than a very few seconds more.

# CHAPTER
## 8

**The** *Bazzaka*
**April 23, 1242 hours**

Abd el-Sikkin had never known such terror. The rounds from the pursuing patrol boats were falling around the *Bazzaka* one after another in a deadly rain of spray and high explosives. At first, he thought their attackers were toying with them, dropping a shell to the left, another to the right, a third in their wake seconds after they'd raced across that patch of sea, trying to frighten them into surrender.

Most of the rounds missed by a wide margin, however, a result of poor marksmanship against a difficult target at extreme range. The two patrol boats were still a long way off—ten or twelve kilometers, el-Sikkin guessed—and they were plunging through the rough water as wildly as was the twelve-meter *Bazzaka.*

Realization struck el-Sikkin like a physical blow. They were trying to *kill* him! No adventure, no vengeance was worth this! Wildly, he turned and stared through *Bazzaka*'s windscreen at the northern shore. He could easily make out the Tarifa lighthouse, perhaps eight kilometers away, but they would never make it that far without being blown from the water. Explosions geysered about the boat every second or so, most missing by over thirty meters, but striking nearer and nearer as the patrol boats steadily closed the range.

Reluctantly, he lowered the pistol. "It is enough," he said. "We must stop."

"Thanks be to God," Kerim said. His face was pale, and sweat was standing in beads on his forehead. Spinning the wheel, he turned *Bazzaka* broadside to the patrol boats and yanked back on the throttle. The cruiser's engines sputtered to sudden silence, and she wallowed heavily in the sea. Three fountains of water gouted into the air one after the other twenty meters to starboard. Something struck the boat's hull with a clang like a sounding gong. "We need a white flag!" Kerim shouted. "Abdul! Get one of the sheets from the cabin!"

Kerim's mate vanished down the steps leading to the cruiser's lower-deck quarters, emerging seconds later with a white sheet torn from a bunk. Four more geysers of water thundered ten to twenty meters beyond the pitching boat. Running up a ladder to *Bazzaka*'s flying bridge, the man began waving the sheet wildly over his head.

The gunfire from the patrol boats fell silent almost at once, and reluctantly el-Sikkin handed the Beretta to Kerim. "You can tell them I forced you," he said. He felt sick. Would they simply shoot him when they took him back? Or would they turn him over to the UIR intelligence people for interrogation?

He remembered his glimpse of the American prisoner in Room 401 and shuddered. He wanted to snatch the Beretta back from Kerim. Better to die now, cleanly, than to endure torture. . . .

\*       \*       \*

**Blue Flight**
**April 23, 1245 hours**

As Morgan Gray's Barracuda neared the surface, he could feel the surge of rough seas above him. Even the most powerful storm disturbs only the top few fathoms of water; a hurricane can be raging on the surface, and fifty feet down the storm cannot even be felt.

"Blue One, Blue Three," Franklin called over the laser com channel. "Feels pretty rough up there."

"Roger," Gray replied. "These minisubs weren't designed for heavy seas."

The wave surge of the water seemed magnified by the SFV-4's twenty-four-foot length. Gray felt a queasy turn in his stomach and wondered if he was about to be seasick for the first time in his life.

He forced himself to concentrate on handling the Barracuda. Tapping touch-sensitive rectangles on the slick, black surface of his programmable instrument console, he opened up a large, central display screen and keyed it to his sail camera.

The SFV-4 Barracuda was designed for underwater work, not for operations on the surface. The ULTRA-C and SUBVIEW imaging systems would work imperfectly, if at all, in the open air, and the rounded canopy enclosing the upper half of his cockpit was completely opaque, no windows, no transparencies to give him a view outside. Since surface ships could be more than adequately tracked for targeting purposes by sonar and by ULTRA-C, he didn't even have a periscope.

However, even for minisubs designed for deep-sea operations, there are always going to be times when it is necessary to maneuver on the surface, and for that the pilot needs to see what he is doing. His cockpit console was programmable; by keying selections on a computer menu, he could designate specific areas as multifunction displays, or MFDs. He enlarged his primary MFD and set it for TV imaging. His sail camera—actually mounted within the streamlined electronics pod affixed to the top of the SFV-4's vertical stabilizer—gave him a wide-angle television picture of his surroundings from a vantage point a yard above and behind his canopy. At the moment, his stabilizer was still underwater, and when he switched on the camera, all he saw on the MFD was a boiling confusion of green light and foam.

"Blue One, Blue Three," Oz called. "It sounds like the gunfire has stopped."

"Affirmative," Gray replied. He pushed the joystick controlling his engine thrust forward, feeling the throb of the sub's pulse jet engines increase. "Hold your position, Oz. I'm going to break the surface for a quick look around."

He could feel it when his stabilizer emerged from the water. A shudder passed through his craft, and the wake at the surface created additional drag that slowed the SFV-4 despite the added engine power. On his monitor screen, seawater streamed off the camera in a wet blur, and then the monitor cleared and he could make out blue sky, green water, and a distant gray jaggedness in between that must be the Spanish coast.

The seas were running at about three feet, he decided. Each wave carried the Barracuda up to its crest, balanced it there for a moment, then dropped it a yard into the following trough. Fortunately, his initial queasiness had vanished. He brought his directional joystick over to starboard, turning the fighter sub to face the last-calculated heading of target Alfa. He should be pretty close at this point, less than a kilometer or two.

There it was! Almost straight east, and at a range of five hundred yards. He touched a control on his console and engaged the camera's telephoto lens, zooming in on the cabin cruiser. It didn't appear damaged, but it was wallowing heavily in the three-foot seas. It looked like a typical pleasure craft with an open deck aft and a two-tiered superstructure—a lower pilot house-cabin and an upper, open flying bridge. Someone was standing on the flying bridge, waving what looked like a white bed sheet.

Checking his sonar, Gray got the bearing for targets Bravo and Charlie: one-seven-zero, almost due south. He tracked the sail camera to the right, until the data line across the bottom of the screen indicated the camera was properly aligned.

There they were, two long, lean, shark-deadly gray shapes, racing northeast at high speed. One had the hull number 304, the other was 307. Both were still several miles away, but with the telephoto engaged Gray could make out men on their decks and see the long snouts of their forward OTO Melara naval guns tracking up and down to compensate for the patrol boats' motion through the waves.

Oz was right. The gunfire had stopped.

"Blue One to Blue Flight," Gray called on the laser communications channel. "Looks like we're too late. Target Alfa has just surrendered."

An instant later, yellow flame snapped from the muzzle of the main gun of one of the patrol boats. Quickly switching his camera back to the cabin cruiser, Gray saw the shell explode in the water astern of the helpless craft as the man with the sheet continued to wave it frantically back and forth. A second explosion erupted closer to the cruiser, followed by a third, a fourth . . .

"On second thought," Gray said, "it looks like our UIR friends aren't taking prisoners."

## The *Bazzaka*
## April 23, 1247 hours

The line of geysers started thirty meters astern of the *Bazzaka*, walking in a ragged line directly toward the wallowing boat. The fifth shell in the series struck the flying bridge above the wheelhouse with an ear-splitting roar and a shock that knocked both el-Sikkin and Kerim to their knees. Splinters, wiring, clots of insulation, and shards of glass spilled across the carpeting on the wheelhouse deck as smoke billowed through shattered windows. Despite the smoke, the interior of the pilothouse was now bathed with hazy light, and el-Sikkin realized that a gaping, three-meter hole had been torn through the overhead.

He could hear the crackle of flames somewhere above.

"Fire!" Kerim yelled. On hands and knees, he crawled to a window seat and yanked the seat cushion away. Underneath were several bright orange life jackets. Grabbing one for himself, he tossed another at el-Sikkin. "Take it! Put it on! We've got to get out!"

Another gout of water hissed into the air less than a meter from *Bazzaka*'s side, and el-Sikkin felt the hull lurch as something sledgehammered it beneath the waterline. The cruiser began listing to port.

Blindly, he groped through the smoke aft, coming out from under the shattered pilothouse superstructure and onto the open afterdeck. He was having trouble fastening the unfamiliar straps and buckles of the life jacket and finally compromised by simply looping it unfastened over his shoulders. As he took another step his foot came down on something long, soft, and slippery and he nearly stumbled. Looking down through smoke-tearing eyes, he made out the bloody crook of Abdul's hand and forearm lying on the deck, the fingers still clenching a tattered scrap of sheet.

More shells exploded nearby, sending a wave of green water sloshing over *Bazzaka*'s transom. He looked about wildly for Kerim and couldn't see him. Then he spotted the pilot's head, surrounded by the bright orange collar of his life jacket, in the water a few meters away from the boat.

Clinging to the starboard side railing on the after-deck, he hesitated. He wanted to jump, but he was paralyzed by fear. He was an indifferent swimmer, and the sea about the cruiser had been churned to white froth by wind and shell blast.

Then the deck rose sharply beneath his feet, cata-pulting him into the sky. He screamed, but the sound of his own voice was lost in the volcanic roar of the explosion; orange flame erupted from the cruiser's fuel tanks and the air was filled with whirling bits of debris. *Bazzaka* vanished in the explosion. . . .

**Blue One**
**April 23, 1247 hours**

It was hard to see the cabin cruiser, for the smoke from the first hit had filled the air around the sinking boat with a thick haze of smoke. Then a second shell struck the cruiser's afterdeck and detonated its fuel tank. A huge, yellow fireball erupted on the surface of the sea, followed by a mushroom of pitch-black smoke shot through with tongues of orange flame. Bits of debris rained down across the surface of the sea hundreds of yards from the blast.

The gunfire ceased at once, but the Moroccan patrol boats continued to approach. They would reach the area where the cruiser had been in less than ten minutes.

"The bastards blew them up!" Gray said, incredulous. "They surrendered and the bastards blew them up!"

Turning his camera back to scan the wreck site, he searched the surface for survivors. That boat had been a pleasure craft, unarmed. What had it been smuggling that required its destruction?

The haze of smoke was thinning now, and he could see part of the wreck, the forward part of the hull, turned turtle and settling beneath the waves. As the SFV-4 crested another ocean swell Gray was able to make out what looked like a man's head bobbing on the surface, thirty feet from the wreck.

"Blue Three, this is One," he said. "I see a survivor. I'm closing on him. Maybe I can pick him up."

"I'm right with you, man."

As he increased power the fighter sub rose higher in the water, until the bulbous curve of the canopy broke the surface in a spray of foam. At fifty knots, Gray closed the distance to the wreckage in seconds. He could see the lone swimmer, who was clinging to a six-foot fragment of wood decking. Were there other survivors? Gray could not see them if there were.

As he slowed, the sub began to sink again. The SFV was a heavier-than-water craft, which meant it rose by generating lift with its wings, precisely like a conventional aircraft.

Like an aircraft, then, he could not stop and hover in one place; if he tried it, he would sink like a rock. Nor could he open his canopy to rescue the swimmer. To do so would be to swamp the little vessel with the first wave to break over the hull, and in any case, the cockpit had room only for one.

Still, he could communicate. The SFV had an external speaker hooked to an intercom circuit, a means for the pilot to talk with maintenance personnel before launch but after the canopy was sealed.

The only question was whether or not the swimmer could understand English.

**The Strait of Gibraltar**
**April 23, 1248 hours**

El-Sikkin clung to a piece of floating wreckage, still dazed by the blast that had flung him headlong into the sea. He shouted Kerim's name, but without result. He was alone, and in minutes the Moroccan patrol boats would arrive.

Movement caught his eye, and he tried to blink away the salt water that stung his eyes and blurred his vision. Something was approaching, something tall and thin and light gray in color. At first he thought he was seeing the dorsal fin of some enormous shark and he nearly fainted. Then he noticed the streamlined swelling at the tip of the fin with a glassy eye on the front, and he realized that the thing was man-made.

But what was it?

It passed him, slicing cleanly through the rough sea. The fin, obviously part of something larger, stood a full meter out of the water. Leaning into a gentle curve around him, it accelerated, and part of the larger structure broke the surface, trailing a white wake.

"Hello!" a voice called to him. "You in the water! Can you understand me?"

El-Sikkin blinked. English! Had he just been addressed by a whale, he could not have been more surprised.

"I . . . I understand!" he yelled back, twisting in the water so he could keep facing this extraordinary apparition. A wave slapped him in his face and he choked on seawater. Was he hallucinating? He didn't think so. The sting of salt water in his eyes and on the burns on his legs, back, and shoulders, the sharp pain in his chest where he feared a rib had been broken, were all too real.

"Grab hold if you want me to pull you out of here," the voice told him. "I can't stop, but there are some handholds on the canopy forward, or you can try grabbing the stabilizer. Tell me when you're ready."

Some of the words were strange to el-Sikkin, whose English was not much better than his swimming skills. Handhold? Canopy? Stabilizer?

Still, he thought he understood what the voice was telling him. As the strange craft brushed past him he could see that the thing's hull was not completely smooth, as he'd thought when it had first surfaced. There were finger holes for small access panels.

"Okay!" he yelled back. "I'm ready!"

The fin cut through the waves twenty meters away, circled, then bore down on him again. El-Sikkin swallowed hard, then braced himself. The thing was approaching with terrifying speed, like a sword sweeping toward him through the water.

UIR Patrol Boat *Commandant Azouggarh*
April 23, 1248 hours

"By the Prophet!" *Qayid* Fahim exclaimed, peering through his binoculars. "What is *that?*"

Cutting through the water near the wrecked cruiser, the triangular shape moved with graceful purpose and speed. It looked like the fin of a shark . . . but it was a hellishly big shark, if so. Studying the thing more carefully, though, he could pick out letters painted on its gray side . . . and numbers. . . .

He knew enough English to recognize the letters "USN" and the unit ID number of a U.S. Navy vessel of some kind.

"It is an American submarine!" he snapped. Turning to his weapons officer, he gave a sharp nod. "You may open fire again, *Mlazim.* Now!"

The forward gun barked again.

# CHAPTER
## 9

**T**he round screamed into the sea thirty yards away, detonating with a crash that rang inside Gray's cockpit. He ignored the shudder that passed through the sub fighter's hull, holding the craft dead on course for the swimmer.

If he cut back much below ten knots, he would sink, but if he rammed the man with stabilizer or prow too hard, he would kill him. And there was another problem as well. The Barracuda's gaping water intakes, one on either side below and aft of the cockpit, were large enough to swallow a man. Gray had to time his approach very carefully, cutting his SFV's power at the last moment and letting the fighter sub coast the last few feet on its own momentum before it began to sink.

Another shell struck the sea, fifty feet away. As dangerous as this pickup maneuver was, it had just become far more dangerous. The patrol boats had spotted him and were doing their best to mark him down.

The gentle throb of the SFV's intakes dwindled as

95

the SFV slid past the swimmer. Gray's starboard wing slipped beneath the man's legs, and then the swimmer reached up and grabbed an access handle recessed into the Barracuda's side just below the canopy seal. The handle was an emergency canopy release, but Gray had already disarmed the mechanism. Pushing the throttle forward again, Gray accelerated the SFV through the water, the swimmer clinging to its starboard hull like a remora on the side of a shark.

Another detonation, this one painfully close. The shock wave rolled the Barracuda heavily to port, and the rescued swimmer almost lost his hold.

Blue Flight had orders not to be conspicuous, but their orders also allowed them to shoot back in self-defense. "Oz! Monk! Douglas!" Gray yelled over the laser circuit. "Weapons free! Weapons free! Get these people off my back!"

## Blue Three
## April 22, 1248 hours

"Roger that, Skipper," Oz called. "I'm on 'em!"

Franklin had been circling at fifty feet, watching the situation unfold through his SUBVIEW display. He'd already positioned himself between the cabin cruiser and the approaching patrol boats, and so he was closer to them than the rest of Blue Flight by a large margin.

The Moroccan patrol craft were still too distant to register visually, but he had a strong fix on them through his Barracuda's sonar as their props churned the water. In his helmet phones, they sounded like a pair of freight trains, barreling down on him at full throttle. The SFV's computer had pinpointed both targets, plotting them as red diamonds glowing against his all-round canopy display.

He brought his helm over and pushed his throttle to full power. The Barracuda accelerated, sluggishly at first, then faster and faster, until it was tearing through the water at eighty knots.

Oz Franklin's SFV was armed with a pair of Mark 62 torpedoes, slung from pylons mounted beneath either wing. More like an aircraft's Sidewinder missile than a traditional torpedo, the Mark 62 was one foot thick and twelve long, needle slim, and driven by a rocket motor burning liquid oxygen and hydrogen that could push it through the water at speeds in excess of one hundred knots. Its three disadvantages were reach, warhead, and noise. Its range was less than one mile—point-blank by the standards of modern submarine warfare—and its warhead was limited to an eighty-pound shaped charge, considerably smaller than the big, ship-killer torps carried aboard full-sized subs. More dangerous still in warfare that depended on stealth, the Mark 62 was extremely noisy, its rocket engine creating a shrill sound like ripping cloth that could be heard for miles underwater.

The Moroccan patrol boats were now four miles distant. At eighty knots, it would take Oz another two minutes to get his SFV in range.

The thunder of the enemy's naval guns rumbled through the water.

## Blue One
## April 23, 1250 hours

As far back as World War II, submarines had been used to rescue downed pilots in the water, but never

had such a pickup been tried with so small a craft.
For the first minute or two, the swimmer had clung to
the disconnected canopy release, but it was clear
from the view on Gray's monitor that he was having
trouble keeping his head above the blast of spray and
wake coming off the SFV's blunt bow.

Gray toggled a switch, and his DS-41 antenna tele-
scoped into the air from the Barracuda's back just
behind the canopy. The DS-41 was an emergency
radio, intended as a distress beacon if the SFV's pilot
was forced to eject the sealed cockpit compartment
from the rest of the craft, ending up bobbing on the
surface awaiting rescue. Now the yard-tall antenna,
normally hidden inside the hull, served as a handhold, allowing the swimmer to straddle the fighter
sub's dorsal spine just ahead of the stabilizer and
hang on with his head well above the white boiling
water.

A trio of explosions fountained off to the right as
the patrol boats tried to get the range. Gray felt blind
and helpless. He could hear the blasts and feel them
as the shock waves slapped the hull of his boat, but
with his ULTRA-C laser and imaging sonars clear of
the water, the interior of his canopy remained blank.
It was like flying blind in a fighter at night or in a
storm. He had to rely on his instruments, and on the
single television image on his primary MFD.

Another explosion, this one to the left, and close.
He battled the controls of his sub fighter, but he was
now more concerned about its low-speed surface handling than he was about enemy fire. The Barracuda
was designed for operating at depth. It didn't handle
well at the surface, especially in rough seas, and from
moment to moment there was danger that the swimmer he'd plucked from the water would lose his grip

and be lost. The rescued man was not wearing a life
jacket. The cabin cruiser's explosion had torn his
clothes to rags, and through his sail camera, which
now showed the back of the man's head and shoulders in the lower part of the screen, Gray could see
the red welts of savage burns, and it looked like he
was trembling as he clung with both arms to the DS-
41 antenna. The guy was obviously weak from shock
and pain.

Desperately, Gray fought to balance the protesting
SFV's speed slow enough to keep from tearing the
swimmer from his insecure life grip, yet fast enough
to keep the minisub on the surface.

In the next few minutes, he learned a very great
deal about the hydrodynamics of the SFV-4B.

## Blue Three
## April 23, 1251 hours

Oz Franklin touched a succession of computer-generated touch points on his console, engaging his
weapons system. The red diamonds of the two targets,
Bravo and Charlie, flicked to circles, each accompanied by a data tag that gave its bearing, range, and
speed.

"SUBVIEW, targeting!" he called aloud. "Target
Bravo!"

The Barracuda's computer responded to his voice,
and a targeting reticle winked on, bracketing the
nearer patrol boat. The range was now two thousand
yards—just a bit more than a mile. He touched the
controls that armed both torpedoes.

On one of his cockpit multifunction displays, a line
winked on and off: WEAPONS ARMED.

"Target lock!" Franklin ordered. "Acoustical!"

TARGET LOCK: B. ACOUSTICAL HOMING. READY.

"Fire one!"

His Barracuda shuddered and gave an upward lurch as the Mark 62 slid from its pylon and screeched into the emerald fog ahead. Franklin could see it on his canopy display, rendered by SUBVIEW as a black needle trailing a blurred contrail of sound. It looked exactly like a Sidewinder missile launched from a fighter.

"SUBVIEW targeting!" he called. "Target Charlie!"

On his canopy display, the targeting reticle shifted to the second ship. He could just make out the shape of the hull now, a long, knife-lean shadow cutting toward him high in the gloom.

"Target lock! Acoustical!"

TARGET LOCK: C. ACOUSTICAL HOMING. READY.

"Fire two!"

His second Mark 62 screamed into the water. "Fox One! Fox One!" he called, the aviator's warning that missiles had been launched.

Weaponless, now, Oz put his fighter sub into a hard, fast bank to port.

**Blue One**
**April 23, 1252 hours**

For Morgan Gray, it had become a do-or-die battle to get this stranger safely ashore, if only because those Moroccan patrol boats so obviously wanted him dead. Since he couldn't exceed about ten knots without losing his passenger, the UIR craft would overtake him in another few minutes.

His only hope was that Franklin, Young, and

Douglas could run interference for him. He was frustrated by not being able to *see* the battle taking place behind him. Until the invention of ULTRA-C and SUBVIEW, modern submarine combat had always been a kind of high-tech blindman's buff, with the sub able to "see" its opponents only through the fuzzy patterns and vague echoes of sonar. Gray, trained in air combat maneuvers in high-performance jet aircraft, was used to *seeing* the enemy, even if as nothing more than a black speck miles away. Wallowing along on the surface, unable to see his pursuers, he thought he had at least a hint of the claustrophobic terror of classical submarine combat.

"Blue Three, Blue One," he called. "Oz, was that you launching?"

"Affirmative," Oz's voice came back on the laser com. "That's two birds on the way."

"Get the hell out of there, then."

"Way ahead of you, Skipper."

"Blue One, this is Blue Two," Young reported. "I'm with Blue Four about two miles from the bandits, Skipper. We'll be in range in less than a minute."

"Roger that."

Another round shrieked over the fighter sub low enough that he could hear it through his sealed canopy. It struck the sea twenty yards dead ahead. His sub bucked as it hit the shock wave, and his MFD showed a cascade of white water. His passenger rode out the tidal wave, head and shoulders hunched down against the onslaught. Another near miss like that and the rescued swimmer would be swept away.

And those Moroccan gunboats were getting too damned close for Gray to circle back for another rescue.

\*          \*          \*

**The Strait of Gibraltar**
**April 23, 1252 hours**

Franklin's first torpedo, running several hundred yards ahead of the second one, was set for passive acoustical homing, meaning its tiny, electronic brain was locked onto the propeller sounds generated by Target Bravo. Morocco's Lazaga-class patrol boats, designed to operate against surface targets, carried neither active nor passive sonar, and so no one aboard heard the first Mark 62 as it screamed in from the northwest and slammed into the hull of the *Commandant Al Khattabi*, some ten feet forward of the vessel's stern.

Eighty pounds of high explosive detonated with a sharp crack. Unfortunately, the torp had come in at a sharp angle, and the shaped-charge warhead wasted much of the blast's effect along the hull rather than into it. The detonation tore a three-foot gash beneath the waterline, sending water pouring into the *Al Khattabi*'s number-one engine compartment, but the hit was far from fatal. Her captain ordered the port engine shut down and the engine compartment evacuated and sealed. There would be power enough to maneuver on the starboard shaft alone, even if the vessel's speed would be sharply reduced.

Unfortunately for the *Al Khattabi*, the detonation had created a thunderclap of sound ballooning out from the stricken patrol boat like a huge bubble. The explosion momentarily deafened the passive sonar ear on Franklin's second torpedo, breaking its lock on target Charlie—Fahim's *Commandant Azouggarh*.

For several seconds, the torpedo arrowed blindly through the water, and then its onboard computer began seeking to reacquire a target lock. The roar of the first explosion had filled the sea with a hissing wall of white noise. Switching from passive to active homing, the Mark 62 sent out a high-frequency pulse of sound, a shrill chirp that struck both Moroccan patrol boats and echoed back, bearing precise information on range and bearing.

With a machine's indifference, the torpedo's brain chose the closer of the two returns. Its stabilizers and trim tabs shifted, swinging the hurtling undersea missile onto a new course as it continued to ping on the now listing hull of the *Al Khattabi.*

The second torpedo slammed into the Moroccan gunboat amidships and not far from the keel. The explosion lifted the three-hundred-ton craft in the water and then dropped her, her back broken. Already listing slightly to port from the flooding aft, the *Al Khattabi* quickly settled in the water. A green wave washed over her stern, staggering her, thundering through open vents and hatches in the deck. Her captain ordered all stop, and then, with a last, wild look around, he gave the order to abandon ship.

Three minutes later, as her crew leaped from the railings of the quickly settling rail craft, the *Al Khattabi* rolled far onto her port beam. Fuel oil and gasoline fumes leaking into engine spaces already half-filled with water compressed, then exploded at the touch of a spark or a piece of hot machinery. Flame engulfed the boat aft of her single funnel, and a moment later, the Exocet ship killers stored in their launch racks aft added their warheads to the thunder and destruction.

*        *        *

**UIR Patrol Boat** *Commandant Azouggarh*
**April 23, 1255 hours**

*Qayid* Fahim had slowed his vessel the moment the first torpedo had struck his sister ship, but he ordered full speed now. "Hard starboard!" he yelled. "Bring us about to one-eight-zero! Now!"

Flame boiled high into the sky as the *Al Khattabi* exploded, rattling marble-sized bits of metal off the *Azouggarh*'s bridge windscreens and superstructure.

A submarine had just put two torpedoes into the *Al Khattabi*. Chances were the unseen attacker was already lining up on his *Azouggarh*, might already have torpedoes in the water and streaking toward his boat.

Fahim was a brave and dedicated naval officer, but there were limits. His orders had been passed to him by the UIR Naval Command Headquarters in Rabat, but Fahim was a Moroccan first, a UIR officer second. He would not jeopardize his command to the whim of a foreigner, even a foreigner in the gold braid and epaulets of an admiral in the UIR.

Worse, his radar operator had just picked up three surface targets, eight miles away and racing toward the battleground of the Gibraltar Strait. They looked like American frigates.

No defector was worth the death of his crew or the destruction of his vessel. The UIR might command his loyalty, but it could never command his fanaticism, nor could it wipe away his responsibility for the lives and well-being of the forty-one men aboard.

His forward gun hurled two more shells at the half-visible American submarine, now less than three miles away, then fell silent. At thirty knots, the *Commandant Azouggarh* raced south for the safety of Tangier.

Behind him, the forward half of the *Al Khattabi* continued to float in a sea turned to flame by a surface scum of burning diesel fuel. Her crew struggled into lifeboats or clung to wreckage as wind and current set them drifting slowly toward the mouth of the Mediterranean.

Three miles to the north, the mysterious American submarine altered course for the approaching enemy frigates.

**Blue One**
**April 23, 1256 hours**

"Blue Flight, this is Blue One," Gray called. "Break off, break off!"

"Blue One, Blue Two. Damn it, Skipper, we're in range! A perfect shot!"

Gray sighed. They'd been lucky so far. One of their two pursuers was settling now by the stern in a sheet of orange flame, the other racing toward the southern horizon at thirty knots. It was tempting to have Young and Douglas pop another couple of fish into the Moroccan gunboat, but such a demonstration would serve no purpose. Other Moroccan military units would have been alerted by the gunboats. Air units or other, larger warships could be on the way from Tangier at this moment.

Better to break off the action now and escape to the north with their drowned-rat prize.

His sonar had detected the approach of three ships from the northeast. His computer identified them as two Perry-class FFGs, guided-missile frigates, and a DDG, a guided-missile destroyer. Gray slammed a flare into his cockpit launcher set into the canopy above and behind his head, locked the breech, and stabbed the firing button. There was a thump, and a red flare arced high and dazzling through the Gibraltar skies. That would get their attention.

"Negative, Blue Flight," he said, answering Young's angry protest. "The cavalry's on the way. Abort your attack and rendezvous with me."

"Roger that, Skipper." Young sounded disappointed. "We're coming in."

But he wondered if they would meet again, his squadron and this sleek, Moroccan greyhound of a patrol boat with a captain who pressed the attack on an unarmed vessel that had already surrendered.

As Gray opened a radio channel with the approaching American ships, he hoped very much that they would.

# CHAPTER
## 10

**Blue One**
**April 23, 1315 hours**

The exhausted Moroccan lost his hold on the radio mast twice in the next few minutes, but both times Gray was able to circle the SFV tightly, bringing the craft again into line with the drifting, semiconscious man and pick him up. Once, the man slipped away underwater and began sinking, too weak even to try to reach the surface again.

Gray submerged, unwilling to lose him now that he'd brought the wreck survivor this far. Underwater, the minisub's SUBVIEW worked again, displaying the silvery-green radiance of the sea's surface from just below the waves. He could see the Moroccan drifting slowly deeper, a stream of bubbles streaming from his mouth. Gently, Gray steered the SFV's blunt nose under his body and propelled him back to the surface, like a dolphin protecting a drowning swimmer.

The U.S.S. *Kauffman*, FFG 59, came alongside minutes later, members of her crew leaning over her starboard railing as they stared down at the drama taking place in the water below. A couple of sailors hurled life preservers into the sea, then jumped in after them. In moments, they were helping the half-drowned man from the sunken cabin cruiser toward their ship.

Gray released a long, heartfelt sigh of relief as his charge was taken off his hands. As he dove back to a comfortable depth, formed up with the other three fighter subs, and outraced the American skimmers toward Rota, he hoped the rescue had been worth the risk. If this Moroccan turned out to be a North African drug smuggler or fleeing criminal, Gray was going to have a problem justifying his effort to save the man to Captain Maxwell. Hell, he was going to have trouble if the rescued swimmer was the Mahdi himself. Gray had managed to put his fighter sub at a serious disadvantage in a fight unwarranted save for the potential intelligence value of the man off the cabin cruiser. In war, the value of an individual life could rarely, if ever, be taken into consideration.

He just hoped the guy was worth it.

The rescue had been possible at all only because the American fighter subs had held one important technical advantage—their ULTRA-C tracking and communications gear, and the SUBVIEW imaging system.

It was a damned good thing, Gray thought, that the enemy had nothing like the new American systems, he thought. If they had, if they'd even possessed simple sonar, the short, sharp skirmish might have had a very different ending.

Perhaps the one advantage the Americans had in this as yet undeclared war with the UIR and their Japanese backers was SUBVIEW, which made vessels like the SFV possible.

How long would it be, he wondered, before the Japanese were able to field something similar? When they did, the American advantage would be ended, and U.S. submarine forces would find themselves fighting for their lives.

## Imperial Navy Submarine *Teigei*
## The Indian Ocean
## April 23, 1415 hours (Time zone Zulu +5)

*Taisa* Komei Tanaka was adrift in wonder. The ocean opened up around him with astounding blue-green clarity, revealing glory upon glory as the huge submarine drove ahead through the depths. The sea was shallow here, less than five hundred meters as it rose from the abyssal depths of the Indian Ocean's Ceylon Plain toward the island-dotted, north-south stretch of the Chagos-Lacadive Ridge. He could make out the bottom as a roughly convoluted surface of darker blue-on-blue rippling past three hundred meters below; streamlined shapes flitted back and forth at the edge of the imager's resolution, momentarily riding *Teigei*'s bow pressure wave before streaking back toward the surface and air.

Tanaka recognized the shapes as dolphins, though there was no color and not enough detail for him to identify the species. The sight of them cheered him, as they'd cheered countless sailors throughout the ages. For the last hundred kilometers, they'd been *Teigei*'s silent, flashing escorts.

To port and ahead, three hundred meters away, another escort moved with the same majestic grace as Tanaka's command, a shark-lean, dark gray shadow. *Teigei*'s hunter-killer escort, the Tyogei-class attack submarine *Umiryu*, had been on station since they'd left Yokosuka eight days before.

At a depth of nearly two hundred meters there was

not enough sunlight from the surface to illuminate his surroundings. If Tanaka had been using his normal, human vision, the sea would have been an opaque curtain of blackness drawn tightly about the two great vessels, as impenetrable as the eternal night of the Shuhodo caverns near his home city of Yamaguchi. But Tanaka was wearing the *Kabuto-no siranui*, and through its eyes, eternal night was transformed into light.

*Kabuto* meant "helmet," the word drawn from the traditional armor of the samurai warriors of centuries past. *Siranui* was a poetical term applied to the phosphorescent foam in the wake of a ship; literally, the word meant "unknown fires."

This "helmet of the unknown fires" was the electronic interface between Tanaka and *Teigei*'s laser imaging system, a high-tech wonder only recently developed in a joint research-and-development project between Toshiba and MITI's Electro-Technical Laboratories. Sea-penetrating blue-green lasers scanned the surrounding ocean from rotating mounts on *Teigei*'s sail and prow; a powerful Toshiba computer converted reflected laser light into a sophisticated computer simulation of *Teigei*'s surroundings, creating fairly detailed images of objects within two to three kilometers, and displaying graphic symbols and data for more distant targets, out to a range of thirty kilometers or more. Images and data were projected by lenses within the helmet directly into Tanaka's eyes. Seated on *Teigei*'s bridge, wearing the heavy helmet, it was as though he were perched high atop the submarine's sail. The illusion was so perfect he imagined he could feel the rush of cold water past his face.

Tanaka was well aware that the *siranui* imager had

recently been developed in the West as well. Several American submarines were known to use something very much like it, a system called ULTRA-C, including the two monster Typhoons purchased a decade before from the Russians and refitted as mother ships for miniature submarines. Reportedly, their new fighter subs had used it in their defeat of Islamic forces south of Cuba a month before.

Not for the first time, Tanaka wondered whether *siranui* and ULTRA-C had been developed independently, or if one nation's secrets had been stolen from the other. It didn't really matter, of course. No doubt, underwater laser imaging was simply an idea whose time had come; lasers and computer imaging made the development inevitable, and so it was inevitable, perhaps, that the world's two most technically proficient powers would develop it simultaneously.

Like two sumo wrestlers, Japan and the United States were testing one another, crouched on all fours within the sacred ring of straw rope, scowling face-to-face, breathing one another's air. Soon, very soon, the head-to-head collision would come, and only Japan would remain within the ring. America, once great, had allowed her greatness to fade and slip through her fingers. The onetime superpower had lacked the discipline, the cohesiveness, the internal concentration of vision and resources and well-focused drive that distinguished the Japanese as a great people.

Someday, perhaps someday quite soon, the bulky helmet of *Teigei*'s *siranui* display apparatus would be replaced by artificial protein computers, called biochips, micro-organic circuitry implanted within the brain and interfacing directly with the human central nervous system. When such technology became available, Captain Tanaka would not simply command the *Teigei*, he would *be* the monster submarine in every respect, brain and nerves, eyes and heart of a thirty-thousand-ton predator prowling the ocean deeps.

Japan would have that new technology first. Tanaka was certain of that. He took both comfort and great pride in the sure knowledge that Japan had the clear lead in the advanced technology that spelled superiority in war. The orbital weapons that had brought the United States to her knees in the Persian Gulf four years before were but one example. The great irony was that the space-based military system had been drawn from America's own dreams, the vaunted "Star Wars" defense system proposed just twenty years earlier. As the Americans had become more and more divided internally they'd abandoned space and the technology that had gotten them there.

Japan had simply picked up the torch the Americans had dropped. Tokyo's Ministry of International Trade and Industry, the government-subsidized research complex known to the West as MITI, was widely acknowledged to be ten to twenty years ahead of the United States in most areas, including laser physics, computer technology, and energy storage. There were some high-tech surprises hidden away within *Teigei*'s massive hull that would certainly come as a nasty shock to the Americans, if and when open conflict came. If it was fated that *Teigei* was to meet the American Typhoon somewhere ahead in the ocean deeps, *Teigei* was certain to emerge the victor.

"Captain Tanaka?"

The voice seemed remote, muffled by the helmet. He glanced at the data readout line superimposed across the top of his private window on the ocean and was surprised to note the time. It was so easy to become lost in this wonder world that comprised seven-tenths of the world's surface.

Carefully, with hands that felt disembodied, Tanaka unfastened the harness that secured the *kabu-to-no siranui* on his head. With a soundless pop, the vision of the undersea world vanished, and he blinked against the harsh, fluorescent lighting of *Teigei*'s control room. His First Officer, *Chusa* Isamu Matsushita, ever-formal and correct in his spotless navy whites, gave a formal bow. "Sir. Please excuse the interruption. But we have reached Point Hatukari."

*Hatukari*: the poem-name for the season's first flight of the wild goose. It designated a featureless point in the Indian Ocean, southwest of India and astride the equator, where *Teigei*'s orders had been left to his personal interpretation. And now it was time to decide.

*Teigei*'s destination was the UIR's great fleet anchorage at Alexandria. Her mission called upon her simply to show support for Japan's Islamic allies in their escalating struggle with America, but Tanaka had considerable latitude in how he carried out his orders. He had a choice, too, in his route to Alexandria—up the Red Sea to the Suez Canal, or the long way around, southwest past the Cape of Good Hope, up the western coast of Africa, and into the Mediterranean through the Strait of Gibraltar.

The southern route would almost exactly double the length of the voyage, twenty-three days as opposed to twelve, but the extra eleven days could purchase a valuable advantage: secrecy. Israel remained a powerful enemy of the UIR despite her isolation in the eastern Mediterranean. The small

Israeli navy included six diesel submarines, and at least two patrolled the Red Sea from their base at Eilat. Between the submarines and the Israelis' numerous patrol boats and corvettes, *Teigei* was almost certain to be spotted. Even if the Jews missed the two Japanese subs, there would be numerous unfriendly eyes, both in the wastes of the Sinai and in space overhead, to record their passage of the shallow Suez Canal.

And Tanaka wanted to preserve the secret of *Teigei*'s presence in the Mediterranean for as long as possible. He had no doubt at all that his small flotilla would soon be engaged with the Americans. The firestorm of words and threats sweeping between Washington and Cairo had gone too far to be contained, and with the clash at Cienfuegos, open warfare had begun that would swiftly engulf not only the United States and the UIR, but their allies as well. World war was inevitable.

But a delay in that final confrontation, however, would allow the situation between Washington and his own government to be clarified. It would allow Tanaka to choose his own battleground, his own time of attack. If there was to be war, he wanted to begin it on ground of his choosing, making the best possible use of his technological superiority.

Tanaka turned his attention back to his waiting first officer. "Thank you, *Chusa-san*," he said. "We will take the southern route."

Matsushita's dark eyes were veiled, expressionless. "The Cape of Good Hope."

Tanaka knew the man's preference for the quicker route. Matsushita was a blunt, direct man, eager to come to grips with the enemy, *any* enemy, and the sooner the better.

"*Hai, Chusa-san.* Come to two-five-zero. Maintain depth and speed. Please pass the order to *Umiryu,* please."

He watched for several minutes, assuring himself that everything in the control room was routine, running smoothly. At the forward end of the long, broad compartment, helmsman and planesman sat side by side, hands on the console joysticks that steered the mammoth submarine. Above their heads, a large television monitor recreated the *siranui* panorama ahead, shades of blue and green rushing past *Teigei*'s blunt prow. Matsushita barked an order, and the helmsman put his stick over to the left, keeping his eyes on the digital compass readout on his console. Ponderously, *Teigei* swung to port, coming onto the new heading.

Yes, Matsushita, the order means an additional eleven days locked away in this Great Whale's belly, out of sight of the sun, Tanaka thought. But it gives us more time to assess the American enemy. I will not underestimate this foe, as so many others have.

Side by side, the two Japanese navy subs sped southwest through the black-emerald depths.

## U.S. Naval Base, Rota, Spain
## April 23, 1630 hours

Gray stood at attention in Maxwell's office. "'Keep a low profile,' I said." Maxwell glowered from behind his desk. "A *low* profile! So what do you do? You surface in the middle of a gun duel, rescue a foreign national under the noses of possibly hostile warships, then *sink* one of those warships when it fires on you! Is that your idea of keeping a low profile, Commander Gray?"

"No, sir. But it did seem like the thing to do at the time."

Maxwell sighed. "Technically, Commander, the United States is not presently at war with the United Islamic Republic. Were you aware of that? Or did you perhaps take it upon yourself to declare war on the Islamics, on your own authority? Possibly you are operating under special orders that I haven't seen? Something from the President, perhaps?"

"No, sir."

"I am aware that the Pentagon regards the current situation as a kind of cold war, an undeclared war, if you like, with the UIR. There are no battles and no casualties. Only . . . incidents."

"Some of those *incidents* still cost lives, Captain." He was thinking of Dominico and Seegar.

"Perhaps. But I will have no more incidents created by officers under my command. Is that understood?"

"Perfectly, sir."

"Good." Maxwell leaned back in his chair, rubbing his chin with one hand. "Just so we understand each other. I'd hate to have to relieve you just when I need you for a big op." He gestured toward a chair. "Lecture over. Relax. Have a seat."

"Thank you, sir. Uh, 'big op'?"

"Actually, it's damned hard to fault you on this one, Gray," Maxwell went on, as if Gray hadn't spoken. "Considering the fact that that Moroccan you fished out of the sea today turned out to be a real prize."

This was the first Gray had heard about the man he'd rescued. "He knew something, sir?"

"I'd say so. Until he defected to us, he was a civilian clerk inside the UIR Command Headquarters outside Tangier. Turns out he knows a fair amount about Islamic troop deployments, weapons emplacements, that sort of thing."

Gray whistled. "Lucky thing we found him, then."

"It's better than that, Commander. Your Moroccan friend saw at least one of your men with his own eyes, there in the headquarters building. Turns out he knows exactly where Dominico and Seegar are being held."

Gray's eyes widened. He felt his heart beating harder. His men! But he hardly dared hope . . .

"And to ease your mind," Maxwell went on, "yes, we're going in after them." He smiled. "You see, I'm not afraid of causing a few incidents of my own. At least, not when the Chiefs of Staff authorize it!"

"When, sir?"

"Tonight."

"That's damned short notice."

"Has to be. We're already running a hell of a risk that someone over there realizes that our friend knew about Seegar and Dominico when he defected, and moves them someplace where we can't get at them."

"I understand, sir."

"I hope so. Because you and your people are going to be in on this."

Gray blinked, then grinned. "I was kind of hoping that would be the case, Captain. I, ah, noticed the SEALs coming in yesterday. I imagine they'll be the shooters, right? But they'll need someone riding shotgun off the beach."

Maxwell nodded. "We still have only a fuzzy picture of the other side's naval strength in the area," he said. "The guy you rescued will be able to help pinpoint some of their assets, but there's still a lot of guesswork involved. SSF-1 will provide escort for the

SEALs to and from the beach. The SEALs have their own means of insertion, but they'll need to keep hostiles away from their operational area. And that, Commander, means you."

"Thank you, Captain." He hesitated, an impish grin tugging at the corner of his mouth. "I trust that an 'incident' or two won't be misconstrued as a declaration of war."

"That, Commander, is up to our superiors. And to the Mahdi. Now get out of here. Round up your people, grab some chow, and meet me in Room 17 at 1830 hours. We'll go over the specifics of your orders with the SEAL team leader then."

"Aye, aye, sir." Gray saluted and left.

Adrenaline pounded through his system. They were mounting an op to get Dom and Cigar out!

The moodiness he'd felt earlier, his anguish at being unable to help his men, had vanished completely. He broke into a trot as he banged through the building's main doors and into the warm light of a Spanish afternoon.

# CHAPTER
## 11

Saadeddin Matar, *al-Qayid min al-Jamahir, al-Mahdi*, President of the United Islamic Republic and Speaker for one billion Muslims, stood in his office on the third floor of Cairo's Presidential Palace, hands clasped behind his back, his hard, dark features flushed with anger. "This happened when, you say?"

Admiral Mohammed Hamada bowed stiffly, the movement causing the rows of medals on his uniform coat to clink loudly, a jarring sound against the usual, oppressive silence of the lush-carpeted office. "Less than two hours ago, *Mahdi*. Word only just arrived."

At Hamada's side, Admiral Abdullah al-Sheikh glanced at his counterpart, then looked away, his hawk's face disdainful.

Matar considered the two admirals for a moment, weighing the suspicion and dislike each felt for the other. The politics of his own position, astride the Muslim world like a colossus, was daily becoming more and more difficult.

Hamada, the president knew, was both Shi'a and

**119**

devout, which meant he almost certainly believed that he, Saadeddin Matar, really *was* the Mahdi, the "hidden Imam," the promised messiah come to restore the lost glory of Islam. Al-Sheikh, on the other hand, was Sunni, a follower of the *Sunna*, the words and deeds of the Prophet, and one who considered Shi'ite fanaticism and saint worship little removed from the hated polytheism of the infidel.

He would have to choose his words carefully. Matar was not a religious man, though he'd found in the firestorm of Islamic fundamentalism the ideal tool for welding together the disparate factions of Islam in the chaotic aftermath of the *Qaumat*, the Great Rising. More than anything else, Matar was a practical man, shrewdly calculating, one who chose his subordinates carefully for the parts they had to play in his grand scheme. Hamada had been handpicked by Matar as commander of the First Fleet precisely because he was Shi'ite and held the loyalty of the thousands of commoner, Shi'ite sailors. His counterpart with the fleet, al-Sheikh, was Sunni, and as such held the respect of the predominantly Sunni officer corps of the navy.

The problem with being a messiah, he told himself, is that you have to be infallible, even in the eyes of those who don't believe in you.

Betraying no emotion, he walked to his large desk and sat down, carefully studying the two men before him. "What measures has General Algosaiba taken?" he asked. Algosaiba was the supreme commander of UIR forces in Morocco. He was also the man in charge of the air and land components of Operation *Janubi-y Saif*, the Southern Sword. He was another Shi'ite, a fanatic who called himself "al-Tariq."

"His forces are now on full alert," al-Sheikh said.

"And he has sent air patrols over the strait. He reports that the sinking of the *Al Khattabi* was almost certainly the work of an American submarine operating out of their base at Rota."

"He is sure of this?"

"According to the general's last report," Hamada said, "he was able to capture several American naval personnel. Submariners, members of a new minisub squadron that has been deployed at Rota. It is possible that the *Al Khattabi* was sunk by these craft."

"American submarines in the Gibraltar Strait," Matar said, thoughtful. It was American submarine forces that had frustrated him the month before at Cienfuegos. "They must be dealt with. Their presence could endanger Southern Sword."

"We could sortie the First Fleet, sir," al-Sheikh pointed out. "Deploy from Alexandria to Tangier and seize control of the strait."

Matar considered this. "I prefer to await the arrival of our . . . friends."

"The Japanese," Hamada said. He spat the word. "*Mahdi*, we must not wait for them. They are not even *ahl al-kitab*. We cannot trust them."

*Ahl al-kitab* translated as "people of the book." The phrase referred to those people—Jews and Christians—who at least believed in the God of Islam even if they had yet to accept the Prophet as His one true messenger.

"It is ironic, my dear Admiral Hamada, is it not?" Matar said with a smile. "Allah's will embraces even the infidel. He has given us this alliance with Tokyo, and who are we to question His gift?"

Hamada's mouth opened, then closed again. Clearly he was not about to challenge the *Mahdi* on a point of theology.

"Indeed, *Mahdi*," Hamada said. "The ways of Allah are mysterious."

"The new Japanese submarines are miracles of technology," Matar continued. "Even if their inventors are blind to the glory of Allah. With Allah's help, we will use them, to our success, and to Allah's glory."

*"Ya sidi, Mahdi!"*

"Transmit my command to General al-Tariq," Matar told Hamada. "He is to maintain vigilance against the Americans, but he is not to move until the First Fleet arrives. With the new Japanese submarines."

With another stiff bow and a military click of the heels of his boots, Hamada turned and hurried from the office. Al-Sheikh remained behind, shifting uncomfortably as his counterpart left.

"Do you dislike my use of the Shi'a's messiah?" he asked the Sunni. He needed this man's loyalty, but the way to al-Sheikh's heart was to make him an accomplice, to take him into his confidence and bolster his ego.

Matar knew the souls of the men he commanded.

"Of course not, Mr. President. If the rabble thinks you to be the Mahdi, then that, too, is a weapon in Allah's hand. Like the promise of Paradise to those who fall in holy battle. No, it is merely the reliability of such men as Hamada and Algosaiba. Their fanaticism can blind them to the realities of war."

He is wondering if my own fanaticism has blinded me, Matar thought. This is his way of searching out my heart.

"We all are fanatics when it comes to our love of Allah," Matar said carefully. "But some men express that devotion in different ways. I value men such as Algosaiba and Hamada, because they value their own lives far less than obedience to me."

Al-Sheikh heard the reprimand in the words, and the challenge. "Sir! I would die for you!"

"I do not doubt that, Abdullah. I would not take you into my confidence if I did not. When the time comes to unsheathe our Southern Sword, it will be Hamada and Algosaiba who overwhelm the enemy with their numbers and with their willingness to die in my cause. But it will be you and those like you who interpret my will with cool heads and reasoned logic. They are my heart, Abdullah . . . but you are my brain. I value both, but I rely most upon you."

"You . . . honor me, my President." He bowed, his own medals clinking against his breast.

"Inform your officers of my intent. The First Fleet will deploy as soon as the Japanese arrive at Alexandria."

"And that will be when?"

"Tokyo has not given us a timetable, unfortunately. I find it unlikely, however, that they would risk their precious *Teigei* in the narrow and shallow waters of the Suez. Likely they are coming the long way around. We can expect them in another two weeks."

"Sir, we could meet them at Gibraltar."

Matar considered this. "No, I think not. We will need to enlist their cooperation in Southern Sword, and for that I will need to speak with their commander. It would not hurt, however, to send a small squadron to Tangier to be certain the American fleet does not impede *Teigei*'s passage. Perhaps two of our Alfas, and some surface ships."

"A squadron is already within a few hours' sail," al-Sheikh said. "At Malta."

"Perfect. You will order them to proceed to Tangier. There, they will be in an ideal position to intercept any aggressive American moves in the strait."

"I will give the order at once, sir."

"Excellent, Abdullah. I know that I can count on you."

At least for now, Matar thought as al-Sheikh saluted and strode from the room. Informants had reported that some Sunnis among the UIR's naval officer corps were unhappy, that they felt that Matar's military moves against the hated Americans had not been strong enough, that the recent operations in the Caribbean should have been better supported, more decisive. Matar had no proof that al-Sheikh was among the disaffected officers, but the man was certainly the key to their continued loyalty. When the time came, he would have to purge the lot of them, and al-Sheikh would almost certainly be among the first to be shot.

In the meantime, putting them into action was the best way to keep them busy. They wouldn't have time for plots or coups if they were happily killing Americans.

And when Southern Sword began, there would be blood enough for anyone.

He touched a control on his desk, and a floor-to-ceiling high-definition monitor covering one wall of the office—a gift from his Japanese allies—switched on. Another keyboard entry, and the screen displayed a map of the United Islamic Republic, a sea of green from the Atlantic to central Asia, with only the tiny, yellow island of Israel to interrupt it.

The United Islamic Republic suffered one serious strategic disadvantage as it struggled to make itself the preeminent global power. Like the long-dead and unlamented Soviet Union, the UIR lacked access to the open ocean. In all of that vast expanse of green revealed on the map, there were no major ports that

were not locked behind the bottlenecks of two strategic choke points: the Red Sea and the Strait of
Gibraltar. To the east, the Red Sea and the Suez
Canal were vulnerable to the Israelis, and until that
particular viper's nest was crushed once and for all,
most UIR naval deployments would be through the
Strait of Gibraltar.

Even if Israel had not been a factor, fleets transiting the Suez Canal and Red Sea debouched on the
Indian Ocean, adding at least a week to their sailing
time to American waters. For operations against the
Americans, again, the Strait of Gibraltar was the preferred route.

But Gibraltar was narrow and exposed, ten miles
wide—half the distance between Dover and Calais—a
congested marine bottleneck open to strikes by the
UIR's western, seafaring enemies, Great Britain, and
most especially, the United States.

Matar thought of General Hassan Algosaiba, the
formidable Tariq. Southern Sword was his idea.
Sometimes, it seemed the tall general really did think
of himself as the legendary Tariq reborn.

In the year 89 of the Hegira—711 A.D. by Western
calendars—the Muslim tide had swept across all of
North Africa, and Tariq, an Arab general, had invad-
ed Spain. Landing at one of antiquity's Pillars of
Hercules, he'd named it the Rock of Tariq. The
Arabic *Jebel al-Tariq* had, over the centuries, become
"Gibraltar." His subsequent victory over the Visigoths
at Jerez de la Frontera had opened the way for the
Muslim invasion of Europe. Not until 870 of the
Hegira—1492—had the forces of Islam been forced
to relinquish the last of its West European bastions.

The *Qaumat*, the Great Rising, had begun a new
age in the golden history of Islam, forging a theocrat-

ic empire that would soon devour the carcass of the
Soviet empire that had preceded it, and which even
now was challenging the might of corrupt and deca-
dent America. Before the UIR's true glory could be
made known to the world, however, the Strait of
Gibraltar had to become an Islamic channel once
again, with the green flag of the UIR flying from *both*
sides of the narrows, from Hacho in the south and
Gibraltar in the north. Rota, a scant fifty-five miles
from Gibraltar, would be destroyed, the hated
Americans purged from the Mediterranean.

   And Tariq's Operation Southern Sword had been
shaped precisely toward that end.

# CHAPTER
## 12

Off the Moroccan Coast
April 23, 0330 hours

For the second time within twenty-four hours, Morgan Gray sat in the cockpit of his SFV-4. Two hundred feet above his head it was a pitch-black night, moonless and overcast. The Barracuda's SUBVIEW took no notice of daylight, however, and the waters beyond his canopy appeared to be their usual, blue-emerald hues. Fish flitted like shadows, and as the bottom rose to meet him he could make out the gentle weavings of seaweed in the current and the long-legged scuttlings of some kind of crustacean.

Three other Barracudas were with him in close formation, piloted by Franklin, Wilder, and Lieutenant Robert Koch. Their call sign for this operation was Sea Eagle.

Bringing up the rear were two larger vessels, smooth, teardrop-shaped craft forty feet long, with tiny, bow-mounted conning towers and gaping water intakes. Powered by the same magnetohydrodynamic impulse drive that propelled the Barracudas through the water, the Electric Boat VR-7A "dry" transport submarine could travel at thirty-five knots, dive to over two thousand feet, and had a range of nearly four hundred miles. Each carried an eight-man SEAL team and all their equipment, plus a crew of two. Their ULTRA-C systems allowed them to use laser communications with other suitably equipped vessels in their line of sight.

"Sea Hawk One, this is Sea Eagle," Gray said, opening the tactical channel to the lead transport. "Do you copy?"

"Sea Eagle, Sea Hawk One." A hard voice came back in Gray's headset. "Copy."

"According to our charts, we're at Point Delta. We are deploying. Good luck, and good hunting."

"Roger that. See you at the rendezvous, Sea Eagle."

He switched channels. "Eagle One to chicks," he said. "Did you copy that?"

"We're with you, Eagle One," Koch's voice replied. "Let's leave these slugs and do some *real* flying."

"On my mark, three, two, one . . . now!"

Like sleek aircraft, the four fighter subs accelerated, leaving their plodding charges astern. Gently, Gray brought his stick left, and Wilder followed. Koch and Franklin broke right, changing course toward the southeast.

"See you fellows around," Gray called as the other two fighter subs dwindled into the green haze to starboard. "Don't get lost."

"Same to you, Skipper," Koch replied. "See you at Point Fox!"

The raid had been designated Operation Cid, after the half-mythical Spanish hero who'd fought Moors in eleventh-century Valencia. Besides Gray's flight of four Barracudas, a second four-sub element, designated Blue Eagle and consisting of Monk Young, Hernandez, Douglas, and a brand-new Lieutenant j.g. named

Charles Blackwell, had broken off from the main group at Point Bravo, angling southeast toward the port of Tangier. Their contribution to Operation Cid would be a diversionary attack against UIR naval vessels inside the harbor moles. Gray checked the time on his console display: 0335 hours. Their attack was scheduled to begin in another twenty-five minutes.

Gray's contingent, meanwhile, had stayed with the two VR-7s all the way to Point Delta, ten miles off the stretch of rugged, seaside cliffs designated as Red Beach. Now, however, Koch and Franklin were splitting off and moving south, to take up a patrol position five miles south of Red Beach, while Gray and Wilder took a similar position five miles north. Together, they would screen Point Echo—the spot on the map from which the SEALs would deploy against Red Beach for the rescue attempt itself. The crumbling stone fortress on the cliff above Red Beach had been designated Red Castle.

It was a risky series of maneuvers requiring split-second accuracy. Each element of the op would be out of ULTRA-C communication range with the others and forced to operate completely independently.

Each fighter sub carried a full warload, two Mark 62 torpedoes slung beneath its belly, plus two more hanging from newly added racks on its stubby, anhedral wings. In addition, both Gray and Koch carried another brand new SFV improvement, a Mark I SSAM. Pronounced "S-Sam," it was a streamlined pod mounted atop their stabilizers above and behind the TV camera/ULTRA-C laser mount. Gray had been glad when Huxley told him that two would be available for Operation Cid. As close to shore as they would be operating, the SSAM just might give them a vital edge.

The collective weight and drag of the extra weapons reduced their top speed to less than sixty knots but gave them greater staying power in a fight. With luck, there wouldn't be any fighting, but it was vital that the SEAL op at Red Beach be covered, just in case UIR gunboats at Tangier or at Rabat farther down the coast decided to make an appearance.

It was the SEALs, Gray knew, who had the roughest part of the mission. He almost wished he could go with them, even though he knew that their success depended on their very special NavSpecWar training and close-combat skills.

No. It was enough to be here, a small part of Operation Cid.

He prayed that Seegar and Dominico were still alive to be rescued and that they hadn't been moved from Red Castle.

**Sea Hawk One**
**SEAL Squad Red One**
**April 24, 0355 hours**

Lieutenant Christopher C. Lewis, the leader of SEAL Squad Red One, made his way from man to man, giving a personal last check to rebreather gear, equipment, and weapons. With each man he came to, he stopped and exchanged a few words, a rough joke, a warning to tighten a strap or to make sure that a buckle was well wrapped with tape to keep it silent. The words were more formality than anything else, a way of reminding each man of their martial brotherhood. Members of SEAL Team Four out of Little Creek, Virginia, they were professionals to the core, every one of them, and they knew their jobs.

The eight of them were crouching in the cramped, humid confines of the VR-7's squad bay, a compartment about as roomy as the back of an Army Bradley APC. Each wore black fatigues and a rebreather, and carried two waterproof satchels containing weapons and explosives. None wore face mask or flippers; flippers were a needless encumbrance, and the glint of light reflected from a mask might give them away. Their faces were heavily smeared with waterproof green paint.

On the squad bay's forward bulkhead, a red light winked on, and the sub's pilot spoke the long-awaited words over the intercom: "Time, men. We're at Point Echo, on the bottom at thirty feet."

Lewis peeled back the Velcro cover of his wristwatch. Zero-three-fifty-eight, a full seven minutes ahead of schedule.

He picked up the intercom mike and held it to his mouth. "Roger that. We're ready for lock out."

The VR-7's lockout trunk was aft of the squad bay, an upright cylinder just large enough for four men and their gear. At a nod from Lewis, the first SEAL in line stooped, opened the interior hatch, and squeezed through, followed by the three men behind him. The inner hatch was locked, a red light warned that the trunk was flooding, and the remaining SEALs heard the hiss of water entering the chamber. Less than two minutes later, the red light changed to green, and it was time for Lewis and the last three men to lock out of the sub.

It was a curious fact, part of the intraservice rivalry that rose from tight budgets and bureaucratic compromises, that for many years the SEALs had not been permitted to have their own submarines.

Lewis had heard that once, back in the early 1900s, the SEALs had been torpedoed in their quest for a "dry" submarine specifically designed for small-scale, covert insertions like Operation Cid. They'd tried to acquire an Italian-made midget called the 3gst9 for the surprisingly reasonable price of fourteen million dollars each, but the move had been blocked by the Navy's submarine faction for the sole reason that SEALs were considered part of the fleet, the naval barony of surface ships, while funding for submarines was controlled by the Navy's submarine command. Turf wars between the various rival Navy factions had raged viciously in those years, especially as the Cold War wound down and the defense budget shrank to a fraction of its former size.

SEALs back then had deployed from full-sized nuclear submarines, or they used so-called "wet" submersibles—minisubs with flooded compartments that forced the SEALs aboard to wear SCUBA or rebreather gear all the way to and from the target. Often, the minisubs were carried in barns attached to the nuke sub's deck, but operations close to hostile shores were often made more dangerous and less secure, simply because the submarine navy insisted on maintaining its monopoly over "real" submarines.

That attitude was changing now, and about damned time, Lewis thought. The *Lincoln* disaster had changed a lot of people's attitudes. Electric Boat's VR-7 had appeared eighteen months after the *Lincoln* had been sunk, and was considered one of the finest submarines of its type in the world. Small enough to get within a few hundred yards of a beach, with range enough to carry a SEAL squad two hundred miles out and back without tiring the men by adding to their time-in-water exposure, the VR-7 had been the answer to SEAL planners' dreams. Controlled by two SEALs in a separate, sealed compartment forward, the VR-7 was piloted by a man wearing the Mark I version of SUBVIEW, the same sort of virtual imagery helmet used aboard *Leviathan* and some other Navy subs, though there were plans for new designs equipped with the Mark II version, with an all-round cockpit display like those aboard the SFVs.

The escape trunk quickly filled with water, and Sanders cracked the overhead hatch. Lewis let the others go first, pulling themselves along the handrail, then followed, moving by feel hand over hand into the inky blackness outside. Using underwater lights strapped to their waists, they unshipped a pair of rafts stowed on the VR-7's deck, inflated them, and guided them to the surface. Squad Red Two, from the second VR-7, joined them moments later.

By 0400 hours, still ahead of schedule, Red One and Red Two—sixteen green-faced men in four black, electric-driven rafts—were cruising silently through the surf toward the rock-bound coast ahead.

**Tangier Harbor**
**April 24, 0358 hours**

Lieutenant Joseph Young, "Monk" to the other aviators-turned-submariners in the Blue Hunters, gently pulled back on his SFV's stick, bringing the fighter sub up through the water until the tip of his stabilizer broke the surface. His main console MFD had been set to display the image from his sail camera, and as the stabilizer emerged from the water the console screen blurred, then cleared, showing the expanse of the Tangier port facility.

Set for starlight imaging, the camera revealed the dock in eerie shades of gray and green, with the harbor lights as dazzling, sun-bright flares. To the right, he saw the long commercial wharf with its ferry terminal and hydrofoil dock. Directly ahead was the main port channel, with moored tankers and freighters and ore ships rising from the dark water like black steel cliffs.

The warships were to the left, on the east side of the harbor area. Under high-power magnification, Young could see soldiers standing on the pier, their faces sharply illuminated by the glow of cigarettes. Most of the ships tied up at the pier were patrol craft and gunboats; according to the Naval Intelligence briefings he'd seen, Morocco's largest warship was a single frigate, a former-Spanish Descubierta-class vessel of 1,270 tons now called the *Lieutenant Colonel Errhamani.*

He'd hoped to find the *Errhamani* in port, but he didn't see her among those quiet ranks of gray naval vessels. He did see something else, though, that gave him pause. He recognized that sharply raked bow and superstructure, the twin turrets aft, the flat casing of a quadruple missile launcher on her forward deck.

A Krivak II! Originally a Soviet antisubmarine warfare vessel, this one must have been one of those ships sold during the 1990s to one of the Islamic states that later joined the UIR. This was no local Moroccan warship. It must be part of the UIR's main fleet, on an official visit from Alexandria.

Young bit off a sharp curse. Why hadn't the Blue Hunters been told that a Krivak was here? Or was it that she'd just arrived at Tangier and word of her presence hadn't yet filtered down the chain from Washington?

Whatever the story, a Krivak II could put a real crimp into Operation Cid. The Moroccan navy had few ASW assets, but Krivak IIs were big, mean, and fast, mounting both antisubmarine rockets and torpedoes and a decent sonar suite. She could spell real trouble for Young's tiny flotilla.

He opened his tactical channel. "Okay, Eagles," he called. "Patch in to my video feed." He touched his console, transmitting the television pictures he was seeing on his own MFD to the other fighter subs. "Looks like we have an unwanted visitor."

"Holy shit, Monk," Hernandez said. "What the hell's a Krivak II doing out here?"

"I don't know and I don't much care. She's target number one for tonight, though. If we don't put her down, we're going to have a problem getting out of here."

"Think there are any more of those sub hunters around?" Blackwell asked.

Various North African states had purchased a number of Krivaks just before the *Qaumat*, Young remembered. The UIR was thought to have at least five or six of them now, assembled from the former navies of Libya, Egypt, and Syria.

"Could be." He considered the tactical situation a moment, then arrived at a decision. "Okay, Blackwell and Douglas, you two come about and head back for the harbor entrance."

"But, Lieutenant—"

"Stow it, Blackie! All we need to do is stir up some excitement in Tangier, and Hernandez and I can do that fine by ourselves. I want you watching our backs. If there are any more ASW skimmers out there, they could come back at an awkward time and trap us inside the harbor."

Reluctantly, the two junior men peeled off from the formation and angled back across the inner harbor, making for the narrow entrance between the two

breakwater moles. Young and Hernandez stayed on
course, slowing until they could barely stay at the surface. Young let his stabilizer slip back beneath the
waves. They were now less than half a mile from the
row of moored warships.

"I make it zero-four-hundred, Monk," Hernandez
said. "Time."

"Roger that. They're not making any noise, so we'll
use laser targeting."

"How do you want to do this?"

He studied the situation. Through his SUBVIEW
imaging, he could see the dark, unmoving shapes of
moored ships in the distance, motionless in the shadows a few feet above a soft and muddy bottom. That
big one, with the bulbous swell of a sonar mounting
at the bow beneath the waterline, was the Krivak.

"I'll take the Krivak with two fish. You hold off
until we're sure she's crippled, then fire at any target
that strikes your fancy. Then we cut and run. It'll be
getting lively then."

"That's a major roger."

"SUBVIEW," Young called out. "Targeting. Laser
designation."

The SFV's computer registered the order on his
central MFD.

TARGET LOCK. LASER DESIGNATION.

PASSIVE/ACTIVE?

"Active," he replied.

DESIGNATE TARGET.

Cross hairs appeared centered on his canopy forward. Holding the Barracuda's course steady with his
right hand, he used his left to grasp a finger-sized joystick on the arm of his seat. With a gentle touch, he
nudged the cross hairs onto the sleek black hull that
he'd identified as the Krivak.

"SUBVIEW!" he called when the cross hairs were in place. "Laser designation, lock *now!*"

His cockpit view went dark as his dorsal ULTRA-C laser disengaged from its steady, flickering sweep of his surroundings and became a target designator for the Mark 62. He could still make out the line of warships as they were imaged by his computer through sonar and the ventral ULTRA-C laser. An intense, blue-green spark of light remained centered on the Krivak's hull.

TARGET LOCK.

READY.

Young squeezed the trigger on his control stick, and his first Mark 62 hissed from his Barracuda's hull. Laser sensors in its nose registered the point of reflected laser light and fed course-correction data to its brain.

Accelerating quickly to one hundred knots, the torpedo rocketed across half a mile in twenty seconds, slamming into the Krivak's starboard hull amidships.

The night over the Tangier docks was transformed by thunder, fire, and water.

And in the harbor, all hell began to break loose.

**North of Tangier**
**April 24, 0401 hours**

As the first deep-throated thunder of an underwater explosion rumbled through the sea, Lieutenant j.g. Charles Blackwell was guiding his SFV between the harbor entrance markers and into the deeper water beyond. "That's it, then, Dave," he told his wingman. "The party's started."

"Yeah, and they're starting without us," the other

pilot replied. He sounded as disgusted as Blackwell felt. "I'd say that's discrimination, wouldn't you, Blackie?"

"Damned straight."

Charlie Blackwell still wasn't sure what he was doing in this new and surreal environment. All his life, ever since he'd learned that his father flew airplanes off carriers, he'd wanted to be a Navy aviator. He'd been three weeks from graduation with the rest of his class at Pensacola when the word had come down from on high: every man and woman in the class had a choice, truck driving, desk driving, or Project Orca.

Truck driving—flying the air armada of U.S. Navy logistical support, sub hunter, EW, and other aircraft— had for Blackwell always been a kind of mark of shame. His mouth quirked back in a little smile as he remembered explaining things to Jeannie, his brand-new wife. There were the hot fighters and attack aircraft, he'd told her, and then there were all the others, the planes aviators flew when they washed up, when they screwed the pooch or somehow proved that they didn't have the almighty right stuff. As for flying a desk . . . well, damn it, that wasn't why he'd joined the Navy. Project Orca? Now, that sounded interesting. . . .

So he'd switched to combat fighter submarine school. Jeannie hadn't wanted him to go. She'd met him while he'd been in the middle of a love affair with high-performance aircraft—possibly that had been part of what had attracted her to the boyish-looking, would-be aviator in the first place—but she didn't like the idea of her husband sealed away in a metal-and-ceramic coffin, sinking into the crushing black depths of the sea.

But, hey, it was a new navy now. Carriers were on the way out, and submarines were the wave of the future. He'd gentled her fears and smoothed them over. They'd transferred to New London for sub school, and that's where he'd met Dave Douglas. The two had become fast friends, graduating first and second in their ten-man class.

Unfortunately, the two of them had arrived at Kings Bay too late to take part in the big battle off Cienfuegos between the *Leviathan* and a squadron of UIR subs. In fact, the last few weeks had been downright boring, filled with simulator training and familiarization runs into the waters off northern Florida. He was tired of training and wanted to see some action. The stories of sub-to-sub combat told by Young and Hernandez and the others had convinced him he'd made the right choice. But when would he get to put his training into action?

Even now, deployed on his first combat mission overseas, he was still being held back out of the fight. What would it take before Lieutenant Young and the other old hands trusted him? Damn it, they hadn't seen that much more service in these undersea fighters than he had.

A warning chirped in his helmet.

"Hey, Dave?" he called, studying his readouts. "I've got a sonar target. Bearing, uh, zero-four-five. Sounds like heavy screws, coming from the northeast, outside the harbor."

"Roger that, Blackie," Douglas replied. "Better call it in."

"Let's find out what it is, first." He keyed a series of connections on his touch-screen console, feeding the chirring sound to his Barracuda's micro-Cray and requesting a probability analysis. The computer made a match with the fighter sub's sound library in seconds, displaying the result on his MFD.

MULTIPLE SOUNDS
BEARING 040 TO 048:
1 KRIVAK II-CLASS ASW FRIGATE
WEIGHT 3100 TONS   SPEED 31 KTS
PROB 87%
ADDITIONAL BKGRND SOUNDS:
2 PAUK-CLASS ASW CORVETTES
WEIGHT 480 TONS   SPEED 32 KNOTS
PROB 67%

Blackwell read the glowing letters on his screen with an icy sinking in his gut. This was a major anti-submarine force, and only the UIR used recycled Soviet warships in these waters. It was impossible to determine range with passive sonar only, but the thready churning of propellers *sounded* close . . . and they were coming closer.

"Blue Eagle One, this is Blue Eagle Three!" he called, hitting the lasercom transmit key. "Blue Eagle One, Blue Three! Do you copy?"

Silence . . . and it took a moment to realize that his fighter sub was now outside the harbor mole, that he was no longer in direct line-of-sight with Young or Hernandez and they therefore couldn't hear him.

"Back to the harbor entrance, Doug!" he yelled over the tactical channel. He turned his SFV to face the threat. "I think these guys mean business!"

"What the hell are you doing?" Douglas called back. "You're heading right toward them!"

"You go back inside the harbor and warn Monk and Hernandez," Blackwell told him. "I'll see if I can draw these guys off."

The sub hunters definitely sounded closer now.

# CHAPTER
# 13

**Sea Eagle One**
**April 23, 0415 hours**

Gray brought his fighter sub to the surface, skimming just beneath the silvered, shifting canopy of the surface. His stabilizer emerged from the waves, exposing the streamlined assembly of SSAM pod, dorsal ULTRA-C system, and electronics array. An antenna rose, questing, tasting the night air.

Good. No radar frequencies, which meant there were no UIR sub hunting helicopters or ships searching for intruders such as them in the area. There was a considerable amount of radio traffic, however, more than was usual for four in the morning. Gray couldn't listen in, since much of the traffic was encoded or scrambled, and even the transmissions broadcast in the clear were in Arabic.

But the voices he could hear sounded excited. Something was happening, and he was willing to bet that the something was Blue Eagle's diversionary attack at Tangier, right on schedule.

He pulled his stick left, putting the Barracuda into a tight circle to port. There was nothing to do now

**141**

but wait, and listen for the inevitable UIR response to the raid.

### SEAL Squad Red One
### April 24, 0432 hours

At the top of the rocky cliff behind the beach, Lieutenant Lewis hugged the rocks, studying the terrain ahead through his night-vision scope as the Atlantic surf boomed and hissed at his back. North, up the coast to his left, the coastline grew rougher until it reached the light at Cape Spartel and the northwest corner of Africa. South and inland, the runway lights of the Tangier-Boukhalf International Airport set the sky afire in his scope.

The SEAL squad's goal was backlit by the airport lights, a medieval pile of stone rising from rock and scrub brush less than fifty meters away. Walls and battlements were black masses against the sky, but beyond, several narrow windows showed lights.

There were countless such relics in long-embattled Morocco. Quite close to this spot were the ruins of Cotta, a Roman city. This castle had been built by the Portuguese around the time of Columbus; early in the twentieth century it had been a Spanish stronghold when Morocco was divided between Spain and France. For a time it had been a hotel, convenient to a nearby tourist attraction called the Caves of Hercules, but competition with the more modern resorts of Tangier, bankruptcy, and finally war, had left it an empty shell.

Until Morocco had been strong-armed into the UIR, and the place had been turned into an army garrison headquarters. Through the starlight scope,

Lewis could clearly make out two UIR sentries sharing a cigarette by the gate on the north wall, the wrought-iron portcullis open behind them.

A tiny sound, the scrape of rubber boot on rock; the here-I-am touch of a hand on his ankle. Carlotti and Feinstein joined him, shadows against the deeper shadows of the night, only their eyes visible through the layers of paint on their faces. The others spread out to either side, silent and invisible, but he could *feel* their presence with senses honed by training and long experience.

Two men were waiting with the rafts on the beach. The rest, signaling with touch and hand sign alone, began fanning out through the night, flitting with swift and deadly purpose from shadow to shadow, no more than shadows themselves. The layout of the old Portuguese fort was as their informant had told them: main road entering at the north gate, larger stone buildings rising within the outer wall. Lights shone inside from scattered windows. There would be fifteen to twenty guards on duty, plus a few officers and men standing night watches.

First to die would be the guards at the gate.

**Blue Eagle Three**
**North of Tangier**
**April 24, 0435 hours**

With his stabilizer raised above the water, Blackwell could hear the radio transmissions—scrambled, of course, but chittering and squealing like demented birds—of the sub hunters as they headed for his position. They'd picked up his stabilizer on their radars, he was pretty certain. Through his EW suite he could

hear the chirp of the radar system code named Kite
Screech, which was the fire director for a Krivak II's
two 100mm naval guns, mingled with the deeper
thrum of its Pop Group track-while-scan missile control radar.

It had him on sonar, too. The Krivak's sonar had
gone active, pinging steadily as the sub hunter raced
toward the lone Barracuda.

Blackwell's sole advantage now was speed. His
fighter sub could muster twice the speed of the
Krivak II and its Pauk-class corvette escorts. But
Douglas had just reentered Tangier harbor to pass
the word to Young and Hernandez. If he raced away
at top speed, the UIR sub hunters might break off the
chase and head for Tangier or, worse, split their
forces, detailing one of the Pauks to chase Blackwell
while the other two blocked the harbor entrance.

So he held his fighter sub's speed down to thirty
knots, just barely maintaining his lead over the sub
hunters as he plowed north into the strait. Their
sonar pinging was coming faster now as they tracked
him, and much louder. They were almost certainly
within five miles now, and they knew exactly where he
was.

Something new registered on his passive sonar.
Blackwell was having some trouble sorting the background noises his microphones were picking up from
the steady chirp!-*pinnng* of the enemy's active sonar,
but his fighter sub's computer picked up the sound,
identified it against its catalog of discrete noises, and
flashed a warning on his MFD.

WARNING: TORPEDO LAUNCH
PROBABLE SS-N-14
SHIP-LAUNCHED ROCKET TORPEDO

The SS-N-14 Silex was an ASW weapon mounted by various ex-Soviet ships, including the Krivak II. Fired into the air, dropped into the sea by parachute, it carried a torpedo payload that would acquire the sound of his wake or home on sound image painted by his pursuers' active sonars. As he watched, the range display changed from 4,800 meters—about three miles—to 4,600 meters.

It was time to get the hell out of here.

But how could he outrun that torpedo and still keep his pursuers from breaking off the hunt and heading for Tangier?

## Objective Red Castle
## April 24, 0436

Through his starlight scope, Lewis watched the attack go down, a dance of death, precisely choreographed, flawlessly performed. Night shadows seemed to flow from stone walls and, in perfect unison, wrapped around each sentry's mouth and nose from behind, dragging heads back to expose white throats to slashing black blades. Each guard struggled in nightmare silence in an assassin's death grip, then crumpled. Shadows dragged bodies and weapons aside to sheltering clumps of brush.

The way was clear.

Each man wore a tiny personal commo unit, an earplug and throat mike with two channels, but commands were reduced to hand signs and coded bursts of static. Lewis gave a verbal order now, however, as one of the SEALs at the gate signaled with two clicks over the tactical frequency.

"*Go.*"

One squad went through the front gate, edging through carefully as point men checked for more sentries or electronic sensors. The other went over the west wall, using padded grappling hooks and black, nylon line to make the ascent.

The courtyard inside the walls was empty, occupied only by parked vehicles. A mongrel dog yapped once, then fell silent as a SEAL dispatched it with a hissing snap from his silenced Mark 22 Mod O pistol, a 9mm weapon nicknamed "hush puppy" for the obvious reason. Another sentry died beneath the slash of a black commando knife . . . and then another.

The invaders closed on the main building, avoiding the patches of yellow light spilling from a few of the windows.

**Blue Eagle Three**
**North of Tangier**
**April 24, 0438 hours**

Blackwell could see the hulls of his pursuers now, black knife shapes visible against the surface of the ocean less than a mile away.

As a fighter pilot, he'd learned by heart the various maneuvers he could use to break the IR or radar lock of an oncoming missile. He was trying to apply them here, now, as the enemy torpedo tracked him unerringly through the depths.

Despite the outward similarities in hardware and technology, however, the sea was a very different combat environment. Everything happened so slowly here, even with a fighter sub capable of outrunning a torpedo.

He wished he had the undersea equivalent of chaff or a flare. Neither infrared nor radar worked here—the water absorbed long electromagnetic wavelengths before they traveled more than a few feet, which was why radio didn't work underwater—but there *were* sound-making decoys that could sucker an acoustically homing torpedo.

Unfortunately, SFV-4Bs were so small that they could carry a decoy *or* a torpedo, up to their maximum of four; since the Barracuda was faster than any torpedo made except for its own rocket-driven Mark 62s, it was considered a waste of good payload to trade a warhead for a noisemaker. Speed and maneuverability were the fighter subs' best defenses.

But Blackwell was rapidly running out of options. He'd been trying to circle around, heading back toward his pursuers while staying ahead of the torpedo. Maybe, with luck, he could brush the thing off against the hull of a UIR ship. At the least he'd give them a good scare and break their sonar lock on his craft by ducking through their mingled, thrashing wakes.

No battle plan survives contact with the enemy, the old saw ran. The Krivak II was dead ahead, but the two Pauk-class corvettes had split off to left and right, effectively boxing him in and guaranteeing that at least one of them would maintain their acoustical lock.

Swiftly, he keyed two of his own torpedoes for acoustic homing, immediate launch. With the sea filled with the sound of explosions, he could accelerate to sixty knots and slip right through the chaos of the shock waves. With luck, the frigate would be crippled or sunk and the Pauks would think he was still in the area, possibly lurking on the bottom, while in fact he was flashing toward the open sea. They would start a search for him, and that would give the other fighter subs in Tangier harbor a chance to escape.

TARGET LOCK   ACOUSTIC HOMING

He squeezed the trigger on his stick, feeling the heavy lurch as the Mark 62 hissed from beneath his wing.

He reset and fired again.

**UIR ASW Frigate _Zauba'a_
North of Tangier
April 24, 0439 hours**

"Captain! Sonar reports high-speed contact! Probable rocket torpedoes, dead ahead!"

Captain Victor Yegorovich Lyko reacted instantly, with an assuredness born of long training and experience. "Come left two-five! Launch starboard decoys!"

"Decoys away!"

He heard the thump of acoustic decoys being fired, and waited, keeping his face an expressionless mask. The men with him on the bridge were excitable and easily distracted, and it was vital that he keep them calm and professionally attentive to their duties.

Ten years earlier, Victor Lyko had been a captain first rank in the Russian navy—an _unemployed_ captain first rank as the accelerating breakup of the old Soviet empire gutted the Russian military and beached many of its finest naval officers. Like thousands of others, Lyko had chosen to become a mercenary—he preferred to think of himself as a *sovetnik*, an advisor—in the pay of a foreign government.

In their eagerness for hard currency, Moscow had sold dozens of weapons systems, submarines, and capital ships to other countries. Some, including two of the Northern Fleet's *Tyfun* ballistic-missile submarines, had even been sold to Russia's old Cold War enemy, the United States, an act that Lyko viewed as nothing less than treason. Most of the former Soviet warships, though, had ended up either with the Japanese or with the growing fleets of the various Mediterranean Islamic states. And when the fundamentalist revolution had swept like a firestorm from the Atlantic to the Caspian, those ships and submarines had become the navy of the United Islamic Republic.

A navy that had desperately needed officers with his training and experience. Lyko had answered their call.

Like most Russians, Lyko had a poor opinion of the Islamics—"sand rats," as he thought of them. They certainly were not sailors, and their lack of military discipline was appalling. If the officer and crew aboard his old *Simferopol* had been this disorganized, he would have shot the lot of them.

But patience and constant drill had gradually begun to reforge the *Zauba'a*'s crew into something approaching a military unit. At least they followed his orders now, without waiting for corroboration from his Islamic counterpart on the bridge, Captain Abdullah el-Ayachi.

"Sonar reports torpedoes are diverting, Captain! *Ya sidi!* They are veering to starboard!" A loud, wet boom thundering in the darkness marked the detonation of one of the enemy torpedoes. Moments later, a second explosion erupted in the night astern of the *Zauba'a*. Two shots, two misses.

"Sonar! Did you get a solid fix?"

"We have him, Captain! Range five thousand meters, bearing zero-two-six relative!"

"Very well. We will employ the RBU."

"*Ya sidi!*"

On *Zauba'a*'s forward deck, immediately below the bridge, twelve 1.6-meter tubes clustered in a horse-shoe-shaped grouping atop their mount elevated slightly and pivoted to starboard.

"RBU loaded and ready to fire, Captain!"

"Fire!"

Two by two, the tubes belched flame and smoke, brilliantly illuminating the forward deck as the *Raketnaya Bombobetnaya Ustanovka* hurled its rockets into the night sky. As soon as all twelve tubes had been emptied, they skewed around sharply and ele-vated to a vertical position, and reloads were auto-matically fed through from the deck below the mount.

Patterned off the ASW hedgehog launchers of World War II, the RBU-6000 could throw a twelve-shot pattern of twenty-one-kilo warheads up to six kilometers. Set to detonate on contact, by magnetic influence, or by depth, they would only explode if they hit the enemy sub, or if the fuse was triggered by the sub's magnetic field.

"Sonar reports splashes ahead, Captain."

That was the first salvo striking the water. Lyko kept his face impassive. "Fire a second volley." Again, flame lit the night.

But before the second volley of warheads had reached the ocean, a dull thud sounded through the darkness.

Captain Victor Lyko allowed himself a smile, as the rest of *Zauba'a*'s bridge crew burst into cheers.

**Blue Eagle Three**
**North of Tangier**
**April 24, 0439 hours**

Blackwell struggled to hold his fighter sub on an even keel. The blast had been close . . . terribly close, and the shock wave had engulfed his tiny submarine like a storm. Shaken, ears ringing, he scanned his console as red lights flickered and MFDs scrolled messages of damage, of systems failure, of disaster.

His propulsion system was out, and his ULTRA-C electronics had been knocked off-line, just for a start. His SUBVIEW projection had gone dead, leaving him in a claustrophobic darkness relieved only by the red-and-amber gleam of his console warning lights.

He was sinking. Like a stricken aircraft, with no engine power the Barracuda would plunge all the way to the bottom . . . about a thousand feet down, at this point in the strait. Sonar . . . was sonar still working? Yes, partially, at least. He could still hear the thrum of the UIR frigate somewhere ahead, though he couldn't get a solid fix. And there was something else . . . the telltale splash of numerous impacts on the surface.

He braced himself for another blast, eyes shut, shoulders hunched forward, waiting, waiting to ride out the next near miss . . . or die. After an age-long, terrifying minute of silence, he opened his eyes and loosed a sigh of pent-up breath.

A miss. None of the warheads had fallen close enough to his sub to explode. With shaking hands, he reached for the emergency eject lever that would release his cockpit and life-support unit and send him rocketing to the surface. No doubt he would be picked up by the enemy, but even internment as a POW was preferable to a cold and lonely death in the thousand-foot depths of the Gibraltar Strait.

Blackwell's rear sonar sensors had been smashed, so he didn't hear the final approach of the forgotten UIR torpedo from astern. Still following him, it had lost his engine noise with the detonation of the magnetically fused RBU warhead, switched to active homing, and zeroed in on the diving Barracuda.

At forty-five knots, the Soviet-manufactured 533mm torpedo slammed into the fighter sub's hull, obliterating the minisub and its pilot with the detonation of over 150 pounds of high explosives.

# CHAPTER
## 14

**Blue Eagle Flight**
**North of Tangier**
**April 24, 0440 hours**

Lieutenant Monk Young had counted three explosions, echoing through the depths from the north. Someone was shooting at someone else; those might have been torpedo explosions.

When the fourth detonation sounded, however, there could be little doubt as to what had happened. His passive sonar detected the unmistakable sound of an air-filled compartment suddenly, explosively filling with water, followed by the creak and ominous *tic-tic-tic* of a metallic shell fragmenting underwater. The sounds were small and quickly stilled; a surface ship or large submarine would have been more vocal in its death, and more prolonged. Though he'd never heard it before, Young knew with cold certainty that he'd just heard the death cry of an SFV-4.

The three fighter subs had just cleared the Tangier harbor moles. Behind them, the sky was alight with a diesel fuel fire blazing at the pierside and by searchlights sweeping the water from the ramparts of the

city walls. Patrol boats dashed madly from their docks
as a siren wailed in the night.

Their mission was accomplished. It was time to
head for the rendezvous. But Young knew that
Blackwell would not be joining them.

"I've got surface screws," Hernandez reported.
"Bearing zero-zero-eight true. Sounds like it might be
another Krivak. There are some smaller skimmers
too."

"I hear 'em," Young said. He felt dull, blunted by
shock and by postcombat letdown into a mind-numb-
ing lethargy. He forced himself to concentrate on his
console readouts. "My war book IDs them as Pauk
corvettes."

"Did . . . did they get Blackie?" Douglas wanted to
know.

"Count on it, kid," Young said. "They're pretty far
out. Looks to me like he decoyed the bastards away
from the harbor entrance to buy us time."

At least, he thought, that's what it'll read on my
after-action report. The kid deserves a medal . . . the
least we can do. Damn. I wonder if he had a family?
He was surprised and saddened to realize that he
didn't know.

They made the rest of the passage to the rendezvous in a dark and unhappy silence.


**Objective Red Castle**
**April 24, 0447 hours**


Four-man SEAL fire teams flitted through the rooms
and passageways of the old stone fort like vengeful
wraiths, striking suddenly and silently and leaving
death in their wake.

Their invasion had proceeded with expert stealth, taking out sentries and night watch personnel one by one with lethal precision. Lewis and three of his men had made it all the way to the third floor before a UIR guard had emerged unexpectedly from an office twenty feet down a red-carpeted corridor, just as MM1 Taylor gently lowered the staring, throat-slashed corpse of another guard to the floor.

The man stared, screamed, then ducked back into the office just as Lewis and Sanders opened fire, Lewis with his hush puppy, Sanders with his H&K MP5SD3 subgun. The cracks and splinterings of 9mm slugs savaging the wooden doorframe were louder than the *hiss-snap* of the SEALs' sound-suppressed weapons, but an instant later, the UIR guard leaned back into the corridor, his finger already clamped down on the trigger of his AKM.

*"Khatar! Khatar!"* the man was screaming. *"Muhill!"* Then the thunder of his assault rifle drowned the shouted warning. Bullets hammered at the plaster in walls and ceiling. Wildly aimed, none came near the Americans. With cool precision, Sanders loosed a calculated, three-round burst from his H&K. The weapon *chuffed* almost gently, and the guard's face exploded, splattering the wall behind him with crimson as his body crumpled in the doorway.

"That's torn it," Taylor muttered. Somewhere in the distance, somebody shouted in Arabic, and another shout answered.

"Never mind," Lewis replied. "Room 401 should be right around that next corner and up the stairs. Let's move it!"

\* \* \*

Objective Red Castle
April 24, 0448 hours

*What was that?*

Bleary with the shrieking need for sleep,
Lieutenant Mike Seegar wondered what his captors
were trying on him now. It had sounded like a burst
of automatic fire, echoing somewhere in the distance.
Dominico? Had they shot Dominico? He started to
turn, and a sharp, burning pain flared in his right
thigh. He staggered.

"No looking around, American! That didn't concern you. Stand at attention! Or do you want us to
beat you again?"

The ordeal, the torture, went on . . . on . . . on. . . .

He'd long since lost track of how long they'd kept
him standing here, face to the stone wall, as teams of
guards took turns keeping him awake and at attention. He couldn't see the window behind him and he
was constantly bathed in the glare of sunlamps that
kept the rest of the room dark, so he didn't know if it
was night or day outside. He had nothing against
which to measure time save the rotations of his questioners, and he suspected that those were deliberately
staggered with uneven periods of interrogation to
keep him off balance and confused. Sometimes they
asked him questions, but mostly they simply kept him
from falling asleep.

He'd heard of this sleep-deprivation technique,
something perfected long ago by Soviet interrogators.
*Brainwashing.* Deprive a man of sleep, hammer at him
relentlessly with questions and physical pain, rob him
of the clues that help him clock the passing hours . . .
Sooner or later, the man will break. Seegar wondered
if he'd broken already. He didn't think so, but his

memory was fogged, his thoughts blurred by exhaustion. In the small eternity of uncounted hours standing here, he'd memorized every crack, every detail of the rough gray stone inches from his nose. The pain—where they'd whipped him and especially where they'd beaten the soles of his feet—had been terrible at first, but even that had receded now to a dull, throbbing ache as his mind screamed for the sweet, warm release of dreamless oblivion. If he could just sleep for a few moments . . .

But each time his eyes closed for more than a second, one of his guards would jab him with an electric prod, the searing fire jolting through a different and unanticipated part of his body each time—knee, side, genitals, foot, stomach, buttocks, genitals again. More than once he'd passed out cold . . . only to come wide-awake again, drenched with ice water from a bucket . . . or worse, with salt water that reawakened every gash and leather-scored sore on his body with white-hot flame.

They wanted to know . . . what was it? About American submarines in Spain, about naval forces stationed at Rota, about minisubs and rocket torpedoes and American attitudes toward the UIR and . . . and other things, things too complicated for him to recall now.

And the things they told him between questionings—that he'd been abandoned, that his friends and family had no clue as to where he was now; that his buddy Dominico had already told them everything they wanted to know, that all they needed from him now were a few simple clarifications; that Dom had been taken out to the courtyard and shot and that he was next if he didn't tell them everything they wanted to know.

The thought that nobody knew where he was right now was the very worst torture of all.

Somewhere in the distance, a bell was clanging. Seegar seized on that sound, a break in the unchanging routine, something new to challenge the lethargic half death that had clamped down on his thoughts. He could hear other sounds now . . . shouts, and the pounding of running boots on carpeted floors. It sounded like an alert. He was aware, as if in a dream, that the guards who'd been standing at his side were gone. One had gone to the door, while another was speaking urgently into a telephone at the desk behind him. A third snatched up the AKM assault rifle slung over his shoulder and yanked at the charging lever. The ratcheting *click-clack* of a round being chambered sounded terribly loud in the tension-charged room. Seegar turned, wondering.

"*U'a!*" the man by the door screamed, and then he was spinning back into the room like a string-cut puppet, arms flailing as he slammed into the desk and collapsed to the floor. The guard with the AKM raised his weapon, then dropped it as a bloody third eye materialized between his other two and the back of his head disintegrated in a scarlet spray.

Uncomprehending for a dazed second, Seegar saw three men in black clothing and combat gear crouched just inside the door, their submachine guns aimed at three different parts of the room, covering every approach. They wore black floppy hats or scarves knotted behind their heads, and their hands and faces were blackened as well, imbuing them with a sinister, nightmarish deadliness.

A fourth man strode past the first three, an automatic pistol with a heavy, cylindrical sound suppressor screwed to the barrel. The sole surviving UIR officer in the room had dropped the telephone on the desk and backed into the wall behind him, hands raised, stark terror branded on his face. "No shoot! No shoot!" he gibbered in hoarse and broken English. Seegar recognized the voice of one of his questioners, unseen until now. "In Allah's name, no shoot! I surrender!"

Seegar swayed, suddenly dizzy. Someone—he didn't see who—caught him and lowered him to the floor. He felt a hand on his face. "Lieutenant Seegar?"

He blinked his eyes open, then closed them again when he saw that black face staring intently into his. "I'm Seegar." His voice cracked. Had they understood?

"Eagle, Eagle Leader," he heard the man say. "Package alpha tango."

"My God, look at him," another voice said. "His feet . . ."

"Shut up. Sanders, Minkowsky. Carry him. We're moving."

"What about that bastard?"

Seegar heard a sharp *chuff*, the sound of something heavy hitting the floor. "Screw him. Let's go."

Movement brought agony, especially to his feet, which felt cracked and swollen. Then blackness closed in and blissfully shut down the pain.

**Sea Eagle One**
**April 24, 0458 hours**

"Sea Eagle, Sea Hawk One. Echo Victor, repeat, Echo Victor."

The radio call snapped Gray to action. For over an hour, he and Wilder had circled at their assigned patrol zones, watching the sky gradually lighten and wondering when the ordeal would end.

The characters "EV" transmitted from Sea Hawk One was the prearranged code for complete success: the SEAL team ashore had rescued two men and were on the beach now.

Scanning the frequencies, Gray studied the radio traffic that continued to fill the air above his hiding place. It had not abated in the past hour, but there was still no local search or weapons radar, still no sign that the rescue flotilla had been discovered. Luck, it seemed, that indispensable ally in war, was with them.

Bringing his Barracuda onto an easterly heading, he aimed his sail camera at the distant shoreline. He could see the castle, backlit by the predawn glow in the sky behind it. A smudge of black smoke hung above walls and towers like a pennant. As he watched, a silent flash pricked at one of the interior buildings, and more smoke appeared. The SEALs were making liberal use of demolitions charges as they withdrew, partly to discourage pursuit, perhaps partly to ruin the place as an army headquarters or to strike at militant Arab pride and morale. He was too far from the beach to see anything as small as a man.

Warning chimed in his headset. Glancing at another of his MFDs, he saw a message writing itself on the screen.

AIRBORNE SEARCH RADAR
TYPE: MUSHROOM
PLATFORM: POSS. KA-25, KA-27
PROB. DETECT: 70%

The SFV-4's electronics suite had just detected the touch of a nearby airborne radar. Mushroom was the

NATO code name for a particular type of ex-Soviet search radar, one designed specifically to hunt submarines by picking up the signatures of their periscopes or snorkels. Though carried by several search or reconnaissance aircraft, the usual platforms were the Ka-25 Hormone A, or the faster and more modern Ka-27 Helix, both naval helicopters flown on antisubmarine missions.

Detection wasn't certain. The fact that Gray's electronics could register a radar pulse didn't mean the reflection was strong enough to be picked up by the source. But seven chances in ten weren't good odds. Someone was probably on the way to check him out already.

After an hour of waiting, things were likely to get hot very quickly now.

**Objective Red Castle**
**April 24, 0459 hours**

Seegar had regained consciousness briefly at the top of the cliffs. The SEALs had brought along two Stokes stretchers, wire-frame, man-sized baskets in which an injured man could be immobilized for transport. He came to as someone was strapping him into the Stokes.

It was almost pleasant. He was lying down, and the air tasted of sea and salt, with a burned, smoky tang to sharpen it. A rumble sounded in the distance, like thunder. He opened his eyes and saw Dominico, wrapped in a blanket and kneeling at his side.

"Dom! Goddamn, you . . . made it."

"The bastards didn't do me like they did you, buddy," Dominico said. There was smoke hanging in

the sky behind his head. Seegar could hear the roar
of flames and, somewhere, the wail of sirens. "Guess
they were keeping me in reserve. You're gonna be
okay, though. These guys are taking us home."

"Home . . ."

It seemed like such an alien concept, one made
unreal by distance, time, and pain.

One of the SEALs jabbed the needle of a morphine
syrette in Seegar's biceps, then used a marker to
record the fact on the aviator's forehead. "You've got
kind of a rough ride ahead of you, buddy," the black-
faced man said. "Just tough it out and you'll be fine."

Then they were lowering him down the face of a
cliff, with lines attached to either side of the Stokes.
The stretcher banged once against the rocks, and
Seegar lost consciousness again.

**UIR Ka-27 ASW helicopter**
**April 24, 0503 hours**

They'd scrambled as soon as word came that Tangier
was under attack, but a careful sweep of the harbor
area and its sea approaches had yielded nothing. The
Ka-27 helo, code-named "Helix" by NATO during the
Cold War, had spent a fruitless hour lowering its dipping sonar into the sea and listening for some trace
of the submarine flotilla the naval command center
claimed was assaulting the port.

Nothing . . . no trace of a hostile submarine. No
trace, at least, if you ignored the fiery testimony of a
frigate tied to the navy pier, sinking by the stern in a
spreading pool of flaming diesel fuel.

Then had come a radio report that a frigate operating several miles north of the harbor had caught

and sunk an enemy sub and that, the Helix pilot decided, was that. Without even waiting for a recall, he swung the ASW helo's controls to port and thundered through the predawn sky toward Tangier-Boukhalf Airport, where he was based with a squadron of navy sub hunters.

"Helicopter Lightning KM Three-five, this is Tangier Military Traffic Control" sounded over his radio headset. "What is your position, over?"

There was no sense in lying. They must have him on their radar screens. "TMTC, this is KM Three-five, map reference three-one-one by three-seven-two. Altitude two-zero-zero meters, speed eight-nine. Returning to base." Aware that he'd had no orders to return, he decided to embellish. "Fuel low. Over."

"KM Three-five, come to two-zero-three and investigate possible sub contact, reference four-zero-five by two-nine-three. This is Priority Red, urgent."

"Affirmative, TMTC. On my way."

Those map coordinates marked a spot off the Moroccan coast just offshore from a local army unit headquarters, he knew, a few miles from Tangier-Boukhalf.

"What do you think it is?" his weapons officer said. He'd been listening in on his own headset.

"Who knows? Probably a false alarm, some trainee scared by a whale. We'll take a quick look, then back to base."

"What's that up the coast? Looks like a big fire."

The pilot's eyes narrowed. It did look like a fire, and right about where that headquarters was. Something funny, there. Submarines didn't start fires ashore. "Hang on," he said. "I'm taking us down for a closer look."

Sea Hawk One
April 24, 0503 hours

The U.S. Navy had long before worked out a technique for recovering swimmers in rubber rafts by submarine. It sounded unlikely but had first been used to recover SEALs on a secret mission off the coast of Cuba in the early 1960s, and it had proven itself numerous times since then when a rescue sub could not immediately surface to take on passengers.

In this case, there were four rafts, carrying sixteen SEALs and their equipment, plus two men in Stokes stretchers. Recovery by air or by surface ship was impractical this close to a major UIR airbase, but there was no way the rescued men—one of them seriously hurt—could be dragged down and wrestled through the airlock of a submerged submarine.

So the SEALs had motored out to the recovery point, then tied the rafts together, lashed tightly two by two and with a one-hundred-foot length of nylon line between the two pairs. The pairs had then separated as far as they could, and waited.

Minutes later, the transport minisub designated Sea Hawk One approached from the east, aiming between the two raft pairs, its periscope, electronics mast, and snorkel all raised above the surface of the water. The projections snagged the long line between the rafts and kept on going. The rafts swung together fifty feet astern of the periscope and picked up speed. In moments, they were racing through the water at fifteen knots, far faster than they could have managed on their own. Towed this way, they could be carried to a rendezvous with a ship or helicopter, or simply moved far enough out to sea that the sub could stop and surface.

The disadvantage, of course, was that the rafts were vulnerable to air attack, as was the sub itself so long as it stayed close enough to the surface to keep towing them. And in the swiftly gathering light of the morning, the SEALs could see the black silhouette of a helicopter sweeping toward them from the northeast.

## Sea Eagle One
## April 24, 0458 hours

Gray had detected that first, feather-light touch of an ASW helo's radar, then lost it. Now the signal was back, far stronger and more certain, illuminating the radar warning threat display on his console. Pivoting his sail camera back and forth, he swept the sky, searching . . . *there!*

It was a Ka-27 Helix, unmistakable with its two sets of contra-rotating props, one above the other, and its big, twin tail stabilizers. It was coming in at less than fifty feet, heading straight toward the SEAL rafts.

"Sea Eagle One, this is Three! I'm picking up aircraft–"

"Roger that, I'm on it. Hold your position." Killing the forward speed on his Barracuda, he let the fighter sub's fin slip beneath the waves. He was pretty sure the helo had not spotted him but was after the rafts two miles to the south. The Helix carried either ASW torpedoes or depth charges. The minisub transport would be an easy target, and if the SEALs survived the explosion, they'd be simple enough to collect later, or to machine-gun in the water.

He had only seconds in which to act, but the four fighter subs of Sea Eagle had been positioned on the SEAL team's flanks for just this sort of situation.

Tapping out instructions on his console, he readied his S-SAM missile pod.

Both the British and the Russians had experimented with antiair missiles fired from housings attached to the periscope masts of their submarines with mixed success. A missile from such a launcher had destroyed an American ASW helicopter during the Cienfuegos operation weeks before. Targeting the blurred, sonar image of the Helix as it thundered past Gray's submerged position, he pressed the launch key.

With a sizzling hiss in a cloud of bubbles, the small, solid-fuel rocket shot from the S-SAM pod atop the Barracuda's stabilizer, broke the surface of the water, and leaped into the sky. Free of the water, its infrared tracking array switched on, locking onto the engine exhaust of the helicopter and sending steering instructions to the missile's tiny, one-track electronic brain.

The helicopter pilot had just a glimpse of the missile arrowing toward him at the tip of a snow-white contrail. Shouting warning, he tried to jink to the right, but an instant later the missile slammed into his engine housing and exploded inside the portside lateral engine exhaust port. The blast ripped through both TV3-117V turboshaft engines, smashed the rotor hub, and severed the control linkages. The Helix hit the water nose-first, then exploded, lighting sea and sky with flaming av gas.

Maintaining their pace with the SEAL minisub, then, Gray and Wilder continued to ride flank for the commando party, behind and a couple of miles north of the rafts. Though radar probed the sea's surface several times in the next hour, there were no further air attacks, and by 0600 hours they were well out to sea and far enough from UIR airspace that an American naval helicopter could meet the party and take Seegar and Dominico aboard. Then the SEALs returned to their minisubs, while the fighter subs detached to make their planned rendezvous with Young's team off Cape Trafalgar.

It was then that Gray learned of Blackwell's death.

# CHAPTER
## 15

**Central Cairo**
**April 24, 0900 hours (Time Zone Zulu +2)**

Saadeddin Matar, *al-Qayid min al-Jamahir, al-Mahdi*, was an imposing figure, tall, commanding, with dark eyes that burned with preternatural brilliance in a face that might have been chiseled from granite. Displayed on the three-story-tall, high-res digital screen overlooking the plaza of Midan el Tahrir, opposite the Mogamma, the city's central government building, and the complex of the former American University in Cairo, Matar's figure had been enhanced to the heroic proportions of some mythic figure of old, a modern-day Saladin astride the world, come to lead his people to victory over the infidel. People filled the broad avenues at the giant's feet, a seething, colorful, thronging mass transforming the Shari el Tahrir and the Shari el Qasr el Ani into densely packed, open-air theaters filled with movement and color and sound.

"*Ikwan!*" the image thundered, and it was the voice of God. "Brothers! We but stand for what is right and just in the sight of Allah!"

Throughout the length and breadth of the vast

**168**

United Islamic Republic, men and women watched smaller versions of that colossus astride Cairo's heart. The Mahdi's broadcast, displayed in Cairo on the three-story screen that had been a gift from the Japanese government to the people of the UIR, was being seen in every city, town, and village from Tangier to Baku, relayed by Japanese communications satellite, displayed on Sony and Hitachi TV sets, simultaneously translated by linguistic software from MITI's Electro-Technical Laboratories in lands where time and distance or language made the Arabic spoken in Cairo unintelligible.

The UIR's reliance on Japanese technology was much on Saadeddin's mind as he watched his own speech, taped in the A'bdin Palace studios hours earlier. The same Japanese technology that made the transmission to all parts of the republic possible in the first place had also enhanced that transmission in subtle ways. Digital manipulation by computer had eliminated flaws and pockmarks from his face, giving it that chiseled-stone look, while the God-flame burning in the eyes had originated in an editing program run by Japanese computer technicians right here in the palace. That thunderous voice, too, was enhanced, given rich and subtle undertones of power and authority that sent a small shiver of religious intensity down Matar's spine as he listened, even though he knew it was his own words he was listening to.

Not for the first time, he wondered if the small army of Japanese diplomats, technicians, and advisers in his capital thought of him as puppet rather than ally and client.

He needed them, there was no denying that. He needed them to supply everything from the weapons of modern war to the computer program that trans-

formed his image from that of a mere human to the
power-cloaked mouthpiece of Allah and the Prophet,
the *Mahdi*, the hidden Imam of legend, the Messiah
of God to the faithful.

Perhaps most of all, he needed them to reach
beyond the borders of the UIR, to the peoples of the
world who had never heard the words of the holy
Quran. Thanks to those Japanese communications
satellites, his words and his image were being beamed
across the face of the earth, a pulpit that Muhammad
himself could never have imagined.

"Brothers!" the image on the TV screen boomed
again, startling in its intensity. "We stand before you
now not as President of the Republic, nor as Speaker
for the faithful. We stand now as speaker for the poor
of this world, as voice of the voiceless poor and dispossessed of all the earth! I say now to imperialist
America, bloated and corrupt and festering in the
decay of her spoils, that the poor and dispossessed,
the trampled and disinherited, are the promised
inheritors of this world and its wealth!

"And to you billions long ground under the racist
heels of the Americans and the Europeans, I say that
your time has come, that you must now rise and seize
the power and the wealth and the glory so long
denied you!"

Had he overdone it a bit? Saadeddin wondered.
That bit about "imperialist America," crafted by one of
his best speechwriters, clanked like a piece of invective
lifted straight from the Cold War pages of *Pravda*, but
if it echoed even distantly in the hearts of the discon-
tented masses of the world, it would be successful.

He was particularly interested in Latin America,
for so long both oppressed and desperately poor.
Two days ago there'd been a bloody riot in Mexico

City's Tlatelolco district, with an estimated five hundred dead. A general rising in Mexico or in South America now could transform the Americas as the *Qaumat* had transformed the Muslim world.

"I call upon you," the image on the screen was saying, "upon the poor, the dispossessed, the hungry of this rich world, whoever you are, whichever face of God you worship, to join with United Islam in holy jihad, to take from the rich and proud who would enslave you, to make yourselves masters of your own destinies!"

How, he wondered, would this message be received in the United States? Some of Saadeddin's advisers had suggested that revolution and civil war were possible there, that this message might be received by the blacks and other minorities as a signal to rise and overthrow their government, but the Mahdi was putting little faith in such wishful pronouncements. The Americans had a long history of uniting in the face of attack from without; only when they were at peace did their squabblings and bickerings and incomprehensible demands for rights without responsibilities threaten to destroy their two-century-old experiment in democracy.

But Saadeddin did hope to reach the Mexicans, and anyone else in Latin America who would hear him. With their landing on the coast of Morocco, the Americans had just thrown down the gauntlet.

It was not to be borne. Their destruction of his submarine force in the Caribbean weeks ago had been a setback to his plans. The actual landing of American troops on Republic soil, however, was more than troublesome. It was a direct challenge to his authority, and one that must be answered. War was now not possibility, but certainty.

Hence this broadcast to a listening, watching world. With war and revolution on her own borders, America would not bother with events in southern Spain. Tariq, now gathering landing craft and aircraft for the planned assault, could carry out his invasion without interference by the Americans.

And the next phase of this war might well be fought across the muddy width of the Rio Grande instead of the narrow Strait of Gibraltar.

On the screen, the titanic image had ceased speaking, and the crowd at its feet were answering thunder with thunder, the roar of their cheers drowning out the news commentator's voice-over.

*"Allah akbar! Allah akbar! Allah akbar!"*

"God is Great!"

And in that thunder, Saadeddin Matar thought he heard the echoes of his certain, final victory.

Soon, he would not even need the Japanese to guarantee it.

**U.S. Naval Station, Rota, Spain**
**April 24, 1500 hours**

"A formal unit commendation ought to be coming through in a few days," Maxwell said, standing by the window in his office with his hands clasped behind his back. He turned, fixing Gray with a gaze warmer than his usual cold proficiency. "Your, um, squadron did an excellent job, Commander. You'll be credited with contributing to the success of Operation Cid."

"Thank you, sir. The men will be glad to hear that."

Gray was sitting in a leather chair across from Maxwell's desk, nursing a mug of coffee. Since his return to Rota early that morning, he'd had a chance to shower and change, but with the rounds of debriefings with fleet, submarine, and intelligence officers, he was now well into his second twenty-four-hour stretch without any sleep, and the effects were beginning to show. He felt groggy, and a bit stupid. The strong Navy coffee was helping to keep the light-headedness at bay.

"I'm afraid I can't promise anything on your recommendation for a Navy Cross for your man," Maxwell continued. "I've passed it on up the line with my endorsement, but I very much doubt it'll fly. There were no witnesses."

No witnesses. Blackwell had died alone, facing impossible odds. Gray suppressed a shudder. He'd just been a kid, twenty-three years old.

"Well, I do appreciate your support, sir. God knows, Lieutenant Blackwell deserved more than a damned medal for what he did. He saved the lives of three of my men."

"Possibly. Medals are piss-poor comfort to a man's family, though. I understand he was married just a few weeks ago."

"Yes, sir." That reminded Gray of one particular duty that still faced him, one that he wasn't looking forward to at all: writing the letters, one to Blackwell's parents, another to his wife. What was her name? Jean? Jenny? It would be in his service record.

He took a sip of bitter coffee, savoring its bite. "What about Seegar and Dominico, Captain? I heard Seegar's heading back Stateside."

"He'll be on a medevac flight out to Bethesda tonight. His feet are in pretty bad shape."

"What the hell did they do to him over there?"

"The Turks call it bastinado. Beating the soles of a

man's feet." He shook his head, scowling. "The doctor's report said his feet were swollen to twice their normal size. Add to that sleep deprivation, beatings, exposure. He'll probably be on restricted duty for quite a while. If he doesn't take a medical discharge."

Restricted duty . . . flying a desk instead of a jet or even a fighter sub. For the flamboyant Seegar, that would be like a death sentence.

"Dominico's in pretty good shape, though, I gather," Maxwell went on. "The bastards hadn't started working on him when the SEALs got to him. He'll be taking some medical leave, but I imagine he'll be assigned back to the squadron after that. If he still wants to."

"That's good. He's a good man."

He hoped Dominico would stay. He needed experienced men adept at translating their aviation backgrounds to the peculiar needs and tactics of undersea combat, especially the tactics peculiar to fighter sub warfare. Seegar had been such a man. His loss would hurt, partly because he'd been a key man in the squadron, but even more because he'd become a personal friend in the days before and after Cienfuegos.

Gray had hardly known Blackwell at all, but he felt the kid's death sharply, as though he'd been to blame.

Objectively, coldly, Gray recognized the guilt that was blurring his own perceptions of himself and the squadron. In an abstract sense, of course, it *had* been his fault that Blackwell had died, since his orders had put the kid where he'd been. As for Seegar, there'd been no way to predict the kidnapping of American servicemen on Spanish territory, but Gray remembered the bad feeling he'd had about that liberty party his first evening at Rota, and the nagging feeling that he shouldn't have let them go to town at all.

With ten years of experience as an officer and almost a full year as Assistant CAG of a naval air wing on the U.S.S. *Roosevelt*, Gray was seasoned enough to know that no military commander can ever accept full personal responsibility for what ultimately are the fortunes of war. Each decision he'd made had been the best that could be made at the time.

But that didn't make Blackwell's death or Seegar's incapacitation any easier to accept.

Maxwell turned and walked back to his desk, picked up a folder, and opened it. "So far as operational orders go, Commander, your squadron will stand down for forty-eight hours. The memorial service for Blackwell is scheduled for noon tomorrow, but other than that, no duty. Take some time off." A smile quirked at the corner of his mouth. "Go into town."

Gray looked up, surprised. "Is that a good idea, sir?"

"Security is being beefed up. Some parts of Jerez and Cadiz will be off-limits, but the Spanish *guarda civil* and their army have both promised to help us. They'll have patrols out, and our own Shore Patrol will be watching for suspicious types or people with guns." He shrugged. "In any case, I doubt that our friends across the strait will try that sort of thing again. The Spanish are more worried about terrorist attacks right now than kidnappings."

"Yes, sir. Actually, I was wondering about having the squadron stand down. It might be better if we . . . stayed busy."

Maxwell nodded. "I understand. The truth of the matter is, I'm afraid, that there's some question about how best to employ you people over here."

"Sir?"

"It's been pointed out that conventional submarines or even automated listening devices could carry out the surveillance of shipping in the strait, with better coverage than SSF-1 can manage."

"*I* told them that."

"You know how the bureaucracy is. They'll change their minds ninety-five ways from Tuesday, then hand you a compromise at the last minute that no one can stomach, won't work anyway, and it's too late to do anything about. Sometimes I think the SEALs have the right idea. When some Pentagon pencil pusher with admiral's stripes tells them to do something they're not equipped to handle or that could be done better and cheaper some other way, some young SEAL lieutenant stands up on his hind legs and tells 'em to go to hell." He paused, and gave a small smile. "That's mutinous and seditious talk, Commander. Repeat it to anyone and you'll be in charge of the iceberg census at Adak."

"They won't get it out of me, Captain."

"As for showing the flag for the Spanish, well, the situation may be changing. Did you get a chance to hear the Mahdi's big address this morning?"

"No, sir. I was in debriefing. I heard it was pretty strong."

"Hmmph. Pretty strong like a twenty-megaton warhead. Washington's going to be sorting through the debris for some time yet. As for over here, it seems there are some politician types in Madrid who feel our presence here might be inflaming the Islamics and heightening military tensions. The episode in Jerez has the Spanish pretty shook up."

"They're blaming that on us?"

"It wouldn't have happened if we hadn't been there."

"I don't believe it. Are they closing down Rota?"

"That's up to the politicians, of course, on both sides of the Atlantic. According to Washington, though, the Islamics are building up for something big over in Morocco. The word is that the SEALs picked up a few souvenirs over there besides Dominico and Seegar. And that guy you fished out of the strait has been an intelligence gold mine too."

"'Something big,'" Gray said, exploring the words. "Like an invasion?"

"It's possible, and just the possibility has the Spanish running scared. The UIR general over there calls himself 'Tariq,' after the guy who invaded Spain thirteen hundred years ago."

"Seems like they have damned long memories over here."

"That they have, Commander. That they have. At any rate, the Pentagon's passed the word down the chain for us to be ready to pack up and move."

"Where?"

"The Gib."

"Gibraltar?" Gray's eyebrows crept up toward his hairline. That was news, for the British so far had been careful to stay out of the growing confrontation between the U.S. and the UIR.

"News of our raid in Morocco was read this morning in Parliament," Maxwell told him. "Operation Cid seems to have tipped things in our favor, diplomatically, at least. London has been staying clear of our argument with the UIR lately, because they've got vital economic interests on the continent, and most of the continent has been tilting toward the UIR. They also have a sizable Islamic minority that they're worried about."

Gray nodded. Islamic riots in London and elsewhere had been much in the news lately.

"Well," Maxwell continued, "now it seems they're digging their heels in. They don't want to be dragged into the UIR's arms by the rest of Europe. They've offered us the use of their naval base at Gibraltar, and starting next week, they'll be conducting joint patrols and exercises with us in the strait."

"It's still not much of a force to stop a UIR invasion, sir."

"Agreed. Though if the Spanish cave in, there may not be an invasion. Or it might be directed at Gibraltar alone. Anyway, the MEU at Rota will be at sea by tomorrow night. As for us, we'll redeploy to Gibraltar, at least until *Leviathan* completes her repairs."

"How's the Big Vi coming along, sir?"

"Ahead of schedule. She'll be ready for sea in ten days, two weeks at the outside. As soon as she can put to sea, she'll be on her way to our side of the pond. The Joint Chiefs feel her presence here might help discourage any, ah, UIR adventures."

"It'll be damned good to see her again, sir."

"I can't argue that. Of course, when she gets here, SSF-1 is going to have its work cut out for it."

"How's that?"

"Let's just say there won't be any question about how best to employ your fighter subs once *Leviathan* is in these waters." Maxwell picked up a folder from his desk and handed it to Gray. "Have a look."

The file, marked secret, contained several related reports. One was an NSA brief relayed to all Atlantic commands, advising them that the Japanese carrier sub *Teigei* and her attack sub consort were now believed to be approaching the Cape of Good Hope.

Their destination—the Caribbean or the Strait of Gibraltar—was still anyone's guess.

A separate sheet, this one courtesy of the CIA, the Office of East Asian Analysis. It contained a sketch and some terse speculation on something officially named "*Zingei,*" but which workers at the Mitsubishi plant where it had been designed called "Stingray."

Gray read the paper closely. "The Japanese fighter sub?"

"We've known they were working on one," Maxwell confirmed. "And if this giant sub they call *Teigei* is, in fact, a carrier sub like *Leviathan,* it stands to reason she's carrying something like our SFVs. Looks like you men'll get a chance to show what those toys of yours can *really* do."

"Yes, sir. What if *Teigei*'s headed for the Caribbean, though?" The UIR still had that sub base at Cienfuegos.

"Then we're in deep trouble." Maxwell's face, suddenly, was bleak. "The Mahdi's speech this morning was calling for jihad . . . not by the world's Muslims, this time, but by what he calls 'the poor and dispossessed of all the earth.' He wants to become the savior of all the world's poor and hungry. That could mean real trouble in Mexico."

Gray understood. A revolution in Mexico could attract UIR support, weapons, even troops. And if Mexico joined the UIR camp, other South American countries would follow, especially if the Islamics had a powerful naval element in the region, courtesy of their Japanese allies.

And the United States still depended on Venezuelan oil.

"The best guess, though," Maxwell continued, "is that the Japanese will go to Alexandria first. They could pick up a flotilla of Islamic attack subs there, maybe escort them across to Cienfuegos. But that means they'll be coming through the Strait of Gibraltar first."

"And we'll be there to meet them," Gray said. "What are we supposed to do? Shoot them or take pictures?"

"There's been no declaration of war, Commander. Until there is, there's not much we can do. I suppose the next move is up to either Tokyo or Washington."

In other words, they would have to wait to see whether Washington declared war on Japan first . . . or whether Japan would declare the war by firing at American subs off Gibraltar.

Gray wondered if this ongoing confrontation with the UIR—not peace, but not all-out war either— wasn't still perceived as some kind of political game by the bureaucrats and politicians back home. They were like playing pieces in some vast and, to them, completely unintelligible game, pawns to be sacrificed at a whim. That thought made him feel nakedly vulnerable; tomorrow, their desire for some minor political advantage might well put him, put his whole squadron, in the same lonely last stand that Blackwell had found.

It was not a pleasant thought, nor was it one he could use to explain Blackwell's death to the man's bride. He found he could not even use it to explain things to himself.

"All we can do now," Maxwell concluded, "is follow orders. And wait."

And that, Gray reminded himself, always seemed to be the toughest part of any war.

# CHAPTER
## 16

**The White House**
**April 28, 1100 hours (Time zone Zulu -5)**

The President of the United States sat expressionless at his desk as a makeup technician lightly powdered his forehead, then pulled away the protective cloth draped over his shoulder and chest like a bib. The White House communications director held up a finger from the other side of the Oval Office, just to the right of the cluster of camera and sound crew personnel gathered there. The camera was already running, the microphone pinned to the President's tie hot. "One minute, Mr. President."

"Thank you, Stephanie."

At his back, warm, morning light spilled through the lightly tinted, bulletproof glass in the window overlooking the Rose Garden. It was a beautiful Washington spring, with the cherry blossoms in full bloom along the Potomac.

*Damn* the Japanese. Tokyo's latest communiqué, presented to the Secretary of State only two hours ago, amounted to nothing less than an ultimatum. Japan would continue to support their UIR allies, regardless of the political consequences. And this less than two days after the Mahdi's "Jihad of the Oppressed" speech. It was almost as though Japan *wanted* war with the United States.

A television in the wall off to his right was tuned to CNN, showing the cable network logo and the computer-generated "Special News Report." The sound was off, a news anchor already delivering the introduction.

The President's eyes shifted to the teleprompter, just beneath the gleaming eye of the camera, where the first words of his speech were already cued up: "My fellow Americans."

A hackneyed phrase. Was it too late to change it?

"Five seconds, Mr. President," Stephanie said, holding one hand to her headset, holding up the other with her five fingers extended. She counted down the rest of the way in silence, "four . . . three . . . two . . . one . . ."

She pointed at the President as the camera's red light winked on.

"My friends," the President said, looking directly into the camera's lens. "One week ago, two American naval officers stationed in Rota, Spain, were kidnapped by members of a paramilitary terrorist unit working at the behest of the United Islamic Republic, and taken to a military base in North Africa. . . ."

As he continued to read his address from the teleprompter, the President was keenly aware of the risk he was taking, both as Commander-in-Chief and as a politician. Congress was divided, as were the President's own advisers. Many felt that war with the UIR now would be a war America could not win, especially if Japan came in on the side of the Islamics.

And yet, to *not* respond somehow to the assault on U.S. servicemen in Europe would be an open invitation to further assaults, to further testings of American resolve.

He couldn't allow it to go that far. Not if the United States was to have any future at all amid the rising sea of hungry, angry, and poverty-racked third-world peoples.

"The empire of Japan has spurned our diplomatic efforts and announced that it will support the UIR both in equipment and in men. Since Tokyo's repudiation of their 1945 constitution six years ago, they have had both the time and the resolve to build a formidable fighting machine, one that they have not hesitated to use abroad. Two weeks ago, we learned that a new, large, atomic-powered submarine flying the Japanese flag was en route to Alexandria in order to bolster the UIR's naval forces.

"I have, therefore," the President continued, "directed the Joint Chiefs to prepare an operational plan for blockading the Strait of Gibraltar to all UIR military shipping and, especially, to intercept this Japanese super-sub and force her to turn back. The friend of our enemy is also our enemy. We serve notice now that we have no wish for hostilities with the empire of Japan, but that if they support the UIR belligerents in their undeclared war against America, then we have no choice but to respond. . . ."

Would a blockade work? The jury was still out on that one. At least it would send a clear message to Cairo that the U.S. wasn't going to stand for any more terrorist kidnappings of its personnel. Admiral Shapley, the CNO, had assured him that submarine technology could identify foreign military vessels by their individual sonar and laser signatures, so the blockaders ought to be certain of their targets in the crowded Strait of Gibraltar.

But would a blockade keep the Japanese out of the conflict, or inflame them enough to drag them into a widening world war? And what if their goal was not Alexandria . . . but the UIR base in Cuba?

"Our submarine blockade of the Strait of Gibraltar will begin effective at nine A.M. local time tomorrow. In this operation, we will be able to count on the assistance of our traditional ally and good friend, Great Britain. . . ."

And what a diplomatic coup *that* had been! The British Prime Minister was already in deep, political hot water over the ongoing crisis of England's participation in a united Europe. It had been Secretary of State Strauss's idea to offer joint military action with the U.S. as a way of proving to the world that Great Britain could still operate independently of Europe. There'd been a huge Islamic protest demonstration in Hyde Park when the news was announced, but so far Parliament was standing firm. If the Spanish closed the U.S. Navy base at Rota, as seemed likely from the latest diplomatic sources, at least the British base at Gibraltar would offer a strategically placed facility from which the blockade could be carried out.

"We do not want war. We would rather live at peace with our neighbors on this shrinking world, with the United Islamic Republic and with the empire of Japan. But in this confrontation, engineered by the foes of America in both Tokyo and Cairo, we cannot back down. We cannot yield. We will not yield. . . ."

The President remembered another blockade ordered by one of his predecessors, back when he was a child of eleven and unable to comprehend the worry he'd sensed in his parents. That blockade, he'd learned much later, had placed American submarines and surface ships between the island of Cuba and the warships and freighters of the then Soviet Union. The world had teetered then on the brink of war, a war avoided only by behind-the-scenes diplomacy and a last-minute course reversal by the Soviet ships. He did not think the Japanese would back down in the face of this blockade, not when backing down would mean loss of face and a public abandonment of their oil-rich ally.

It was, the President thought, not unlike a colossal game, move and countermove, with nations and cities and entire populations as playing pieces, with the entire world as a board.

And with stakes far higher than any ever wagered before in history.

**Imperial Navy Submarine** *Teigei*
**Cape of Good Hope**
**April 28, 2110 hours (Time zone Zulu +2)**

*Taisa* Komei Tanaka reread the message flimsy in his hands, searching for hidden shades of meaning or intent. Once each day, *Teigei* neared the surface and raised an antenna, listening for orders broadcast from home. Rarely was there more than cursory news, an occasional intelligence intercept, or orders that were masterpieces both of vagueness and micromanagement.

The message, relayed by satellite from Imperial Naval Headquarters in Yokosuka, was from the Japanese Intelligence Service. The last such message had warned of possible hostile American activity in the Strait of Gibraltar. This one told him to expect it, and included the text of the American president's blockade speech from that morning.

It also directed him to take "every necessary and prudent precaution," and was signed "M. Yoshida, Vice Admiral, Chief of Staff."

Take every necessary and prudent precaution? Did that mean he was to avoid combat with the Americans, or be ready to blow them out of the ocean before they even knew he was there? Run the blockade, or turn about and try the Suez passage? His orders were ambiguous, and the warning next to useless.

Perhaps, though, it was a sign that his decision to take the Cape of Good Hope route had been karma, a fated decision leading inevitably to his long-expected contest with the Americans. Tanaka found himself looking forward to that encounter more and more each day. If Japan, indeed, was in the ascendency over the West, delay would serve little purpose. Perhaps open combat between Japanese and American forces in the Gibraltar Strait would simply hasten the Americans' fall.

Leaving *Teigei*'s communications center, he returned to the submarine's bridge, where *Chusa* Matsushita sat in the command chair with his head encased in the *kabuto-no siranui*'s high-tech clutter.

"Take us back down, Commander Matsushita," he said. "Make our depth two hundred meters."

"Depth two hundred meters, yes, Captain." The First Officer's voice was muffled by the helmet he wore. With the tangle of cables trailing from the base of the helmet and suspended from the overhead and with his face hidden, Matsushita looked like some great, anonymous puppet slouched carelessly in a chair between performances.

"Where is our consort?"

The shining, blind head turned to the left, looking down. "*Umiryu* is still on station, Captain. Three hundred meters to port, traveling at a depth of two hundred meters."

"Very well. Carry on."

"Yes, honored Captain."

Walking aft as Matsushita began passing orders to the ship's diving officer, he stepped through the oval doorway and into the main passageway aft. He could feel the steel deck tilting sharply beneath his feet as he entered *Teigei*'s hangar deck.

The name for the compartment, derived from the terminology of aircraft carriers, seemed out of place for a submarine, but it was apt. A dozen Mitsubishi *Zingei* rested there in massive support gantries, poised like high-performance aircraft, ready to take flight. Each was a flattened disk, slightly elongated fore and aft, with paired stabilizers above the twin MHD propulsive units that bracketed the narrow, one-man cubicle in the center. In operation, the pilot lay on his belly inside the tiny craft, piloting through the *kabuto-no siranui* on his head.

*Zingei*. The name meant "swift-moving whale." If *Teigei* was a carrier-sub, the *Zingei* were what she carried, swift combat minisubs designed to operate in small and deadly groups much like attack aircraft.

This was the future of submarine technology. For over a century, submarines had been tightly sealed metal coffins groping blindly through the darkness a few meters beneath the surface, limited in speed, in maneuverability, and in endurance—fumbling alien intruders from the world of sunlight and air above. These sleek craft, poised on their cradles nose to tail in two lines leading to the hangar deck's twin launch-tube locks astern, were a new step in the evolution of submersibles, creatures of the sea and alien to the world of men.

They shared much in common with the American SFV-4s. Tanaka had seen intelligence reports on the American fighter subs and knew that the Mitsubishis were superior—faster, more maneuverable, deeper diving, swifter climbing. Its pilots and designers had already given the craft a pet name, *Ei*.

Stingray.

The squadron had been named *Kiku*: the Chrysanthemums. The pilots were lined up on the narrow stretch of steel deck between the lines of fighter subs, engaged in calisthenics. Lieutenant Takeo Shioya faced them, leading them in jumping jacks.

"Exercises at so late an hour, Takeo?" he said, smiling.

Shioya barked an order, halting the group, then walked over, mopping his face with a towel. "*Hai*, Tanaka-*sama*," he said, delivering a precise bow, then grinning at his superior. Despite the differences in both rank and age, the two men were close. Shioya was the son of Tanaka's sister, Kazuko, and had been the older man's protégé since his appointment to the naval academy at Yokosuka. "The time doesn't seem to matter as much down here, where we never see the sun."

Tanaka nodded toward the waiting men. "You intend for the Chrysanthemums to be ready for the Americans, *neh*?"

"We are ready now, Tanaka-*sama*." His eyes widened as he read some hint of Tanaka's thoughts behind the older man's mask, and he drew a sharp hiss of air in through clenched teeth. "So! You have heard something, Uncle-*san*? It is to be war?"

How eager the young are for war, Tanaka thought with a touch of sadness.

But then, war with America was not only inevitable, it was already cold and steel-edged fact.

The Japanese had an aphorism that explained their feelings in the matter: Business is war. By that way of thinking, the two nations had been at war since the end of the *last* war, when the American occupiers had tried to remake *Nippon* in their image. It had been a bloodless conflict, and a victorious one, a war in all but the shooting that the Americans seemed patently unable to comprehend. By the late 1980s, Japan had actually owned, outright, vast chunks of the American economy—banks; motion picture industries; electronics and computer megacorporations; incredibly, huge downtown areas of major cities including Los Angeles and New York City; much of the beachfront property of California; well over half of the public land composing the state of Hawaii. . . .

By my ancestors, Tanaka thought wonderingly, what kind of people are willing to sell their own lifeblood, their own heritage, their own souls? To sell them to an acknowledged rival, an outsider, an enemy?

The inevitable backlash had begun in the 1990s. Rioting mobs had murdered Japanese nationals in the streets and burned Japanese businesses. Laws had been passed limiting foreign ownership of American businesses and land. Ultimately, Congress had simply expropriated property owned by foreign nationals and corporations, a desperate move that had deepened the rift between East and West.

The shock waves felt through the world's economy had guaranteed that the war would soon shift from the arena of business to the literal battlefield. The Japanese Diet had sealed that shift by finally repudiating the old constitution of 1945, the one that had stated, in its infamous article nine, that "the Japanese people forever renounce war as a sovereign right of the nation. . . . Land, sea, and air forces, as well as other war potential, will never be maintained."

There was keen irony. For how long had the Americans themselves urged Japan to take a greater part in her own defense?

Well, the nation now was second to none in military might; its army was still small, but this time, Imperial Japan held the edge in technology, from her orbital missile defense systems to these sleek, Stingray fighter subs arrayed in *Teigei*'s hangar bay.

Still, in armed conflict *men* would die, not corporations or the points traded on the stock exchange. Somehow, the younger generation never seemed to quite grasp what a real war would mean. Perhaps that had been the greatest loss in sixty years of enforced demilitarization.

"There is no news," he said, dragging his attention back to Shioya's wide-eyed question. "And no declaration of war. But I have just received a communication from headquarters. It appears likely that we will encounter the Americans in the Strait of Gibraltar."

"Indeed?"

"The Americans have declared a blockade. They do not wish us to help our Islamic allies and have announced their intent to close the strait to us."

Shioya's eyes danced. "So, *Beiko*-Komei!" he said, addressing the older man by the familiar title of Uncle. "But after the battle at Tangier, perhaps our Arab allies will not need our help after all." According to the intelligence reports broadcast from Tokyo, Cairo was claiming three American submarines sunk by Islamic ASW ships off Tangier.

"I do not trust the numbers they report, nephew. I never do. The Americans remain a formidable foe."

"Yes, sir. But we are better."

"You will have your chance to prove that, Takeo. The American president has ordered a blockade against Islamic and Japanese vessels in the Strait of Gibraltar. And we are going to run that blockade." He stiffened, raising his head and withdrawing, for the moment, into the cold persona of a superior officer communicating with a junior. "Lieutenant Shioya, you will prepare for me a detailed plan for an offensive sweep through the Strait of Gibraltar. Assume that we must make an opposed passage, running the American blockade."

"*Hai*, Tanaka-*sama*." Shioya was all proper respect and discipline once more. "But suppose the Americans do not oppose us?" He sounded almost worried at the thought.

"It is always wisest to assume the worst," Tanaka said gently. "And perhaps we can get in the first blow, before they are fully prepared to meet us, before they are even aware of our presence."

Shioya seemed to hear the gentle rebuke. War was not something to rush into headlong. Not something to *invite*. "Yes, sir."

"I would like to see your plan in three days, Takeo-*san*." He glanced past the lieutenant's shoulder at the waiting line of fighter sub pilots. "That is all, for now. But, tell them that I am counting on each of them."

"I will, sir."

"As I am counting on *you*, nephew." Smiling, he turned away.

*Teigei* had leveled off once more. Behind him, the young pilots of the *Kiku* squadron were at their calisthenics again.

Preparing to greet their karma.

**H.M.S.** *Truculent*
**Strait of Gibraltar**
**May 5, 1425 hours**

The last of Great Britain's Trafalgar-class nuclear attack submarines, H.M.S. *Truculent* was just over 280 feet long and had a submerged displacement of 5,208 tons. Her captain, Commander John Sylvester Kingsly, was short, bearded, and pugnacious, a British career naval officer who'd been delighted at the news that England was at last taking a stand against Cairo's threats and political strong-arm tactics. H.M.S. *Truculent* had been patrolling the strait for the past week, silently stalking and listening for UIR traffic.

He'd also been warned of the possible approach of the *Teigei*, a Japanese carrier submarine spotted off the Japanese coast three weeks earlier and believed to be heading for the Med. Nothing had been seen of the giant undersea vessel in all that time, but American intelligence believed she must be taking the long route around Africa and through the Gibraltar Strait, since there'd been no sign of her transiting the closely watched Red Sea or the Suez Canal.

Kingsly's orders were vague regarding what he should do if he encountered *Teigei*. He had no explicit orders to sink her, but he had been told to turn her back, if possible, and to stay in close touch with Whitehall in case there were further orders.

Turn her back? Whoever had written *that* inane set of orders must never have set foot on a real, modern ship of war. As for staying in close touch, that was simply not the way of submarine combat, not when surfacing to broadcast position and status was an open invitation to an enemy who could strike without warning and with deadly accuracy from well beyond the horizon.

But then, London was still jittery about her new, public military alliance with the United States. Each set of orders he received convinced Kingsly that the senders were concerned more about their personal asses than about the threat of confrontation south of Gibraltar's famous rock.

Kingsly stood for a long moment, studying the officers and ratings at their stations in *Truculent*'s control room, sensing the gentle thrum of the boat's pulse-jet engine through the steel deck. *Truculent* was eleven years old and long overdue for refit. Modern for the wars between East and West contemplated by her designers two decades before, she had none of the blue-green laser gear that the Americans—and, reportedly, the Japanese—were experimenting with. Against the Alfas and Akulas of the UIR, she would be able to give a good account of herself. But against a modern, undersea terror like the *Teigei*, well, he had his reservations. Combat might well become an engagement like blindman's buff, where one side was blindfolded, reduced to moving and striking by sound alone, while the other could see and elude the blind man with hilarious ease.

He would have to rely on the American fighter subs if it looked like the Japanese were going to try to force the blockade. A four-sub patrol was usually at sea, close enough that they could respond in a few minutes, if need be.

"Number One," he called suddenly.

"Sir!" His first officer was Lieutenant Commander David Walker, a lean and gangly officer new to submarines.

"I'd like the current position of our allies, please."

"Sir." At the plot table, Walker gestured to the colored marker lines ruled on acetate overlaying a detailed sounding map of the narrows between Gibraltar and Ceuta. "We are here, Captain, just on the thirty-sixth degree of latitude, nine miles due east of Point Marroqui. At last report, the American patrol was here, five miles to the southeast, between our position and Point Leona."

"And when was this last report?"

Walker looked nonplussed. "I'm . . . not sure, Captain."

"I want an accurate plot. Now."

"Aye aye, sir. At once."

"Bridge!" a voice called from the loudspeaker on a nearby bulkhead. "This is Sonar!"

Kingsly picked up an intercom microphone and held it to his face. "Sonar, this is the captain. Go ahead."

"Sir, we have a contact, bearing three-five-eight, relative. Sounds like twin screws, sir, and on a closing course."

A contact, and almost dead ahead, coming into the strait from the west. *Teigei?*

"Very well. Stay on them." He released the microphone switch. "Belay that order, Number One," he said. The only way to communicate with the American subs was through active sonar, and that would give *Truculent*'s position away. If that was *Teigei* up ahead, they needed stealth now. "But we'd better hope to God the Yanks are on their toes, or we've got trouble."

"Yes, sir."

"I'll have battle stations, Mr. Walker. Silent routine, if you please."

Seconds later, the battle alert signs were winking soundlessly in every compartment on the boat, and the men were moving to battle stations with practiced efficiency and speed.

*Truculent* probed slowly through the dark toward her unseen prey.

# CHAPTER
## 17

*Ei* Strike Force
Strait of Gibraltar
May 5, 1430 hours

Lieutenant Takeo Shioya lay in the embrace of his fighter sub's cockpit harness, his attention on the image painted in liquid light on the inside of his helmet. As he turned his head, the helmet display shifted as well, allowing him to look in all directions, seeing what normally would be hidden by watery darkness.

The colors were muted and blurred, for Shioya had ordered the fighter subs' *siranui* lasers switched off. Operating solely on passive sonar, the fighter sub imaging system would be handicapped, but it would not give away their position to the enemy.

The *Zingei* fighter sub force numbered seven, over half of *Kiku* squadron's total complement. They were spread out in a wide V, the open mouth facing east and measuring eight kilometers, tip to tip. All were at a depth of three hundred meters, almost on the bottom and bucking the cold, deep current spilling out of the Mediterranean, but the powerful throb of the Mitsubishi MHD propulsors kept the sleek machines

**195**

moving forward at a smooth and steady forty knots. *Teigei* trailed the Stingrays, ten kilometers astern and at half their present depth.

Shioya's craft was at the point of the formation, trailing the other six as they pushed against the current, moving steadily east. In the rush of enthusiasm that had followed the renunciation of the old constitution, most of Japan's military men had developed a passion for studying the histories of war and combat tactics. Shioya's plan, approved by his uncle, had been based on the classic envelopment of the Romans by Hannibal at Cannae twenty-two centuries earlier. The trick was to bring the prey unsuspecting into the jaws of the V, a maneuver that demanded both keen sensors and superior speed and maneuverability on the part of the Japanese force.

He could see the positions of the other six fighter subs in his helmet display, marked by his computer as points of bright green light against the murky, blue-green darkness. What Shioya could not allow himself to forget was that this was a war of maneuver in three dimensions, unlike the two dimensions at Cannae. By entering the Strait of Gibraltar at three hundred meters, the fighter subs were less than fifty meters above the bottom at this point. To the blockaders at Gibraltar, positioned closer to the surface, they should be invisible against the sonar clutter off the bottom, while the defenders would be silhouetted against the surface.

He checked his weapons once again. Each Stingray fighter carried two Type 96 *yari*, or spears, long-range, jet-powered torpedoes that could be either wire-guided or cut free to home on acoustical signatures or laser guidance. Each had four times the reported range of the American Mark 62s, and a warhead nearly twice as large. In addition, each Stingray carried four smaller, solid-fuel rocket torpedoes much like the American Mark 62. Designated *tanken*, or daggers, they'd been designed to destroy other fighter subs, and were powerful enough to damage a larger submarine if given the chance.

"Stingray Leader, this is Stingray Six" sounded in Shioya's helmet headset. That was *Chu-i* Ishiguro on the north tip of the V, his rank corresponding to that of an American lieutenant j.g. The tactical laser communications channel was on a computer-controlled network, too tightly beamed for any eavesdroppers to detect unless they chanced to pass between two of the Japanese subs. "I have a solid contact, bearing zero-eight-five, range twelve kilometers. Not screws. It sounds like an impeller."

"So?" Shioya considered this. "An American fighter sub?"

"It is possible, sir. But the contact sounds larger than that. Much larger."

"Very well. We will close and identify. All Stingrays, come left nine-zero degrees. Maintain intervals and speed." The maneuver would shift the entire V formation north, positioning it directly ahead of the target. Shioya directed his computer to open a laser com beam with *Teigei*, describing the situation to the mother sub in crisp, measured phrases.

"Very well, Stingray Leader," *Teigei* answered, seconds later. Shioya started. It was his uncle's voice. "Proceed with the plan. Do not fire, however, unless you are fired upon."

"Stingray Leader understands. Out."

Lieutenant Shioya was still weighing his uncle's evident distaste for war. The older man was no coward, of that Shioya was certain, but he did seem to harbor a marked reluctance for battle. Perhaps *Beiko*-Komei simply feared that the enemy would back down at the last minute.

He hoped that would not be the case.

**H.M.S. *Truculent***
**Strait of Gibraltar**
**May 5, 1432 hours**

"Definite submarine, Captain," the sonar officer told Kingsly. On the big screen above the sonar console, parallel cascades of sound tracings glowed in the compartment's eerie, subdued light, like dark, inverted Vs stacked one atop the next. "And a big, damned mother to boot. But we can't match her to anything in our library."

Kingsly knew sonar well enough to identify some of the separate sound patterns at different frequencies displayed on the screen—a piece of heavy equipment, probably a pump motor of some kind; the high-pitched throb of turbine shafts; the *crackle-pop* of cavitation, caused by vacuum pockets forming and collapsing behind turning propeller blades as the unseen craft moved forward. The sound was also being piped over a speaker in the compartment. Kingsly could hear the low-voiced *thrum-thrum-thrum* of a ship's screws.

Evidently this target's sonic signature had never been recorded before, for there was nothing in *Truculent*'s sound library that matched it. It sounded to him a little like a Typhoon, big—very big—with two shafts. Speed maybe thirty or thirty-five knots.

But it was different, too, in a way that Kingsly could not put into words. "You checked against the American Typhoons?" Maybe the Yanks had made some modifications to their new toys.

"Yes, sir. No joy."

"*Teigei*, then," Kingsly said. It could be nothing else. "Range?"

The sonar officer pursed his lips. "Less than thirty miles. More than fifteen. Can't be more precise than that, you know, sir. Not until we're closer."

Kingsly nodded. *Truculent*'s excellent Type 2020 sonar had a passive range of thirty nautical miles, but unless she went active—sending out a pulse of sound to measure the precise distance to the target—there was no way to measure a precise range.

Of course, going to active sonar meant giving away his own position, and Kingsly wasn't ready to do that just yet. He envied the Americans and their ULTRA-C lasers. Still, fifteen miles would put the contact north of Tangier and moving into the strait. It seemed a reasonable guess, at least from which to begin working up a solution for intercept.

He picked up a microphone. "Bridge, this is the captain."

"Walker here, sir."

"Bring her to all stop, Number One."

"All stop, aye, sir."

*Trafalgar*, the first of the Trafalgar-class submarines, had been driven by a conventional, seven-blade screw. All subsequent vessels in the series, however, were driven by pump jet, a low-rev, high-pitch propeller turning against stator vanes in a shrouded duct. The arrangement, compressing water and blasting it astern as a jet, was far quieter than ordinary screws, but it was noisy enough that Kingsly had elected to switch it off and drift with the deep, outflowing current. Perhaps he could learn something more about the target.

Perhaps the target would make the first move.

*Ei* **Strike Force**
**Strait of Gibraltar**
**May 5, 1432 hours**

"The target sounds like a pump jet, Lieutenant," *Chu-i* Ishiguro announced. "My library identifies it as probable British Trafalgar class."

"Trafalgar, eh?" Shioya was excited. "Stay on him." British submarines could die in a trap as easily as Americans. The range was narrowing, down now to just under eight thousand meters.

"Lieutenant!" Ishiguro sounded worried. "The quarry has gone silent!"

"Steady, *Chu-i*," Shioya said. "Continue closing."

"He may have heard us, sir."

"Perhaps. But we will get closer." He wanted to *see* the other submarine's hull in his helmet's display. At the moment, the target was marked simply by a red diamond adrift against a hazy, blue-green backdrop, revealed to passive sonar by the continuing rumble of coolant pumps and machinery feeding its nuclear power plant. He was tempted to switch on his *siranui* lasers and paint the other vessel's hull, but it was too early yet, too early by far. "Reduce speed to ten knots. Continue on course."

Their speed reduced, the seven Japanese fighter subs sank lower in unison, their smooth bellies gliding scant meters above the mud and rock of the floor of the strait.

"White Star Three, this is White Star One. Do you copy? Over."

"Copy, White One. Go ahead." Lieutenant j.g. Frank Wilder heard the tension in Monk Young's voice and felt an answering shiver. He was less certain than ever that he belonged out here. *Down* here, three hundred feet beneath the surface of the water.

"White Three, we've lost *Truculent*. How about zipping ahead for a look-see?"

"Roger that, White One." He pressed his throttle forward, felt the building power of his Barracuda's impellers. "On my way."

The patrol code-named White Star was currently some six miles southeast of the British attack sub, but Wilder was in the eyeball slot, positioned two miles ahead of the other three SFV-4s where he could act as spotter for the others. Monk Young was in command. With him were Oz Franklin and a new kid, Lieutenant j.g. Jason Costello.

Wilder was nervous. Hell, everybody in the Blue Hunters had been nervous, ever since their UIR enemies, until then faceless and impersonal, had become all too real back in that whorehouse in Jerez. The other guys in the squadron had questioned him endlessly about those black-garbed commandos, and Wilder himself had become something of a hero because he'd been there, and survived.

He didn't feel like a hero. The memory still gnawed at him, a sullen glow of shame that would not be quenched. He'd *run* . . . and left Dom and Cigar to be captured. God, he'd seen Cigar's feet when they'd

loaded him aboard the medevac flight for
Washington, and he'd nearly vomited right there on
the tarmac.

The flight surgeon at Rota had questioned him
closely afterward. Post Traumatic Stress Disorder—
PTSD—could be as crippling as enemy bullets.
Ultimately, he'd decided that the best thing he could
do was to get back in the saddle at once. He'd volunteered for Operation Cid, circled his patrol zone off
Red Beach with Gray, but come no closer to action
than watching Gray shoot down a UIR helicopter.
Then he'd learned that Blackwell had been killed
outside of Tangier, and later that afternoon he'd
seen Cigar on the stretcher at Rota's airfield.

If PTSD could be crippling, so too could survivor's
guilt. Wilder didn't recognize it as such, but he'd
started brooding during the forty-eight-hour stand-
down after Operation Cid, a wearing, low-level
depression that continued after the unit transferred
from Rota to the British naval base at Gibraltar. Since
then, he'd volunteered for more and more of the
ongoing patrols into the strait, driving himself and
his SFV-4 until he'd almost killed himself by missing
an engine flood valve warning light on his console,
losing power, and sinking to the bottom of Algeciras
Bay off Gibraltar's south mole. After that,
Commander Gray had ordered him to take another
forty-eight hours off, an enforced R&R period that
had done nothing to improve his spirits.

This was Wilder's third patrol since going back on
the duty roster. Blackie's death and Cigar's torture
had receded in his mind, he thought, until awareness
of them was little more than a dull ache.

But he was finding that he now hated the Islamics
with a depth and a completeness he'd not known

was possible . . . and if the Japanese were determined to help the Islamics against Americans, well, he hated them too. If *Truculent* had gone silent, it almost certainly meant the Brits had picked up a contact somewhere to the west. Surface traffic through the Strait of Gibraltar continued to be heavy, with a ship passing overhead every few minutes. A contact piquing *Truculent*'s special interest must be something unusual.

*Teigei*, perhaps, or an Islamic sub.

Wilder pressed his throttle full forward, accelerating his Barracuda to sixty knots.

**H.M.S.** *Truculent*
**Strait of Gibraltar**
**May 5, 1435 hours**

Kingsly pressed a headset against his ear, listening for the faint *swish-thrum* that Lieutenant Jenkins, the sonar officer, had reported. There it was . . . quite faint, but definitely there.

"What do you think?" he asked Jenkins. "Doesn't sound like a torpedo."

"If I had to guess, sir, I'd say it was one of the Yank fighter subs. But it's definitely ahead of us, and it may not be alone. I keep getting traces of . . . something else. Other contacts, maybe. No screws, but something moving through the water, and that same swishing sound. Might be MHD induction."

"And Alfa?" That was the designation for the large contact they'd been tracking for the past several minutes.

"Still there, sir. Still on course. No change in heading or revs."

"Okay. I think it's time we got a clear picture of what's out there." He reached for an intercom mike and squeezed the trigger. "Bridge? This is the captain."

"Bridge here." Walker's voice came back.

"Have engineering stand by for full revs. What's our warload?"

"Tubes one and two are loaded with Mark 24s, sir. Decoys in three and four."

"Very well. Stand by." He turned back to Jenkins. "Let's go active on the 2020. One pulse."

"One pulse, aye, sir."

The sonar officer pressed a button on the console.

*Ei* Strike Force
Strait of Gibraltar
May 5, 1435 hours

*Chu-i* Noburo Ishiguro was closest to the enemy target, close enough that his *siranui* computers were already painting the shape of her hull in his helmet, a dark gray cigar shape at an estimated range of six kilometers.

Control of most of the combat functions of his Mitsubishi fighter sub was handled through his helmet. He handled pitch, yaw, and thrust with two joystick controllers that he manipulated through touch, but targeting and fire control orders were fed through his helmet. When he looked at the discretes glowing against his helmet display, infrared sensors inside the helmet mechanism measured his eye movements; a hard and deliberate double blink would engage the minisub's sophisticated computer controls. He could also operate the craft through voice command.

He selected the glowing icon for torpedo arming and blinked twice. "You have target lock," his computer's voice told him. "Acoustical homing."

The targeting discrete bracketing the approaching British submarine changed shape, indicating a positive lock for both of his *yari* torpedoes. He was ready to fire now, on command.

He engaged his tactical laser communications, letting his computer identify the *Ei* formation leader and project a tightly beamed burst of laser light between the two fighter subs.

"*Ei* One, this is *Ei* Six," he called. "I have a positive targeting lock and am—"

Then the sonar pulse hit.

To Ishiguro's eyes, it was as though the target had exploded in flaring white radiance. As with the American ULTRA-C, the minisub's *siranui* imaging system used data from both sound and laser to paint its electronic scenes of the surrounding ocean, but the *Ei* minisubs were still operating on sonar only, to avoid giving away their position to American ULTRA-C sensors. The sharp *chirp-ping!* of the target's active sonar momentarily overloaded the *Ei*'s sensitive sonar receivers, blinding them in the same way that pointing a video camera at the sun will burn out its electronics, at least temporarily. The background of sea and distant submarine were blanked out, leaving only the targeting and operational discretes glowing inside Ishiguro's headset. Reflexively, he blinked against the light . . . and blinked again.

By chance, he'd been staring at the launch-one icon. He recognized his mistake as he felt his fighter sub lurch upward, freed of the weight of one of its massive *yari* torpedoes.

"Torpedo one, launch," his computer's voice told him.

As his view of the outside world cleared he saw his torpedo streaking toward the British sub.

**H.M.S.** *Truculent*
**Strait of Gibraltar**
**May 5, 1435 hours**

"Range to Alfa, thirteen-point-two nautical miles," Jenkins reported. "And we have multiple small targets close in, bearing—"

"Torpedo in the water!" a junior sonar operator cried from his station at the console. His hands went to his headphones as he listened. "Bearing zero-zero-three, relative, speed six-three knots and accelerating!"

"On speaker," Kingsly snapped.

Jenkins touched a keypad, and Kingsly could hear it, a sharp, hissing sound, growing rapidly louder. He snagged the intercom mike. "Bridge, Captain! Ahead full! Left full rudder! I want one hundred fifteen percent on the reactor, now!"

"Ahead full, left full rudder, aye, aye! Going to one-one-five on the reactor!"

The deck canted sharply beneath his feet as *Truculent* swung to port.

**Imperial Navy Attack Submarine** *Umiryu*
**Strait of Gibraltar**
**May 5, 1435 hours**

*Chusa* Shigeru Oshida, captain of the Tyogei-class nuclear attack sub *Umiryu*, sat in his bridge chair, his head encased in his *kabuto-no siranui*, the blank-visaged imaging helmet that revealed to him the depths around him.

One hundred ten meters long, with a submerged displacement of almost seven thousand tons and a crew of 108, the *Umiryu* was a close match in size, shape, and mission to American Los Angeles–class attack subs, but she was newer than any of the L.A. boats and was invested with far more sophisticated technology. She'd been designed from the keel up with *siranui* scanning and imaging gear, and her pump-jet engine could drive her at forty-five knots, twenty percent better than even an upgraded Los Angeles sub's best speed.

Oshida was fiercely proud of *Umiryu* and eager to test the sub and her crew in battle. He was aware of Captain Tanaka's reluctance but had dismissed it as the natural desire of a squadron commander to exhaust every nonviolent means of battle before committing the lives of his men to combat. Oshida respected that view but privately knew that nothing less than outright war against the Americans would destroy their arrogance, that nothing less than war could erase the shame of Hiroshima, surrender, and the travesty of a constitution forced on a helpless nation by the conqueror MacArthur.

With good fortune, Oshida thought, *Umiryu* might be among the first to strike a blow for Japanese honor.

For that reason, he was unhappy with the orders given him by Tanaka. According to plan, the *Umiryu* was trailing nearly ten kilometers astern of the *Teigei* and, like the Mitsubishi fighter subs, was at three hundred meters, gliding only a few scant meters above the bottom of the strait. Her sail *siranui* laser had been shut down to avoid detection by the blockaders; only her keel laser was operational, continuing to paint highly detailed panoramas of the rugged bottom. Through the *siranui* helmet, Oshida could see the seafloor spreading out on all sides of the deep-traveling attack sub. It was rocky here, punctuated with sheer-sided massifs, canyons, and jagged prominences that reached for *Umiryu*'s belly like knife blades. In such surroundings, even an American sub equipped with ULTRA-C would have a tough time separating the Japanese killer sub from the tangle of rock and broken-sided canyon walls; *Umiryu* was effectively invisible, held in reserve against the possibility of an American attack.

In reserve! With *Teigei* in the lead, as bait to draw out the American blockade!

Yet Oshida would do his duty. His training, his dedication to his profession, were too great to allow otherwise. But if the leash restraining him slipped the least little bit . . .

He heard *Truculent*'s sonar ping first, distorted by distance and by his surroundings, and doubted that the enemy had spotted him. From his perspective, *Teigei* was ahead and above him, viewed stern-on, tiny with distance but clearly visible by the twin, conical wakes trailed by her propellers as she moved through the water. Beyond, visible only as pinpricks of light on his helmet, were the British sub and seven Japanese *Zingeis* rising to meet it.

Then there was another target, identified by *Umiryu*'s computer as a Japanese torpedo. Excitement galloped in his head and heart. The battle had begun!

"Stand by, Engineering!" he called. "I want full reactor power on my command! Mr. Iwata!"

His First Officer's response was sharp and immediate. "*Hai*, honored Captain!"

"Are all tubes loaded?"

"*Hai*, honored Captain!"

"Then battle stations, Mr. Iwata. Silent routine. Inform the torpedo room to stand by."

*Umiryu* skimmed past a towering, undersea cliff, preparing for battle.

**Barracuda Flight**
**White Star Three**
**May 5, 1436 hours**

Frank Wilder saw *Truculent* two hundred yards ahead, a great, dark whale shape slowly swinging to port. He'd heard the sonar ping, of course, though his SFV-4 had not been in the path of the directed beam and had not had its electronics blinded by the pulse. His Barracuda's sonar had picked up multiple echoes, however, echoes that his micro-Cray computer had converted into a cascade of data. A huge submarine was coming bow-on, eight miles ahead, the Japanese *Teigei* without a doubt. Six . . . no, seven more targets were rising from below, between *Truculent* and *Teigei*, hard to see against the clutter of the rocky bottom, but as clearly revealed in *Truculent's* brief sonar pulse as if they'd been illuminated by a searchlight. That single pulse had provided data enough for his Barracuda's micro-Cray to tag each target and continue to track it, following them now by passive sonar and the backscatter from his ULTRA-C lasers.

He could also see the enemy torpedo, racing toward *Truculent* at a speed that would intercept the British sub in another four minutes.

"White Star, White Star, this is White Star Three!" Wilder called. "*Truculent* is under attack!" He keyed in the computer command that would transmit the tactical data he was receiving now to the other fighter subs, now some four miles astern.

Without waiting for orders, he goosed the Barracuda's engine, hurtling past *Truculent* a few meters off her starboard side. Her massive hull and towering sail drifted past to Wilder's left like a dark gray sea cliff, and his ULTRA-C lasers painted the oncoming Japanese submarines until they shone like fluorescent beacons against the murk.

With odds of seven fighter subs to one and a torpedo already running, Wilder hesitated, wondering what to do next.

# CHAPTER
# 18

**Barracuda Flight**
**White Star Three**
**May 5, 1436 hours**

Lieutenant j.g. Frank Wilder was torn. He wanted to angle his Barracuda toward those oncoming Japanese fighter subs, but the threat posed by the torpedo to the H.M.S. *Truculent* was not something he could ignore. The British sub was turning, but sluggishly, sluggishly, her engine still not up to full speed scant moments after she'd been quietly adrift on the current.

With a bitter, bitten-back curse, Wilder kept his SFV-4 on course as he streaked past *Truculent*'s vast, rounded bow, heading straight for the enemy torpedo. Commander Gray had evolved tactics for dealing with wire-guided torps at Cienfuegos, and he'd suggested ways for taking out other types of torpedoes during the weeks after the squadron's return to Kings Bay.

Homing torpedoes have only a few ways of tracking a target. Recent developments in blue-green laser technology allowed some to home off of reflected laser light, like the laser-guided ordnance used by aircraft during and after Vietnam, but those were expensive and still relatively rare. Air-to-air missiles could be laser-guided, they could use infrared tracking, homing on a target's engine exhaust, or they could use either passive or active radar homing.

Neither infrared or radar homing worked at all underwater, however, for the water itself absorbed both heat and all but the very longest radio waves before they'd traveled more than a few feet. As with so many other aspects of submarine technology, homing torpedoes used sound to track their targets, either in passive mode, homing on the sounds the target made, or in active mode, broadcasting loud, high-frequency pings and following the reflected sound waves like a closing on an acoustically pinpointed moth.

As Wilder swiftly closed the gap between himself and the torpedo, he scanned it with his ULTRA-C. There was no sign of the slender, trailing thread of a control wire, which meant it was running free, controlled by its own electronic brain and not by a human operator aboard the firing sub. It was not actively pinging, at least not yet, so it was almost certainly homing on the thrumming sound of *Truculent*'s pulse-jet engine.

With growing urgency, Wilder stabbed at the glowing, touch-sensitive surface of his console, isolating the noise of *Truculent*'s engine, digitizing and reproducing it, downloading it to his SFV-4's active sonar suite. The process took an agony of seconds to complete, and by the time he was done, the torpedo was one mile away. With Barracuda and torpedo closing at a combined speed of 150 knots, they were now less than twenty-five seconds apart.

Wilder touched the sonar active key, and the Barracuda began transmitting *Truculent*'s engine sounds, but magnified, packed into a narrow beam and blasted at the torpedo like a searchlight. With the computer holding the cone of sound on target, he pulled the SFV's stick back and to the right, turning hard to starboard and rising swiftly toward the surface.

The torpedo, its acoustic senses assaulted by sound at the same frequency as its original target, was effectively jammed. Tracking on this louder, nearer sound source, its computer brain kicked its control surfaces over. At almost seventy knots, it swung left and rose toward its new target.

**H.M.S.** *Truculent*
**Strait of Gibraltar**
**May 5, 1437 hours**

"Bloody hell, where did *he* come from!"

Jenkins's irreverent exclamation brought Kingsly around just as he was leaving the sonar compartment. "What do you have?"

"One of the Americans, Captain! He just dusted off our starboard side, zeroed in on that torp, and started making a noise like . . ."

"Like what?"

"Like us, sir! Tight-beamed, but I'm getting some back scatter. He's playing bloody decoy! Sir."

Kingsly turned and strode back onto the control-room deck. He was sharply aware of the dozen or so stiff, white faces, all looking to him. "Heading!" he snapped.

"Heading now two-one-four magnetic, Captain," the diving officer called out. "Still at left full rudder, turning to port."

"Right full rudder."

"Right full rudder, aye, sir."

"We'll slip past the minisubs," he said, half aloud, visualizing the tactical situation in his mind, "and come in on the mother ship from the south."

Again, though, he wished he had the American ULTRA-C. He had the eerie and quite accurate feeling that they could see him, while he could not see them.

## Imperial Japanese Submarine *Teigei*
## Strait of Gibraltar
## May 5, 1437 hours

Captain Tanaka was in *Teigei*'s control chair, his head in the cool embrace of the *kabuto-no siranui* as the flotilla began its run of the Gibraltar Strait. He'd ordered all *siranui* lasers shut down save those on tight beams for communications, or directed toward the bottom for navigation. Even so, *Teigei*'s computer had painted a fairly detailed panorama of the surrounding ocean, building it up solely from passively acquired sound sources and from that single active pulse from the *Truculent*. He could see *Truculent* as a computer-imaged shadow, drifting off toward the right, as the torpedo launched by *Ei* Six rocketed high and to the left. Had the launch been deliberate, or an accident? Even now he wasn't sure, but he knew better than to try to straighten things out now. The British would launch torpedoes of their own any second. In fact, he suspected that their move toward the south was a clumsy attempt to get on his flank.

Selecting communications from a menu displayed to the side of his view, he opened a laser com link with *Ei* One.

"Take out the British submarine," he told his nephew. "We'll run past at full speed." Shifting frequencies, he keyed in to the *Umiryu*, still several kilometers astern. "*Umiryu*, *Teigei*. Stay with us, and watch for an attack from the rear."

Tanaka distrusted the reports he'd received indicating that the Americans had been forced to leave Rota, now some 145 kilometers to the northwest, up the Spanish coast and well astern of the Japanese flotilla. The light force in front of him might be a decoy, something to lead him into a trap, while the real blow fell on him from astern.

"*Teigei*, this is *Umiryu*." The harsh voice was Oshida's. "Message received. We are with you."

"Commander Matsushita!"

"Yes, honored Captain!"

"Flank speed. Full ahead!"

Tanaka found himself thinking of the dolphins as *Teigei* accelerated into the strait.

**Barracuda Flight**
**White Star One**
**May 5, 1437 hours**

Lieutenant Joseph "Monk" Young had been known as an "iceman" back when he was in VFA-157, flying F/A-18 Hornets off the *Abraham Lincoln*. Along with Seegar, he'd been stationed aboard the Honest Abe in 2002, and only the fact that they'd been flying CAP at the time had saved them when a hurtling chunk of metal had shrieked out of the sky, transforming a multibillion-dollar supercarrier into a flaming, sinking mass of junk.

He was still an iceman in the cockpit, more engineer

than warrior as he gentled his SFV's controls, but beneath his outward persona he hated the Japanese with a seething, white-hot fury that only rarely cracked through his icy exterior. He'd lost a lot of friends and shipmates when the *Lincoln* died, and most of the only family that had ever mattered to him. His parents had died in a car crash when he was twelve; after that, he'd been raised by an unwilling, drunken, and abusive uncle. Young had enlisted in the Navy at eighteen just to escape the house, but he'd quickly qualified for a Navy-sponsored college program, then gone on to OCS at Annapolis and flight school at Pensacola.

A j.g. when the *Lincoln* went down, he'd won his lieutenant's bars when he'd returned to the States. Three years later, he'd volunteered for Project Orca, knowing that sooner or later he'd be facing the Japanese again . . . and he had a better chance taking them on in a submarine than aboard a lumbering, vulnerable carrier.

"White Star, this is White Star Leader," he called over the tactical channel. "Spread out, men. Extended formation. Cover *Truculent* from those fighter subs."

"Wheeoo!" Franklin called out. "Let's rock-and-roll!"

The three fighter subs accelerated hard, boosting to nearly eighty knots in less than a minute.

**Barracuda Flight**
**White Star Three**
**May 5, 1439 hours**

*How long do I have to keep seducing this thing?* Wilder glanced back over his shoulder and saw the red-diamond highlighted blip of the Japanese torpedo, still doggedly pursuing him up through the sea. If the thing lost its lock on him, it was probably programmed to begin circling, either reacquiring its original target, or beginning to emit active sonar pulses, and homing in on the largest, closest new target. If the damned thing would just run out of fuel . . .

He'd considered leading it back toward the big Japanese sub, but he doubted that he'd be able to break the line of enemy fighter subs now drifting toward the *Truculent*. He reconsidered his position now. As long as he was letting the damned thing chase him, it was keeping him out of the battle, and the rest of his flight clearly needed all the help they could get. If he could lose his unwanted companion in the midst of the Japanese force, so much the better.

"Stay with me, fella," he told the torpedo, now clinging gamely to his tail at a range of less than one hundred yards. He brought his stick over to the left and pushed it forward, letting the SFV's nose drop sharply. "We're gonna get back in there and mix it up!"

**Barracuda Flight**
**White Star One**
**May 5, 1439 hours**

Young saw two of the Japanese fighter subs less than a mile ahead and slapped the arm switch for his torpedoes. Were they going to fire again? They appeared to be lining up for a broadside shot at *Truculent*, but he couldn't be certain that the first shot hadn't been a mistake.

He hesitated. . . .

"*Siranui* lasers . . . switch on!" Shioya cried. Instantly, three beacons of light winked to life on each *Zingei* fighter sub, one on each dorsal stabilizer, a third on the belly. Seen through his helmet, the surrounding water displayed a glorious, crystal clarity, as each mote of debris, each eddy in the water took on life and form.

Ahead, fully illuminated now, the vast, gray whale shape of the British *Truculent* plowed forward through the depths, passing his position from left to right. Laser ranging gave Shioya the precise distance: 924.4 meters.

Selecting one of his menu icons with a glance and a double blink, he switched his computer control to voice activation. He wanted to feel this launch. "Targeting!" he called, staring at the image of the British attack sub before him. "Lock on, acoustical homing, torpedoes one and two."

"You have target lock," the computer's voice replied. "Acoustical homing."

"Fire one!"

With a piercing hiss and a lurch, the first torpedo slid free of Shioya's fighter sub, rocketing into the distance on a frothing contrail of sound made visible by the computer.

"Fire two!"

His second torpedo whooshed from beneath his hull, following the first. Over his headset, he heard Nakamura echoing his launch order with an order of his own: "Fire one!"

"Break left," he told the others, pulling his own

hand controller hard to port as he spoke. "Watch for the American fighters!"

He could see them now, hurtling in from the east like stub-winged missiles.

With a glance, he armed his four *tanken* mini-torpedoes.

**Barracuda Flight**
**White Star One**
**May 5, 1440 hours**

"They've fired!" Young screamed. "They're firing at the Brits!"

Was there anything that could be done? There wasn't time now to try Wilder's trick with the sound mimicry. At least four Japanese fighters had just launched, from distances ranging from over a kilometer to less than five hundred meters. Running time for those fish would be seconds, and the American subs were too far from the fight to get between the torps and the target in time.

Young's cool broke, the fury blazing like a furnace. "Get them! *Get the bastards!*"

And then the Barracudas were among the Japanese fighters, twisting and turning in a duel to the death.

**H.M.S.** *Truculent*
**Strait of Gibraltar**
**May 5, 1440 hours**

Altogether, seven Japanese *yari* torpedoes were loosed at H.M.S. *Truculent.* Captain Kingsly ordered decoys

launched as soon as his sonar officer reported the
first torp in the water, but the running time was so
short that the order was never carried out.

The first three struck almost simultaneously along
her starboard side, in her rounded bow, beneath her
sail, and farther aft, just forward of her stabilizers.
The eighty-five-meter-long hull was engulfed by the
triple explosion, which tore off her bow, punched
through her control-room bulkhead, and shredded
her tail section in a single, convulsive detonation.

Moments later, Shioya's torpedoes slammed into
the central third of the hull as it began settling
toward the bottom, scattering debris like rain
through the dark water and sending *Truculent's*
nuclear power plant and its casing plummeting like
a stone into the depths. By the time the last two torpedoes reached the area, there was no longer any
target.

What was left of H.M.S. *Truculent*, and the ninety-
eight officers and men aboard her, was already well
on its way to the bottom.

*Ei* Strike Force
**Strait of Gibraltar**
**May 5, 1440 hours**

Shioya was taken aback by the fury of the American
attack. The thunderous detonations from *Truculent's*
funeral pyre were still echoing through the deep as at
least three SFV-4s plunged through part of the
Japanese formation.

"Target lock, Dagger one, two, three!" he cried.

One of those dancing, stubby aircraft twisting past
his bow was circled by a red ring. Data flickered

across his vision, giving range, bearing, speed, and angle on the bow.

"Fire one!"

His first Dagger shrieked from beneath his hull, trailing sound like smoke.

"Fire two!"

The second sub killer followed the first. Their range was sharply limited, less than two kilometers.

But at a range of four hundred meters, he could hardly miss.

**Barracuda Flight**
**White Star Four**
**May 5, 1440 hours**

Lieutenant j.g. Jason Costello had been with the squadron for less than a week, too brief a time to have learned more than the names and handles of the others in the squadron.

Technically, he was a replacement for a man he'd never met, another j.g. named Blackwell, but he'd been assigned a slot with the Blue Hunters long before Blackwell had died off Tangier.

Replacement or not, he was raw and inexperienced, not yet comfortable with his transition from fighter jock to sub driver. "Costello! Break right!" sounded over his headset, but he'd already lined up on one of the saucer-shaped Japanese fighters, so he held his course for a second too long, trying to lock on.

The *tanken* slammed into his Barracuda just behind his cockpit, cracking his life-support capsule and splitting the canopy open.

At a depth of 512 feet, the water pressure was almost 230 pounds per square inch. The mercury-bright stream smashed into the back of Costello's head with sufficient force to slam his head forward into his console. Unconscious, then, he did not see the flickering array of red lights warning of failed systems and shutdowns.

He was probably dead sometime before the shattered Barracuda fluttered to the floor of the strait, where the pressure hit a quarter ton per square inch and popped his already weakened canopy like an eggshell.

Barracuda Flight
White Star Three
May 5, 1441 hours

Wilder had lost the Japanese torpedo. As he'd dived for the swirling undersea fight, it seemed to lose interest, falling away and drifting toward the bottom, its fuel expended.

By the time Wilder entered the combat, White Star Four had already been hit and was arrowing into the depths, trailing black oil and silver bubbles. Wilder dropped smoothly onto the tail of one of the sleek, odd-looking saucer shapes, but before he could lock on, the enemy fighter pulled up and away, twisting out of his reach in a tight and graceful barrel roll.

He locked onto another, more distant fighter, one that seemed to be trying to get onto Oz Franklin's tail. He triggered his Mark 62, and the torpedo shrieked through the water, swinging to meet the target's shifting course, then merging with it in a blossoming flower of thundering white noise.

"Splash one!" he yelled, then laughed out loud. The old aviator's battle cry of an air-to-air kill sounded strange when the combatants were already two hundred feet beneath the waves.

Then one of the diving saucers was on his tail, angling in from above, and no matter how hard he twisted and turned, the other craft stayed glued to his tail, two hundred feet astern.

The explosion jarred him like a hard punch to the face. Stunned, blinking, he tried to focus on the red lights flaring across his console display. Power was out . . . steering out . . . engines and MHD impellers dead. . . . Then there was a hissing snap, and his console lights went out as though someone had just yanked the plug.

There was no sense in riding a wreck to the bottom. Wilder grabbed the ejection ring and pulled. For a heart-stopping moment, nothing happened . . . and then with a deep, hollow-sounding boom, the Barracuda's life-support pod broke free from the shattered hull and rocketed toward the surface.

**Barracuda Flight**
**White Star One**
**May 5, 1442 hours**

Young saw Wilder's escape pod break free and hurtle toward the sky. Only he and Franklin were left now, against six Japanese fighter subs.

"Oz!" he called. "Head for the bottom!" Among the rocks and canyons below, they might be able to avoid the maneuverable and deadly saucers that seemed almost impossible to pin down.

"Roger that!" Franklin called back. "It ain't very healthy around here. The Surgeon General really ought to have somethin' to say about that!"

They fell with the fluttering wreckage of Wilder's Barracuda, hoping to evade detection. Fortunately, the battle had scattered the Japanese, and none seemed to notice their maneuver.

In the distance, though, the two large Japanese submarines were looming out of the darkness like thunderheads.

Could the two Barracudas nail them . . . or even just one? Young wanted to kill the *Teigei* so badly he could taste it, but he was down to one torpedo left, same as Franklin, and if they maneuvered for a shot, they'd be spotted and cut down by that saucer wolf-pack long before they could acquire and shoot.

Helplessly, he watched them sweep past a mile and a half to the north.

**Imperial Navy Submarine *Teigei***
**May 5, 1443 hours**

The battle was over. The Japanese, with overwhelming superiority in firepower and numbers, rumbled down the strait, unstoppable, unapproachable. On *Teigei*'s control-room deck, Tanaka sat in his command chair and listened to the exultant victory cries from his scattered pilots.

"*Teigei*!" Oshida's gruff voice called. "This is *Umiryu*! Two of the enemy fighter subs are hiding on the bottom. If you deploy your fighter subs in the area under my direction, we can flush them out, or destroy them."

Tanaka thought for a minute. A clean sweep would be sweet . . . but it was more important that he get his command intact to Alexandria. One of his precious *Zingeis* had been destroyed. The others had been scattered by the dogfight across half the strait, and enemy sub hunters could appear at any moment. He dared lose no more, dared not risk *Teigei* or *Umiryu* when the Americans had yet to show themselves in full force.

"Negative, *Umiryu*. They are of no concern to us. Maintain course and speed."

"But—"

"Let them go! We will deal with them later, when we return."

*When we return.* There would be another meeting. And Tanaka was determined to destroy whatever was left of the blockading American submarine fleet then.

# CHAPTER
## 19

**Off Cape Trafalgar**
**May 9, 1030 hours**

"Homeplate, Homeplate," Gray called over the Barracuda's ULTRA-C communications channel. "This is Blue Hunter with six guppies, inbound at Devils two-point-one, range twelve thousand. Request vector for docking approach."

"Blue Hunter, this is Homeplate ReCon," a voice said over his headset. ReCon—Recovery Control—was the submarine equivalent of the Primary Flight Control aboard an aircraft carrier. "We have you at zero-nine-five. You have approach clearance. Come right five and descend to Devils two-point-five. We'll take you aboard three to port, three to starboard."

"Right five, Devils two-point-five, roger. Here we come." He shifted channels to his squadron frequency. "Okay, gentlemen, you heard the man. Let's line 'em up and take 'em in."

The six Barracudas had left Gibraltar hours earlier for their rendezvous here, ten miles south of Cape Trafalgar. Three more were on patrol at the moment, five miles south of the Gib, but the remainder of Blue

Hunter Squadron was with him now as they slid into the approach vector that would put them aboard the U.S.S. *Leviathan*.

The American Typhoon had finally made it, four days too late to have participated in the Japanese running of the Gibraltar blockade. Her battle damage from Cienfuegos was completely repaired now, though, and she'd been deployed to Gibraltar as mother ship to the Barracuda fighter sub squadron.

Or what was left of it. Gray felt a tight, tense anticipation as he held his SFV-4 on its new course. Of twelve SFV-4B fighter subs that had been shipped to Spain just seventeen days earlier, he had nine left, and Chief Huxley and his maintenance crew had been working like demons with their limited stocks of spares and backup modules to keep all of those running.

Worse, he'd started with twelve pilots, counting himself, lost three—Seegar, Dominico, and Blackwell—received one replacement—Costello—then lost him as well. Dominico was expected to return from medical leave in another few days, but that would still leave him with only ten men.

Worse, old hands Hernandez and Koch and newbies Douglas and Mackey, while as experienced as the rest of the squadron at piloting SFVs, had not yet been in a sub-to-sub battle. Torpedoing a Krivak II in Tangier harbor didn't count; the deadliest enemy of any submarine was always another sub, and the SFV-4s had been designed from the start for ASW combat. When the Japanese fighter subs and their giant mother craft reappeared, Gray would have only six men experienced in antisub maneuvers—five if Dominico didn't make it back in time.

His one hope was that the Japanese pilots were in almost the same shape. Their single undersea dogfight had been the brief engagement in the strait four days before, and they'd outnumbered the American fighters so badly that only a few had been directly involved in anything other than the mass torpedo launch against the H.M.S. *Truculent*. Gray was going to have to rely on the combat experience of five of his men, and on Japanese overconfidence, to make up for the enemy's superiority in numbers.

At least, now that *Leviathan* had arrived, he would no longer be forced to throw his fighters out against the enemy four at a time so that he could rotate fighter subs and crews. The huge carrier sub could stay on station, maintaining the blockade *all* of the time, and with keener senses than the Barracudas could carry. When the Japanese reappeared, the entire squadron would be able to deploy, rather than those few that happened to be on patrol at the time.

Five minutes later, he throttled back as the huge shadow of *Leviathan* loomed out of the murk, her sail and ventral ULTRA-C lasers brilliant beacons against the gloom. In her wake, two more whale shapes, long and lean and representing a fraction of the Typhoon's tremendous bulk, followed like guard dogs. They were *Leviathan*'s escorts, the Los Angeles-class attack subs *Charlotte* and *Oceanside*.

"Blue Hunter, this is ReCon. We'll take port side first. Send in your first three."

"Roger that." He brought his fighter sub into a long, slow circle south of *Leviathan*, a holding pattern like the marshal stack for an aircraft carrier. Young, Franklin, and Wilder would recover first.

He thought about Joe Young as the young lieutenant started his approach. Monk had been subdued these past few days, less than his usual, wryly humorous self, and Gray wondered if he should say something about it. It struck him that he didn't know his men as well as he should, even those like Young who'd been with the squadron since Cienfuegos. He knew Young harbored a burning hatred for the Japanese, born in the flames that had engulfed the U.S.S. *Lincoln* four years before. The deaths of Blackwell and Costello must have affected him much as they'd affected Gray.

Gray remembered Franklin's rejoinder, back at Rota, that he should get out more. That, he thought ruefully, was true. How could he command men whose backgrounds he knew only through the dry entries in their service records and annual fitness reports?

He'd had the chance to get drunk with them at Rota and refused it. Hell, if he'd accepted, maybe it would have been *him* shipped back to the States, his feet bandaged and broken, and would that have changed anything?

That kind of thinking, he knew, would get him nowhere at all. Commander T. Morgan Gray was only reluctantly beginning to accept a hard and bitter truth, that whatever the politicians might say, he was now in the middle of a war. As a Navy officer, he'd trained for this eventuality all his life, first as an aviator, then as a submariner. It seemed strange that the reality should catch him unprepared, but perhaps that was the way it always was with Americans, even professional warriors, caught by the outbreak of war.

The problem was reacting to the challenge, and not letting the surprise kill you.

Three of the twenty missile hatches lined two by two down that long, long deck forward of *Leviathan*'s sail were already open, and the capture nets, looking like wire-frame Stokes stretchers extending from the circular openings in the deck, had been unfurled. The recovery was carried out with practiced efficiency, each of the first three fighter subs coming in one after the other from *Leviathan*'s starboard side, each following a laser guide beacon toward an extended capture net hanging over the Typhoon's port side, pulling its nose way up as it crossed the big sub's deck in a deliberate stall that let it drift belly-first into the net's embrace. Magnetic grapples clamped home, and the capture net was drawn slowly back into the launch tube, swallowing the SFV-4 tail-first.

Then it was time for Mackey, Koch, and, finally, Gray to be taken aboard to starboard. Here were two more men, Gray thought, whom he didn't know well enough—Mackey, one of the three longhair newbies recently arrived from Kings Bay, and Bob Koch, an old hand who continued to shave his scalp bare as one of the original Bald Eagles. They made their final approach from *Leviathan*'s port side, capturing to starboard.

Gray went in last, leaving the holding stack for his approach vector off *Leviathan*'s port side.

"Okay, we've got the best for last," the cheerful voice of ReCon announced over his headset. "Hunter Leader, Homeplate is on heading zero-nine-zero, speed five knots. Depth two-seven-oh. Pressure one-two-oh, psi. Call the ball."

The "ball" was another holdover term from carrier aviation, applied now to the white light affixed to the top of the mesh capture baskets that guided the Barracudas into the net.

"Blue Hunter Leader, ball," he replied. "Ten knots on one-eight-three, range four-zero."

He was approaching *Leviathan* from the north, keeping the white light centered in a red cross hair projected onto his canopy. A second light, a green one, winked on just below the first.

"Blue One, we have you on the LAG. Cut speed to eight knots, adjust left to one-eight-one."

LAG—the Laser Approach Guide—allowed *Leviathan*'s approach control to precisely direct the SFV into the capture net. He adjusted his course and speed, then watched *Leviathan*'s forward deck loom huge on his SUBVIEW, her sail a sheer wall to his right. The capture net expanded to fill his forward view. Then, cutting back on his throttle and pulling the Barracuda's nose high, he went into his approach stall, dropping the SFV into the waiting capture net.

"Home Plate, Blue Leader, touchdown," he called.

"Roger that, Blue Leader. Good trap." With a shudder and a dull rumble of machinery, the net drew the SFV erect, tail-down, and hauled it back into the gaping maw of the missile tube. Water shrieked and boiled around him as the tube was emptied by a blast of high-pressure air. Then, with a clang of steel on steel and the hiss of equalizing pressures, Gray's canopy banged open, and hands reached in to help him get free of his harness. It was awkward getting out, for he was now lying on his back, head down, feet wedged into the cockpit's well deck beneath his console and elevated above his head, as though he'd been seated in a reclining chair tipped back onto its spine. Someday, he thought, they would design a carrier sub from the keel up instead of recycling an old Russian boomer, one that didn't have to rely on what once had been missile launch tubes to deploy and recover her fighters.

Or had one already been designed that way, with *Teigei*? Yeah, that monster must have been engineered as a mother sub from the start. He wondered what her launch and recovery deck was like.

"Welcome aboard, Commander," a familiar voice said as the recovery crew pulled him through the

launch tube access hatch and onto *Leviathan*'s steel
mesh missile deck. Rising to his feet, Gray looked up
and saw the grinning face of Commander Bill Parker,
*Leviathan*'s exec.

"Good to be aboard," he replied. They shook
hands.

Had it only been three weeks since he'd seen
Parker last? It seemed like a lifetime.

"The captain wants to see you, Morgan," Parker told
him with a jerk of his head aft. "In the wardroom."

He plucked at his sub suit, a modified flight suit
designed to keep him warm in the often chilly SFV
cockpit. "Okay. Do I have time to change?" He'd
been wearing this one for hours, and felt less than
presentable.

"Afraid not. We got a laser com, flash priority,
early this morning. I think something's up, and it
sounds hot."

"Then I'd better not keep him waiting," Gray said.
He sighed. A shower and a clean uniform would have
been nice, but those could be luxuries aboard a submarine, even one as large and as well equipped as
*Leviathan*.

Especially in the middle of a war.

He followed Parker aft from the missile deck.

In the few short weeks since his deployment to
Spain, Gray had almost forgotten how large *Leviathan*
was. The ex-Soviet ballistic missile sub—a "boomer"
in American submarine parlance—was 558 feet long
and 75 feet wide, and her submerged displacement of
over thirty thousand tons made her as massive as a
World War II aircraft carrier. Where most submarines consisted of a single pressure hull inside an
outer hull or skin, *Leviathan* had four separate pressure hulls, each connected to its neighbors by airlock

passageways that could be sealed off at need. The two main pressure hulls, resting side by side beneath *Leviathan*'s outer skin, had begun service as the inner hulls of two Delta-class missile subs. They included the missile decks stretching forward of the boat's sail, a reversal of the usual aft-deck arrangement, and one that made the big Typhoon more stable both while maneuvering and during launch operations. Another pressure hull forward housed the torpedo compartment with its eight, bow-mounted tubes.

The fourth pressure hull rode the paired main hulls like a saddle in the bulging deck fairing set beneath *Leviathan*'s long, low sail—the "conning tower" of earlier generations of submarines. It included *Leviathan*'s control room, the nerve center of the entire boat, as well as ancillary facilities such as Recovery Control, the communications suite, and the massive Cray Series IV supercomputer that manipulated the torrents of laser and sonar data that became *Leviathan*'s SUBVIEW imagery.

*Leviathan* was large enough that she felt far roomier than, say, an American Los Angeles–class attack sub. The wardroom was still all but filled by the Formica-topped table in its center, but there was room enough for a small coffee mess of its own. A television monitor on one bulkhead displayed a SUB-VIEW image repeated from the sub's control room—a vaguely seen ripple of dark bottom terrain one hundred yards beneath *Leviathan*'s keel.

Several officers were already seated around the table as Gray and Parker walked in. One of them was Captain Maxwell . . . correction, Gray told himself, *Commodore* Maxwell, though he was still wearing his captain's eagles on his uniform. The others were officers on either Maxwell's or the Captain's staff.

Captain Leonard K. Ramsay, a small and wiry man in blue coveralls adorned with *Leviathan* and Orca unit patches, was pouring himself a cup of coffee when Gray walked in. "Welcome aboard, Commander," he said. "I hear you people have been busy."

"You could say so, sir. We're damned glad to see you. Mounting patrols four fighters at a time, we about got run down the other day."

"Commodore Maxwell here briefed me on the action. I'm sorry to hear about Costello."

"Yes, sir."

Gray nodded to Maxwell, who'd been given the brevet and temporary promotion and flown out to *Leviathan* early that morning with orders to take command of the entire flotilla—*Leviathan*, *Charlotte*, *Oceanside*, and the Blue Hunters. The last CO of Submarine Flotilla 1, Rear Admiral Delacroix, was now in Norfolk, assuming a new challenge as head of COMSUBLANT, the command structure for the Navy's submarine forces in the Atlantic.

"Good morning, Commodore," Gray told him. "Congratulations on your promotion."

"Thank you, Commander." He gave a wry grin. "So far it's all of the headaches I had before, and none of the perks."

Gray and Parker took their seats as Lieutenant John DuPlessis, *Leviathan*'s intelligence officer, passed out manila envelopes, each containing fax-quality black-and-white reproductions of two photographs.

"The first photograph," DuPlessis said without preamble, "was taken by one of our PHOTINT satellites three days ago. It shows the inner harbor at Alexandria."

Gray picked up the photo and studied it with a practiced eye. Though it looked like an aerial photograph, shot obliquely across a large harbor and the sprawling waterfront and city beyond, it had been transmitted from a spy satellite orbiting some two hundred miles above the earth. The detail was crisp and clear, the magnification sufficient to show specks that were almost certainly people. A higher magnification, he knew, could have read license plates or the largest headlines of the newspaper in a man's hands, but a lower power had been selected to show the entire military harbor area.

"Note, in particular, the middle background," DuPlessis said. "You can make out *Teigei* and her consort, which the CIA now believes is the nuclear attack sub *Umiryu*.

"*Teigei* and *Umiryu* arrived at Alexandria, as expected, late in the evening of the sixth. Look at the lower right-hand part of the photo now, at the waterfront."

Gray looked at the indicated portion of the image. Four long, low shapes were tied to the piers extending into the harbor. He immediately recognized what he was looking at—the unmistakable profiles of Alfa-class attack submarines.

The Alfa, first built by the Soviet Union in 1972, was widely known as the first of a new generation of high-speed attack submarines. Powered by a revolutionary liquid-metal-cooled reactor, the Alfa could reach forty-five knots or better, better than anything possible in the West for over twenty years. Two hundred sixty-seven feet long, with a submerged displacement of over 3,600 tons, the Alfa had been designed to make short, high-speed dashes from Soviet ports to attack American boomers or carrier groups. With the collapse of the Soviet Union, the Alfa had become one of the new Russian republic's best sources of hard currency. Several had been sold to Japan and, later, by the Japanese to the new United Islamic Republic. *Leviathan* had faced three UIR Alfas at Cienfuegos, sinking one of them.

Here was evidence of four more—possibly including the two that had escaped Cienfuegos—moored to the pier at Alexandria.

"The second satellite photo," DuPlessis continued, "was taken this morning and relayed to us through TENCAP. I don't think I need to elaborate."

TENCAP—Tactical Exploitation of National CAPabilities—was a satellite-based network that allowed military commanders in the field to access spy satellites directly, downloading reconnaissance data only minutes old instead of waiting for it to wend its way through the military and intelligence bureaucracies in Washington.

In this second photo, with a date-and-time line indicating that the image had been captured less than two hours earlier, all six submarines—the four Alfas and both visiting Japanese subs—were gone. Their berths at the waterfront were empty.

Commodore Maxwell broke the silence that hung over the wardroom for several bleak moments.

"It appears," he said, "that the UIR is sortieing with a large portion of their attack submarine forces, and that they are being accompanied by this new Japanese carrier sub. We don't know their mission, but we can assume that they are approaching the Strait of Gibraltar rather than leaving the Med via the Suez Canal. If that is the case, they will be here no later than early tomorrow morning.

"Gentlemen, I would be quite interested in hearing any thoughts anyone here might have."

# CHAPTER
## 20

**Imperial Navy Submarine *Teigei***
**May 10, 0645 hours**

**T**eigei slipped silently through the waters of the Mediterranean, surrounded by her escorts like a queen attended by her courtiers. On the surface, the sea was touched with golden morning light, but three hundred meters down, only the submarines' laser beacons pierced the dark, dazzling stars illuminating a night that had been absolute for the past five and a half million years.

On board, in the *Kiku* pilots' ready room, Lieutenant Shioya was sitting in one of the wooden desk-chairs that filled the small compartment, drinking tea and giving his latest set of orders some hard thought.

. . . SINCE THE ENCOUNTER IN THE GIBRALTAR STRAIT, IT MUST BE ASSUMED THAT A STATE OF UNDECLARED WAR EXISTS BETWEEN THE UNITED STATES OF AMERICA AND THE EMPIRE OF JAPAN. OFFICERS AND CREW OF IMPERIAL WARSHIPS NOW SERVING IN SUPPORT OF THE EMPEROR'S ALLIES IN THE MEDITERRANEAN SHOULD CONSIDER THEMSELVES TO BE ON A WAR FOOTING. . . .

**237**

Though he'd thought about it often during the three-week passage from Japan, Lieutenant Shioya was only now adjusting to the revelation that his country, no matter what the politicians might still be saying at home, was at war. Despite the obvious forebodings of his uncle, it was a heady, warm, exciting feeling, the sure knowledge that the years of his formal naval training, his months of practice with the maneuverable little Mitsubishi Stingrays in the Inland Sea, the regimentation and study and discipline that had made him an officer of the Imperial Navy, were bearing fruit at last. The brief skirmish with the Anglo-American blockading force in the Strait of Gibraltar had provided the merest foretaste of what he knew would come soon now, the chance to guide thirty tons of high-tech, state-of-the-art military hardware against the enemies of his nation and his emperor.

At the front of the ready room, Lieutenants Ogata, Tokuyama, and Tsuru, three of his fighter sub pilots, were enthusiastically involved in a discussion of their recent visit to Alexandria. Tsuru was describing his encounter with a belly dancer at a nightclub in El Gumruk, while the others laughed and pounded on their chair desktops. Shioya smiled as he eavesdropped on Tsuru's outrageous exaggerations but did not join in. For him, his visit to Alexandria had not been entirely successful.

They'd arrived at Alexandria harbor the day after the fight in the strait. Shioya had never been anywhere outside of Japan before, and the noisy, exotic bustle of the UIR's chief naval port had at first filled him with a young traveler's wonder and wanderlust. After *Teigei* and *Umiryu* had berthed in the sheltered enclosure of the city's inner harbor, he'd joined the other off-duty officers and men of the two Japanese submarines and gone ashore in Alexandria—El Iskandariya as the locals called it. The people had lined the pierside and cheered wildly as he and his brother officers had strode ashore, celebrating their victory over the American blockade. As he'd wandered the city like any camera-carrying tourist, the spired domes and minarets of the Abu el Abbas el Mursi Mosque, the crenellated massif of Qaitbai Fort overlooking Eastern Harbor, the teeming and undisciplined throngs of Arab merchants in the bazaars all contributed to his heady and mildly disoriented daze.

That initial rush of enthusiasm had quickly paled, however, and Shioya decided that he didn't really care for this ancient city of Alexander. The mingled stinks of garbage and crowds of unwashed humanity in the streets were repellent, the beggars and the sellers of everything from rugs to drugs to young boys too insistent by far, too willing to crowd close with a directness of eye contact and groping hands that was shockingly rude. Prices were high, the food was strange, and the women he and his friends engaged for the evening's amusement were not nearly as skilled as the ladies of Tokyo's legendary willow world. Several officers claimed to know where liquor could be obtained for the right price, but their attempts to find it failed. The unavailability of alcohol ashore was like a blanket over the festive spirit of the occasion, and Shioya finally returned to *Teigei* early.

On the way back to the waterfront, he'd encountered a mob whipped to shrieking, tearful frenzy by shouting, fist-clenching mullahs. As near as Shioya could make out, they were demonstrating against the Americans, the British, and the Spanish, but somehow the religious invective against the unbelievers, the loudspeaker-boomed chants of death to the enemies of the Mahdi and the Prophet seemed to be directed against *all* foreigners. Shioya was wearing his dress uniform, but he didn't trust the crowd's ugly mood, or the demonstrators' ability to distinguish between various types of foreigners. Mobs, he knew, could be shortsighted to the point of blindness, and Shioya did not speak enough Arabic to persuade them otherwise if they decided that he was a valid target. With the districts of both El Gumruk and Ras el Tin thronged by angry, chanting demonstrators, he'd had to take a long and cautious detour to get back to the comfortable familiarity of *Teigei*.

Perhaps he'd been overreacting. His comrades had returned later, with no incidents beyond the inevitable jailing of a few crewmen who'd somehow found hard liquor in Islamic Alexandria and gotten into fights.

Nevertheless, he'd been delighted when the new orders had come through three days later. *Teigei*'s liberty parties ashore had been recalled and the great submarine had cast off from the Inner Harbor docks and slipped quietly northwest into the Mediterranean. There she and the *Umiryu* had been joined by *Muqarrar*, *Nasib*, *Ralib*, and *Sar*, four Alfa-class attack submarines that comprised the backbone of the Islamic Mediterranean fleet.

. . . THE UNITED JAPANESE-ISLAMIC TASK FORCE WILL PROCEED TO THE STRAIT OF GIBRALTAR, AND THERE SECURE LOCAL CONTROL OF THE SEA IN SUPPORT OF ISLAMIC GROUND FORCES PARTICIPATING IN OPERATION SOUTHERN SWORD. . . .

Which, translated, meant they would have to destroy the Anglo-American blockading force so that the armada of landing craft and transports now being assembled by General Tariq along the Moroccan coast could make its crossing to Gibraltar.

After five centuries, the Moors would return to Iberia.

Shioya felt much happier about helping Japan's Islamic allies fight the Americans when he didn't have to actually live and work with them. There were Japanese naval advisers aboard the Islamic subs in the small flotilla making its way west, and he didn't envy them their assignments one bit. The cultural differences between the Middle East and the Orient were in some cases so profound it was difficult to find any common ground at all.

It was easier to maintain his enthusiasm at sea as his squadron went through the final maintenance checks and countdowns for the next deployment of the *Ei* fighter subs. Though not even his uncle was saying much, the rumor spreading through the mother sub held that an American carrier sub, *Leviathan*, had been spotted at Gibraltar in satellite photos. If so, the climactic confrontation with the Americans was hours, possibly minutes away. Tanaka had already given a speech to the men of the fighter sub squadron, informing them of Tokyo's decision to help the UIR directly in their fight against the Americans in order to secure the promise of continued cheap oil for Japanese cars, homes, and factories.

It was not, Shioya reflected now, a particularly noble reason to go to war—fighting for oil rather than, say, for freedom or to repel a foreign invader. But if Imperial Japan no longer instilled in its warriors the ancient codes of bushido and the samurai, it did still teach them to follow orders, to accept the knowledge, the *certainty* that those in charge knew best, and to accept the discipline of self and of community that had already won Japan's economic war against the West, and that would now win for them a military war as well.

Still, his brief visit ashore in Alexandria had made Shioya question some deep and basic part of himself.

Was he, after all, so eager to go to war?

A lighted warning panel set high in the forward launch deck bulkhead began flashing, the silent signal for battle stations.

"Attention *Kiku* Squadron, attention," Tanaka's voice said over the compartment's speaker system. It was not loud—nothing ever was aboard a submarine—but it commanded the instant attention of every man in the squadron. "The target has been sighted, and navigational data is being fed to your crafts' onboard computers at this time. Please man your craft. . . ."

There was a scramble of moving bodies and scraping chairs, and the *Kiku* squadron pilots were surging in a mass toward the passageway leading aft to the hangar bay. Shioya allowed himself to be carried along.

Now, he knew, was not the time for doubts, not when doubt could spell the split-second difference between life and death. In the hangar bay, service technicians were already opening the narrow hatches in the stern of each disk-shaped fighter sub as the pilots trotted into the room, pulling on gloves and communications "Snoopy hats" as they came. "*Banzai!*" a white-garbed technician shrilled, raising a clenched fist.

"*Banzai! Banzai!*" The old battle cry echoed through the hangar deck, haunting, like the ghosts of battles long past. Shioya wondered if the noise was too much, if it would communicate to the sea and the listening enemy, or if the squadron would be reprimanded for this breach of discipline.

Then he decided that it didn't matter, and joined with the rest of *Kiku* squadron, letting the chant sweep him up like a current, carrying him over each submerged reef of fear and self-doubt.

"*Banzai!*"

"Ten thousand years!"

"*Banzai! Banzai! Banzai!*"

**U.S.S.** *Leviathan*
**Strait of Gibraltar**
**May 10, 0645 hours**

Gray wiggled a little in his seat, trying to get more comfortable. These long minutes when he was sealed inside his tiny fighter sub, flat on his back and unable to move while waiting to be hurled into the sea, were always the worst.

"We have a target update for you, Commander," a voice said in Gray's headset. "Bearing zero-eight-five magnetic, range estimated at thirty miles, speed forty knots. Too far to tell yet, but it sounds like they're coming loaded for bear. Murph says he can hear at least six sets of screws."

"Murph" was Sonar Technician 2nd Class Ron Murphy, a man who more than once had demonstrated an uncanny ability to draw the maximum amount of information from a few scraps of distance-blurred sound.

"Primary targets have been designated Foxtrot through Kilo. Foxtrot matches the sonar profile for the big submarine that came through here the other day. Golf is her escort, type unknown but probably similar to our Lima-Alfas." That was Navy shorthand for a Los Angeles–class attack sub. "Murph thinks the other four targets sound like Alfas."

Gray gave a low whistle. Five attack subs . . . plus however many fighters that mother boat could put in the water. "Roger, I copy that," he said. "What about surface traffic?"

"We have numerous targets, as usual." Even with a war in the making, the Strait of Gibraltar remained a high-traffic zone. "Target Lima is the closest. She sounds like a bulk carrier. Target Mike may be an escort."

"Okay, Flight Control, Hunter One copies," Gray said. "Let's get on with it."

"Resuming preflight," the voice continued. "Laser power."

"Go."

"Sonar."

"Go."

"ULTRA-C integration."

"Go."

"Indicators."

"Set for launch configuration."

"Engine."

"Power on. Pressure at nine-seven. All go." He flicked a switch and heard a deep, throaty hum from somewhere behind his back. The Barracuda trembled slightly at the touch of restrained power. "MHD powered up and spooling."

"Hull."

"Green. Integrity good, intakes open."

"Weapons."

"Warload safed."

"Waterfoils."

"Folded, unlocked, ready to deploy."

"Stand by to flood tube."

"Ready."

"Roger. Flooding Tube Two-one."

He felt the SFV-4 shudder as seawater rushed in around the cradled fighter sub, filling the launch tube. He completed his final instrument check, scanning the console for any telltale red lights or computer alarms.

"Clamps released," said the voice in his headset. "Deck hatch open. Depth is five hundred fifty feet, speed zero-four knots, pressure two-four-five psi."

"Confirm hatch open," Gray said, reading the telltale on his console. "Blue Hunter Leader ready for launch."

"Roger, copy. We read Blue Hunter One, ready for launch in three . . . two . . . one . . . *launch!*"

Acceleration nudged his back, and he sank into his padded seat. The Barracuda rose in a billowing cloud of bubbles, sliding clear of its cradle and emerging in the open water above *Leviathan*'s deck. He switched on his SUBVIEW as he cleared the hatch and the ocean exploded around him, an emerald glory of light and color filling the normally opaque inner dome of his canopy.

At his back, *Leviathan* was a dark, smooth-sided island adrift in azure light, her paired, forward-deck missile hatches like the vertebrae of some vast, prehistoric monster of the depths. The view was spectacular, but Gray ignored it until his Barracuda's fins unfolded, deploying to their operational positions. Putting his stick over, he let the heavier-than-water craft fall past *Leviathan*'s massive hull, picking up speed in the dive until compression built in the fighter sub's intakes, kicking on the MHD impellers and engaging the SFV-4's hydrojet thruster with a high-pitched, pulsing keen.

To the east, the approaching enemy force registered as an indistinct red blur on his canopy display. They were too distant for details, such as the presence of fighter subs, to register, but that was good. With luck, Japanese sensors had not yet picked up the launch of the Blue Hunters.

One by one, the other SFVs burst from their missile tubes in shimmering clouds of bubbles, gracefully unfolded their waterfoil wings, and took up their positions in a loose three-three-and-three formation. As the last fighter sub launched, Gray tipped his control stick forward, easing his nose down. The others followed.

On his cockpit display to starboard, he picked out the stub-winged Barracuda bearing the number 105 on its blunt prow, diving in step with him toward a bottom lost in murky blackness.

Dominico's minisub. Dom had returned from his medical leave the day before. Gray had offered to leave him off the duty roster, to give him a day or two to settle back into the routine at the Gib, but the j.g. had almost angrily refused. It took no tremendous leap of insight for Gray to see that the young man was wrestling with some guilt of his own. Why Seegar, he was wondering, and not me?

Gray knew what he was feeling. The rest of them—Young, Koch, Wilder, Hernandez, Douglas, Franklin, Mackey—they all had their own reasons for being here, and their own private thoughts in these last minutes before combat. The hell of being the skipper of a small, tight unit like this one, Gray reflected, was the fact that the odds were long indeed against all of them coming back. Who would be lost this time?

Monk Young, reckless in his old hatred of the Japanese? Dominico, trying to prove something to himself after walking out of Tangier alive and whole? Wilder, still smarting over having run away when Dom and Seegar had been captured?

There were at least as many emotions among those pilots as there were men, but Gray was pretty sure that all of them shared at least one in common.

They all were afraid. Used to combat in the open skies, they fought now in the claustrophobic depths where the slightest mistake meant instant death. No amount of training or experience could completely prepare a man for that.

The bottom was registering on his cockpit display now. The depth in this part of the Strait was just over eight hundred feet. Punta del Carnero, at the mouth of Algeciras Bay, was five miles to the north; Punta Leona, on the Moroccan coast, was seven miles to the south. Just ahead, according to the graphics now glowing on their cockpit MFDs, was the sheer drop-off that once, five and a half million years before, had been shrouded in the mist-thunder of the torrents pouring over Gibraltar Falls.

"Okay, people," Gray said over the laser link. "I've got a positive track on the bottom. Set for computer lock, autopilot control. Acknowledge by numbers."

"Hunter Two, set." That was Monk Young.

"Three, go." Koch.

"Hunter Four, computer lock go." Dominico, his voice betraying his tension.

"Hunter Five," Franklin said. "I'm cool and go."

"Six, go." Hernandez, sounding tense, and maybe a bit eager as well.

"Hunter Seven," Wilder said. "Come back to me. I'm having some trouble with the damned computer."

"Rog."

"Hunter Eight." That was Mackey. "I'm go."

"And Nine." Douglas. "Ready to go."

"Hunter Seven, this is One. How's that computer problem?"

"Damned thing's not accepting the autopilot command."

Gray thought fast, scanning his own instrument board for inspiration. If Wilder couldn't get the computer to engage according to the mission profile, he'd have to abort. That would leave the squadron short one precious SFV, and could compromise the maneuver that was unfolding now in the darkening depths far beneath *Leviathan*'s keel. If the approaching enemy subs heard the sounds of the fighter being taken aboard . . .

"Check your autopilot sequencing," Gray suggested. "The autopilot select has to be on——"

"Shit! That was it," Wilder said, obviously angry at himself. "Okay, computer locked, autopilot set. I'm go for the mission."

"Good. Don't let it rattle you."

"Roger that. Sometimes these machines are smarter than I am."

"And sometimes they're so dumb we forget we're dealing with machines. Okay, gang. We're coming up on the cliff now. Take a last look around, then go passive on all systems."

The top of the sea cliff was just visible as a shadow against a darker void. The laser light reflected from the bottom bounced back various readings, most from crags and broken rock along the cliff face, but it looked like the cliff dropped five hundred feet straight down, then tumbled away at an approximate thirty-degree slope for another five hundred feet at least. The average depth of the Gibraltar Strait was about 1,200 feet, but here, where the Atlantic had once spilled over the lip of the Mediterranean Valley's western rim, the bottom was nearly 1,800 feet beneath the surface.

"Hunter Leader," Gray called for a final time, informing both the rest of the squadron and the listeners back in *Leviathan*'s Combat Control Center. "I'm shutting down."

With a down-spooling whine, his impellers fell silent, and Gray's SFV was plunged into a profound and icy silence. He switched off the craft's ULTRA-C lasers as well, and the image projected across the inside of his cockpit display went black.

Almost black. His micro-Cray computer was still processing information, but drawing data from passive sonar alone. The battle four days earlier had proven that the Japanese had ULTRA-C lasers too, or something just like them, and it had to be assumed that their sensors could pick up the blue-green laser frequency used by the American subs. By shutting down their ULTRA-C network and keeping quiet, Gray's squadron had just become invisible.

Of course, that also meant they could no longer see their surroundings in detail. They were not completely blind, however. *Leviathan*'s great screws continued to throb in the distance, illuminating the American Typhoon as a vague, cigar-shaped blur almost directly overhead. Those sounds echoed from the bottom and the rocks as well, highlighting them in shadows of blue on blue. Background noise was now crisp and distinct through the Barracuda's external microphones: the snap and crackle of shrimp, the mournful whoop of a distant whale, a cacophony of bleats and whines, hisses, clicks and grunts from a teeming menagerie of undersea life. The computer interpreted these as a background glow that, as his eyes became adjusted to the dim light, seemed to brighten even as he drifted deeper into the abyss.

For he was going down. By shutting down the SFV-4's MHD impellers, he'd turned the stub-winged craft into an undersea glider. Heavier than water, he could not remain at the same level without thrust to provide lift any more than an airplane could, but his forward velocity through the water was sufficient to let him bank and turn and even ride the outflowing current as he dropped. His computer was doing most of the piloting at this point. When he'd locked in the computer, minutes before, he'd downloaded a last, ULTRA-C glimpse of the cliff below, and the Barracuda's autopilot was now flying on its electronic memory, weaving the SFV back and forth across the face of the cliff. At his current rate of descent it would be hours before he reached the bottom.

All they needed was another fifty minutes, for the Islamic-Japanese fleet was already visibly closer, illuminated by the sounds of its own multiple wakes. With one eye on the approaching fleet, the other warily keeping track of the sheer rock face of the sea cliff, Gray rode his Barracuda into greater and greater depths.

# CHAPTER
# 21

**Imperial Navy Submarine** *Teigei*
**May 10, 0711 hours**

Captain Tanaka sat in *Teigei*'s control room, his head encased in the *kabuto-no siranui*, studying the tactical situation unfolding ahead with a professional's calm detachment. The American blockade was still too distant for the lasers to image details, but he was certain that the three red blips now glowing side by side in the distance ahead of *Teigei* represented the American carrier sub *Leviathan* and two attack sub escorts. They appeared to be spreading apart now, maneuvering for a better position in the face of Tanaka's overwhelming superiority in numbers.

"Sonar, Bridge."

The reply crackled in his headset. "Sonar here, sir."

"Has there been any sign of the American fighter subs?"

"We picked up some noises about ten minutes ago that could have been a fighter sub launch, Captain . . . or it could have been one of the American subs flushing a ballast tank. It is difficult to tell at this range."

"If the Americans have already deployed their fighter subs, I want to know where they are and what they are doing."

"Yes, Captain."

Tanaka was not too worried. Fighter subs were noisy; their magneto-hydrodynamic drive systems made more racket than a conventional screw. They should be visible soon.

He opened a squadron communications channel. "*Teigei* to all units," he said. "*Umiryu*, you will take the lead. *Muqarrar* and *Nasib*, to the north. *Ralib*, *Sar*, to the south. We will close upon them from three directions and crush them."

One by one, the other submarine commanders in the flotilla acknowledged. To his right, he saw the great, gray shadow of *Umiryu* sliding past, taking up a screening position several hundred meters ahead of the carrier sub. Oshida had been disgruntled at being kept out of the action four days earlier, but this battle plan should satisfy even him. The four Alfas, rumbling as they pressed their liquid-metal-cooled reactors to the limit, split left and right, two and two. Those old Russian subs, Tanaka thought as he watched them, looked more like whales than *Teigei* did; their hulls were shaped like elongated, slightly flattened teardrops, and their sails merged smoothly with their decks, like blisters, or as though they'd somehow been grown from hull metal instead of welded on. It gave them an organic look as they swung their tails toward *Teigei* and dwindled into the distance.

*Muqarrar* and *Nasib*: Determination and Destiny. *Sar* and *Ralib*: Vengeance and Victory. Tanaka's Arabic and English were both good enough that he was able to translate the names into Japanese, then into English. With a mild shock of surprise, he realized that the English translations were oddly alliterative. He'd not been aware of the fact until now, and he wondered if there was some hidden, spiritual meaning to the martial words.

Probably it was coincidence, he decided, and meaningless. Still, the world of spirits is close to any traditional Japanese, and those names could be taken as signs. Strange that he'd not noticed it before. *Determination. Destiny. Vengeance. Victory.* Tanaka frowned. He was determined, certainly, and he was convinced that his destiny, his karma, lay here, with these men and these machines. But vengeance? Despite the fact that he planned to kill as many of them as possible, he did not hate the Americans and had sworn no oath of vengeance. And as for victory, well, only time would reveal the meaning to that part of the chant.

It wouldn't be much longer now.

**U.S.S.** *Leviathan*
**May 10, 0716 hours**

"Commodore?" a voice called from the bulkhead speaker in *Leviathan*'s combat center. "Ramsay here. Their formation appears to be dispersing."

Maxwell glanced up from the plot table, a glowing, translucent surface on which *Leviathan*'s computer had projected a two-dimensional representation of the seabed, the targets, and the three American subs. He picked up a microphone and keyed in the numeric combination that would connect him with Captain Ramsay's helmet. "We see it, Captain," Maxwell replied.

The red blips marking the UIR sub contacts were breaking into three groups of two. Foxtrot and Golf were staying in the center, coming straight ahead at forty-five knots with Golf in the lead. Hotel and India were moving toward the north, while Juliette and Kilo were moving south.

Other contacts scattered across the plot table could probably be discounted. Contacts Alfa through Echo were almost certainly civilian surface traffic, plotted earlier but now nearly off the board. Contacts Lima and Mike were unknowns, both on the surface and both to the east of the Islamic-Japanese force. According to *Leviathan*'s sonar department, Lima sounded like a transport or a big freighter, while Mike was probably an escorting warship. They could be ignored, at least for now.

Maxwell leaned with both hands against the edge of the plot table, watching the situation unfold and only half listening to the murmur of conversation among his staff officers on either side.

Derek Maxwell still wore a captain's four stripes on his shoulder boards. His promotion had not yet been confirmed in Washington, and the title "commodore," a naval rank usually reserved for wartime, was at this point a courtesy aboard a vessel that could only have one captain. His promotion was likely to be temporary; if he screwed up now, it would be very temporary, assuming he and *Leviathan* survived.

He raised the microphone again, this time keying in a combination that would transmit his commands across the blue-green laser links to *Charlotte* and *Oceanside*, *Leviathan*'s Los Angeles escorts. "This is Maxwell. *Charlotte*, come left to block contacts Hotel and India. *Oceanside*, you go right and cover Juliette and Kilo. Both of you, keep your distance, and maintain your position on *Leviathan*. Captain Ramsay, I think it's time we came about. Let's see what happens when they think we're running away. Make it half speed."

"*Leviathan, Charlotte* copies" sounded over the speaker.

"*Leviathan, Oceanside*, we copy."

"Plot, Control Room. We're coming about one-eight-zero." In reply to his command, the deck tilted beneath his feet as the huge Typhoon went into a hard-left turn.

Maxwell was a submariner, had been one ever since 1978, when he'd graduated from the Naval Academy and put in his request for sub school at New London. Like most men of the Silent Service, he'd maintained a friendly disdain for the "skimmer navy" and especially for naval aviators with their high visibility in the popular imagination and their high levels of funding and congressional support in Washington. In 1988, in a mission still so secret it was unknown to all but a handful of Pentagon planners, he'd taken a Los Angeles attack sub into the tightly restricted Soviet waters of the White Sea, one of the so-called strategic bastions where they deployed their Typhoon SSBNs.

For Maxwell, the advantage of submarines in any political confrontation was the very fact of their invisibility; back in those tense, sometimes frightening days of the Cold War, a carrier patrolling the Barents Sea off the Norwegian coast would have been an intolerable provocation; a nuclear sub in the same waters was not. The Soviets had known American subs patrolled their coastal waters—as they patrolled the seas close to American shores—but if they couldn't pin one down, there could be no incident. For years, U.S. and Soviet submariners had played a protracted, deadly game of hide-and-seek, tracking and shadowing one another in an escalating and *mostly* bloodless war of nerves and technology.

The Soviets were gone now, but their legacy lived on in the proliferation of their submarines to other maritime nations around the globe, especially Japan and the new UIR. Worse, though, in Maxwell's mind, the technology was changing even more rapidly than world geopolitics. Blue-green laser tracking and scanning, virtual imaging, shipboard supercomputers, the use of rocket torpedoes and fighter subs all heralded a new age in undersea combat, one that was changing the role of the Silent Service.

Studying the colorful map display for a moment, he looked up at Commander Barclay, his chief of staff. "I don't see the guppies, Bar."

*Guppies*—a good-natured put-down of the new SFVs. Barclay, a heavyset, stocky, bull-necked man, shoved a stubby forefinger at the map, less than half a mile from *Leviathan*'s position. "We lost them when they went silent, but this is the edge of that cliff, Commodore," he replied. "They should be lying low somewhere right along here."

"Pray God the Islamics don't look for them too hard, or they won't stand a chance."

Maxwell still didn't entirely like the idea of the new minisubs, and he didn't like bringing carrier people in to run them. Admiral Delacroix, his predecessor in this command, and quite a few other senior people both at sea and in Washington were having trouble coming to grips with the new technology. Maxwell had always considered himself a flexible, adaptable individual; you *had* to be, living aboard a submarine. But each day brought revelations and changes that seemed more and more like the stuff of science fiction.

How could a man keep up with it all?

He was particularly concerned now, knowing that his task force's survival in the next few minutes was riding almost entirely on the nine fighter subs of Blue Hunter Squadron. The one bright part in the whole situation was the character of SSF-1's squadron commander. Gray might be a former aviator like the rest of them, but he was a thoughtful man who exercised his command with authority and competence. He'd obviously been shaken by the loss of several of his men in the past few weeks, but he hadn't let the fact cripple him with either indecision or recklessness.

The blocks of printed data displayed next to the red blips marked Fox and Golf suddenly changed, flashing warning. They were accelerating, leaping forward like hounds in pursuit of a hare.

"Uh-oh," Barclay said. "Looks like they're taking the bait. Here they come."

"How long until they're in torpedo range?"

"Depends on what they're packing, Commodore. They're still twenty miles off. If it's standard Soviet Type Cs, range eight miles, we got some time. If they're loaded with Type 65s, they could've launched ten minutes ago."

The U.S. Mark 48 ADCAPs carried by *Leviathan* had a range of twenty-five miles, but in modern undersea combat, with countermeasures and decoys, the chance that they would get through was slim. Better to wait for a sure shot at close range. In the meantime, it was up to *Leviathan* to draw her pursuers into position.

"What about their fighter subs?"

"No way to tell at this range, sir. They may have already launched them."

He considered the display a moment more. The Islamic-Japanese squadron was closing the range rapidly.

"Right, men. Let's see just how eager they are to catch us." He picked up the microphone again. "Control Room, Plot. Come to full speed."

"Full speed, aye aye, sir. Making revolutions for thirty-five knots."

*Leviathan* was now fleeing her pursuers, racing toward the west. The chase, part one of a carefully choreographed ballet, had begun.

Part two would begin when the first torpedo was in the water.


**UIR ASW Frigate Zauba'a**
**May 10, 0717 hours**

Captain Victor Yegorovich Lyko held his powerful Zeiss binoculars to his eyes, sweeping the horizon from one beam of the UIR frigate to the other. North was the familiar promontory of Gibraltar; south, to the right of the low, purple headland of Mount Hacho, lay the steeper ruggedness of Jbel Musa—yet another of the mountains dubbed "Mount of Moses" that seemed to dot the Islamic world from one end to the other. His lip curled in an amused sneer at the thought. Did the locals really think Moses had made it this far west when he left Egypt for Palestine? Perhaps the old boy had simply gotten lost.

Swinging back to the right, he examined the water ahead of the *Zauba'a*. There was plenty of surface traffic out there, including what might be some American or British ships lurking in Algeciras Bay, but nothing closer than ten kilometers. To port and astern, the transport *Hettein*, loaded with UIR troops for the coming assault on Spain, plowed along at the fringe of *Zauba'a*'s wake. Lyko had escorted the ex-Egyptian rustbucket all the way from Alexandria, and he was looking forward to shaking free of her and seeing some action.

He steadied the binoculars, peering at the stretch of empty water dead ahead. Sonar had reported possible multiple contacts in that direction minutes before.

The ex-Soviet mercenary expected to see nothing significant through the binoculars, but he knew the sight of his stout and massive frame on the bridge, dutifully studying the ocean in *Zauba'a*'s path, would have a steadying effect on the men. Word of the sonar contacts ahead—the American submarine forces almost without a doubt—had caused an explosion of harsh-whispered speculation among officers and crew alike. Some remembered *Zauba'a*'s kill in these waters sixteen days before and were eager to score again. Others were fearful; none knew what to expect in this unprecedented undersea clash, or what part *Zauba'a* would be called upon to play.

"Captain, Sonar," the bridge speaker squawked.

"This is the captain. Go ahead."

"Sir, the contacts ahead are turning away. We're hearing cavitation and high-speed engine noise. They may be running."

"Range and bearing."

"Range, roughly thirty-two thousand meters," the Islamic sonar operator said. "Bearing now from three-four-five to zero-one-zero, relative. We are tracking at least three separate targets."

"Very well. Stay on them."

Three targets: the American carrier sub and its two Los Angeles escorts, and they were fleeing from the

Japanese-Islamic submarine fleet. He felt his anticipation growing.

Lyko had hunted Los Angeles subs more than once, hunted them relentlessly in the frigid, ice-rimmed seas north of Polyarnyy and the North Cape. That had been long ago, when he'd still commanded his beloved *Simferopol*, before the end of the Cold War and the shocking disintegration of the Soviet empire. He'd also escorted the huge Soviet Typhoons in and out of their secret bastions in the White and Barents seas, and he knew just how silent and elusive those giants could be.

Tracking and killing the three American subs was not going to be easy, especially when his own sonar personnel were not up to the standards expected of the Russian navy. The targets they were following now were vague and ill-defined, their exact positions more guesswork than science even if he used active sonar.

His best chance, Lyko knew, would come if one of the Americans was damaged. Then the flutter of water past torn hull plates, the cavitating thump of a bent screw, even the mutter of shipboard machinery or voices transmitted to the outer hull by a failed bit of insulation, could let him pinpoint the target and hunt it down.

"Helm!" he snapped. "Come left five degrees." That would put him in good position should an Islamic torpedo score.

It felt good, he thought, to have this one last chance against his old enemy.

"Weapons Officer!"

"Sir!"

"I want the RBU-6000 cleared for action, the ASW torpedoes armed and ready to fire."

"*Ya sidi!* At once!"

Yes, it felt very good indeed.

**Imperial Navy Submarine *Teigei***
**May 10, 0717 hours**

"Captain Tanaka! They are running away!"

Tanaka had already noted the change in the American disposition. The Los Angeles subs had been moving north and south, evidently to screen *Leviathan* from the UIR Alfas. *Leviathan* herself, moving ahead dead slow, had swung wide to port, coming onto a reciprocal course taking her west, away from the Islamic-Japanese flotilla. Now even the escorting attack subs were starting to turn away, presenting their tails to the advancing *Teigei* and *Umiryu*.

Perfect! It was the moment he'd been waiting for. He opened a communications channel. "*Kiku* squadron. This is Tanaka."

"*Kiku* squadron here, Uncle," Shioya's voice sounded in his ear. "We are ready to launch."

"It is time, nephew. Remember. I am counting on all of you."

Shioya replied with a polite phrase, something meaning, roughly, that Tanaka was giving him too much honor.

No, nephew, he thought. I very much fear that what I give you is death. Outnumbered as the Americans were, they could fight hard when they had to, and it would not do to underestimate them.

Why was it always the young who died for the mistakes of their elders?

"*Gokigenyo*," he told his nephew. "Good luck."

Moments later, the first of the *Kiku* fighter subs

hissed from the paired launch tubes emerging from *Teigei*'s aft deck. Key to the timing of the launch was the knowledge that *Leviathan*, with her superb sonar, was now moving *away* from *Teigei* at full speed. That meant that *Teigei* was now in the Typhoon's baffles, that broad, cone-shaped area astern of a submarine where sound was masked by the churning of its own wake. *Teigei* could loose her fighter subs unheard.

The Los Angeles escorts, more distant and not yet fully turned away, might hear . . . but chances were that their attentions were focused wholly on the Islamic Alfas, even now slipping around on the Americans' flanks.

There was a chance, a very good one, that the high-speed approach of Shioya's Stingrays would go completely unnoticed until it was too late.

But it was only a chance, and there was still the unknown potential of the American fighter subs. The *Ei* fighter subs must be considered expendable.

He watched with a dark foreboding as the eleven disk-shaped fighter subs of *Kiku* squadron formed up ahead of *Teigei*, then accelerated, flashing to almost one hundred knots in a sudden rush of speed and power.

The outcome of this contest might well rest with them.

## UIR Submarine *Muqarrar*
## May 10, 0719 hours

Kilometers to the north of the unfolding clash between *Leviathan* and *Teigei*, Captain Anwar Nazer stood in the control room of the UIR submarine *Muqarrar*, surveying the bustle of white-uniformed men around him. These old Alfa-class attack subs were as cramped as fish in a tin, and Nazer, a tall and gangly man, had to stoop slightly, his hands braced against an overhead strut.

Eight years before, Nazer had been in the forefront of the *Qaumat*, grabbing an AK-47 and leading a clique of Egyptian naval officers in the mutiny aboard the frigate *Najim al Zafir*, then joining the mobs storming Alexandria during the bloody *Lail min al Qaumat*, the Night of the Rising. His leadership in the fighting at Alexandria's governorate had won him promotion and a place on the Mahdi's planning staff. His pride at a headquarters assignment quickly soured, though, especially after the armies of Russian mercenaries and Japanese advisers began arriving. Had the *Qaumat* been fought and won, uniting Islam from the Atlantic to Central Asia, only to have *foreigners*, infidels and unbelievers, command the ear of the Mahdi? Nazer had requested a combat assignment and received it, command of the attack submarine *Muqarrar*.

He'd never commanded submarines before, but with Japanese orbital weapons capable of striking down anything that roamed the surface of the seas, clearly it was submarines that would dominate the world's oceans in the future. He'd attended submarine school at Alexandria Naval Academy and taken command of the UIR attack sub *Determination* early in 2004.

Turning, he fixed his hard stare at the grizzled, unshaven Russian adviser sharing his control room and bit back his distaste.

Most UIR submarines had either a Russian or a Japanese military adviser aboard. Stepan Gromyko was only a *starshy leytenant*, a senior lieutenant, and

Nazer counted himself fortunate in that he'd been saddled with a Russian instead of a Japanese. He hated all foreigners, but in his opinion the Japanese were the worst. He was also lucky that the adviser was his junior in rank; there could be no nonsense of the two of them sharing a command, as had happened in some of the UIR's vessels. *Muqarrar* was *his* boat, Nazer's, and no one else's.

Gromyko was supposed to be useful because he'd once served in Alfa subs in the Red Banner Fleet and would be able to pass on tactical advice in combat, but Nazer doubted it. The Russian lieutenant was in his forties, an old man, especially for such a low rank, and rumor had it that he was an alcoholic as well.

An alcoholic in a nation where alcohol was forbidden, Nazer suppressed a chuckle. Gromyko must think he was serving time in hell. So long as he stayed out of the way . . .

"Well, adviser," Nazer said, smiling. "How does it feel to be sailing into combat against the Americans?"

Gromyko appeared to be chewing on the words, trying to understand Nazer's clipped Arabic. "It is we should make careful," he said at last. His Arabic was slurred, the grammar atrocious. "With only sonar to hear."

Nazer decided the Russian must be warning him that without the Japanese laser imaging system, his Alfa would be at a serious disadvantage against the American subs.

"Don't be afraid," he told the Russian with a malicious grin. "Soon we will be close enough to *smell* them." He slapped his fist against his open left palm. "Then we will destroy them!"

"Captain, Sonar!" a voice cried out.

Nazer spun. The Alfa's sonar suite was in a partitioned corner of the control room, aft, behind the periscopes. "What is it?"

"The targets are fleeing, Captain. The Typhoon has reversed course and is accelerating to thirty knots. The two Los Angeles subs are following."

"Is danger, extreme," Gromyko said, urgently, insistently. He reached out and grabbed Nazer's arm. "Without seeing small American fighter submarines."

Disgusted, Nazer snatched his arm away. He was convinced that Gromyko was still drinking, though how the Russian had found a drop of liquor anywhere in the UIR was a mystery. Perhaps he'd somehow smuggled in his own.

"Sonar!" he snapped, keeping his eyes on the Russian. "Begin active sonar ranging."

"Yes, sir!"

The sharp *ping* of the sonar pulse rang through the hull. With their fancy laser imaging gear, the Americans could see the Alfa clearly, so there was no sense in giving up accurate intelligence in the interests of staying hidden.

"Bridge, Sonar. Range to the nearest Los Angeles now fourteen kilometers."

"Any sign of the enemy fighter subs?"

"Negative, Captain."

"Continue active ranging. Alert me the moment we are in range. Weapons!"

"Sir!"

"Ready all tubes. Wire-guided. Stand by!"

"Sir!"

"Engineering!"

"Sir!"

"Reactor to one hundred fifteen percent. I want full speed now!"

"Sir!"

He felt the Alfa's power throbbing behind the aft bulkhead and in the steel grating beneath his boots. He wanted the honor of the first kill, and he would not be preached at by an alcohol-fogged Russian mercenary.

"Bridge, Sonar! Range to nearest contact, now twelve kilometers. We are in range."

"Very well." He paused, running through the calculations in his head. *Muqarrar* carried twelve Type C torpedoes, wire- or acoustically-guided sub killers capable of traveling at forty-five knots. At that speed, it would take them over ten minutes to cover twelve kilometers. He needed to be closer, lots closer before he could launch and know he would make a kill.

"Weapons, stand by!"

# CHAPTER
## 22

**Blue Hunter Squadron**
**May 10, 0724 hours**

T he cliff towered less than twenty yards off
Gray's port wing, a surrealist's flowing surface,
at once molten and frozen, the rim smoothed
by the torrents that had scoured it clean five and a
half million years before. He kept his hand on his
SFV's control stick, though at this point his computer was guiding the craft's deadstick glide through
the depths. He was still surrounded by blackness,
creating the illusion that he was spiraling deeper
and deeper into some cavernous pit, but enough
laser light from the approaching Japanese subs, plus
reflected sound from numerous sources, combined
to give his micro-Cray data enough to construct a
dim picture, in faint shadows of blue and gray, of
the slowly rising wall of water-smoothed rock beside
him.

At a depth of 1,300 feet, Gray and the other
Barracudas of Blue Hunter Squadron were over
halfway down the sheer face of the undersea cliff,
and the sub fighter pilots had a splendid view of
the two Japanese submarines. Less than five miles

away now and moving out of the east, they were illuminated both by the laser beacons mounted on their hulls and by the rumble of their engines as they pushed ahead at full speed, like a pair of gleaming morning stars in the blackness. Almost directly overhead, a crescent-shaped formation of disks passed over, eerily like a flight of flying saucers out of some science-fiction epic. As they raced ahead at eighty knots, their wakes were like miniature tornadoes churning at their tails, and the shock waves created as their streamlined hulls displaced the water in their paths were visible as cone-shaped contrails glowing in refracted laser light.

Would they see the American Barracudas, now five hundred feet below them? Like the Barracudas, they'd switched off their laser beacons, enabling them to get closer to the SUBVIEW-equipped *Leviathan* without being detected. With no scanning lasers to directly illuminate the SFVs, they probably wouldn't see them, but there was still the risk that scattered laser light, from the approaching Japanese mother sub, could be picked up by the Japanese sensors and translated into revealing imagery.

Seconds later, the Japanese fighters vanished behind the lip of the sea cliff. Gray pondered the situation. The plan, as worked out hours before with Maxwell and Ramsay, called for him to wait until the big Japanese subs had already passed the cliff . . . but to remain flexible should the enemy launch its fighter sub contingent. It was tempting to rise now from hiding, sweeping up and over the cliff and hitting the Japanese fighter subs from behind before they could attack *Leviathan*.

But that would leave *Teigei* and her escort still coming, still a serious threat to the badly outnumbered Americans. Better to wait and catch the big targets, as originally planned.

The question was, would *Leviathan* be able to survive an assault by those fighters, while Blue Hunter tangled with the *Teigei?*

Gray didn't know, and what he didn't know might well kill them all.

## U.S.S. *Leviathan*
## May 10, 0730 hours

Captain Ramsay had swiveled his seat on the bridge around so that he could look—through the computer reality displayed within his helmet—directly astern. It was growing increasingly difficult to see anything behind *Leviathan,* for the turbulence of her own wake was distorting even the shimmer of laser light from the two center contacts, Foxtrot and Golf, and sound was completely lost in the rushing cataract spilling from her own props.

But according to the computer projections, it was time to come about.

"Plot, this is the captain," he said softly, speaking into the pencil mike in his SUBVIEW helmet.

"Maxwell here. Go ahead, Captain."

"Commodore, the computer says it's time."

"Affirmative. Bring us about again, Captain. Keep a sharp watch out for enemy fighters."

"Roger that. They should have launched by now, if they're going to." He switched channels. "Helm, this is the captain. Come about, left full rudder, reciprocal course. Let's hear the tires squeal."

"Captain, Helm, aye aye. Coming hard left one-eight-zero to new course, zero-eight-five."

He felt the deck cant suddenly beneath him and instinctively reached for his armrests. It was one mark of the evolution of modern submarine warfare that the chairs the helmsman and planesman sat in on the bridge, as well as his own seat, all came equipped with seat belts. Somewhere in the distance, muffled by the SUBVIEW helmet, he heard something fall with a metallic clatter. A clipboard not secured, possibly, or someone's forgotten coffee mug. No matter. The time for silence was past.

"Engage ULTRA-C," he ordered. Instantly, the waters around his head brightened to their accustomed pale emerald glow as lasers on *Leviathan*'s sail and keel illuminated the surrounding sea.

As *Leviathan* went into her turn the distance-blurred patches of red light marking the contacts astern swung to Ramsay's right, clearing the blue-gray fog of the Typhoon's wake. New contacts appeared, strung across the blue-green backdrop between *Leviathan* and her pursuers like Christmas-tree lights on a string. Fresh data flickered across his helmet display, giving ranges, courses, bearings, speeds. The Japanese fighter subs were two miles away and closing at one hundred knots.

"Captain, Sonar!" sounded in his helmet. "Multiple contacts—"

"I see them!" he snapped. Damn! They were closer than he'd expected . . . and *Leviathan* had not turned enough to make a shot effective yet.

Come *on*, girl, he told *Leviathan*, not realizing he was speaking aloud, broadcasting his words to the sonar crew. "Move your fat ass. . . ."

**UIR Submarine** *Muqarrar*
**May 10, 0730 hours**

Captain Nazer glanced at the clock mounted on the control room bulkhead. "Range to the nearest target!" he demanded.

"Range four kilometers. Sir, target's aspect is changing. I think he's turning to meet us!"

Four kilometers, almost point-blank for an attack sub. "Fire tubes one and two!"

He heard the hiss of first one torpedo, then the second, sliding from the Alfa's bow tubes.

"Torpedoes one and two running, Captain. We have positive wire guidance."

Nazer glanced again at the clock, noting the position of the sweep second hand. Traveling at forty-five knots, the Type C torpedoes would travel four kilometers in three and a half minutes.

**U.S.S.** *Charlotte*
**May 10, 0731 hours**

"Captain, Sonar! Torpedoes in the water! Bearing zero-one-four, magnetic, speed four-five knots, range three-six-zero-zero!"

Commander Bruce Katkowski, "Bruce the Cat" to his crew, though never to his face, looked up from the control-room plot table. "Very well." He kept his words, his expression bland, though his heart was beating hard enough now that surely the entire crew could hear it.

His mind raced. *Thirty-six hundred yards, forty-five knots. Running time . . . make it three minutes thirty. . . .*

"Captain?" his executive officer said. Perspiration glistened in the man's mustache and on his forehead.

"Maintain the turn."

"Aye, aye, Captain. Maintaining turn."

He needed the torpedoes to come just a little closer. . . .

## Imperial Navy Submarine *Teigei*
## May 10, 0731 hours

"Captain! Sonar! Two torpedoes are running, bearing three-one-zero. It sounds like *Muqarrar* has just launched on the American!"

Tanaka turned his head to the right, scanning the sea northwest of *Teigei*. The two Alfas and the Los Angeles sub were marked on his display, but as fuzzy points of light too distant for details to be made out.

The battle had begun. Looking forward again, he could see *Umiryu*, several hundred meters ahead. Beyond, the broken edge of an undersea cliff rose in stark relief, the top of its worn and current-smoothed face illuminated by *siranui* lasers aboard *Teigei* and *Umiryu*, but plunging swiftly into blackness below. And beyond that, partly blocked by *Umiryu*'s bulk and by the spread-out line of contacts marking the fighter subs, *Leviathan* was giving up her run for safety and coming about once again, returning to the fight. The third American sub and the last two Alfas were almost lost in the distance to the south.

"*Umiryu!*" he called. "This is Tanaka. Come north to give *Teigei* a clear shot!"

Clumsily, the Japanese attack sub began drifting to the right. In another moment, *Teigei* was sweeping across the cliff, the bottom rising precipitously, then leveling off one hundred meters beneath her keel. Range to *Leviathan* was now just twelve kilometers.

*Kiku* squadron was almost at the target. Could *Teigei* fire without hitting the Stingrays?

"Weapons Officer!" he called, using his eyes to select options from the menu on his helmet display. Targeting cursors bracketed the American Typhoon, indicating a solid weapons lock.

"We are tracking, Captain," his weapons officer's voice announced. "Acoustical lock, range six thousand meters."

"Fire!"

"Firing one." *Hiss!*

"Fire two!"

"Firing two." *Hiss!*

Trailing churning streamers of sound, the torpedoes streaked one after the other into the emerald gleam of the sea.

**U.S.S. *Leviathan***
**May 10, 0732 hours**

Sonar warned him when *Teigei* fired, but Ramsay's full attention was on the approaching wave of Japanese fighter subs. "I want a spread of four torpedoes, remote detonation on my command. Fire one! Fire two! Fire three! Fire four!"

With a rapid succession of shuddering hisses, four torpedoes punched out from the open tubes stretched like a gap-toothed grin across *Leviathan*'s huge, rounded bow. On his helmet display, Ramsay watched as the blips marking the speeding torpedoes spread out, each accompanied by a data line giving range, course, and speed. In scant, flickering seconds, the torpedoes approached the nearest fighter subs; when the ranges matched, he gave the order.

"Easy . . . easy . . . now! Detonate!"

Signals raced down the slender fiber-optic cables threading out behind each torp. Four balls of white fury expanded, touched, then mingled half a mile off *Leviathan*'s bow. The explosions sent a shudder through the Typhoon's length, and for a moment Ramsay could see nothing ahead at all.

## Blue Hunter Squadron
## May 10, 0732 hours

With his head craned as far back as it would go, Gray watched the two Japanese submarines pass overhead, the attack sub in the lead and a little to the north, the *Teigei* trailing. Just before the mother sub reached the edge of the cliff, she fired a torpedo and then, a heartbeat later, she fired a second. Seconds later—too soon for *Teigei*'s torps to have hit their target—a rumbling thunder boomed down through the depths, the mingled detonations of several warheads at once.

Hidden in the lee of the cliff, Gray had no way of knowing how far or close *Leviathan* might be, but clearly the battle had just been joined. He waited another few seconds, until *Teigei*'s long, cigar-shaped bulk slid past the top of the cliff. Instantly, with the Japanese laser beacons blocked, the region around the Barracudas was plunged into blackness absolute.

No matter. It was time. He switched on his Barracuda's ULTRA-C, the laser array suddenly transforming night into blue-green radiance. In its glow, he quickly spotted the other eight Blue Hunter minisubs, scattered across the face of that towering cliff like dust motes before a fall of pleated curtains.

Next, his fingers tapped out a combination of commands on his console as he nudged the control stick forward, dipping the Barracuda's nose. For long seconds, he dropped, ending the long glide down the face of the cliff with a sudden dive. Pressures built as he keyed the engine command. Nothing . . . again nothing . . . this kind of cold start at high ambient pressure had never been tried in practice. Theoretically it should work, but then, theory often failed when faced with reality.

He tried again. . . .

### *Kiku* Squadron
### May 10, 0732 hours

Lieutenant Shioya was again trailing his formation, a ragged line stretching half a kilometer end to end. The range to the American carrier sub was down to a kilometer or less when four torpedoes emerged from the line of open bow doors across its bow.

Simulations and maneuvers carried out in Japan's Inland Sea had suggested that wire-guiding something as ponderous as a Mark 48 ADCAP torpedo, 5.84 meters long and traveling at fifty-five knots, into a target as small and as maneuverable as a Mitsubishi *Ei* fighter sub would be all but impossible. A fighter sub could easily slip to one side to let the torpedo pass, and be long gone by the time it circled around for another attempt.

But the spread of torpedoes from the *Leviathan* weren't targeting individual fighter subs. Detonating just ahead of the attack formation, they tore huge, hollow spheres in the water and the Japanese fighter subs, hurtling forward at eighty knots, hit those expanding shock waves like bullets slamming into concrete.

Wrenching at his control stick, Shioya sent his saucer twisting to port as the sea turned silver in front of him. The shock wave gripped his Stingray and shook it like a dog worrying a bone, and his hull rang like a bell struck by a sledgehammer. Shioya was slammed against the side of his cockpit and his helmet cracked against a support strut.

For several crucial seconds, he could see and hear nothing at all.

**UIR ASW Frigate *Zauba'a***
**May 10, 0732 hours**

For a moment, blast followed thunderous underwater blast, and raising frothing domes of white water in patches scattered across the surface of the Mediterranean, domes that heaved, trembled, then burst open in geysers of spray. Clearly, a struggle of titanic proportions was raging in the depths beneath *Zauba'a*, a high-tech marine battle to the death between unseen forces.

Captain Victor Yegorovich Lyko swung his Zeiss high-powered binoculars to the southwest, training them on a cascading rank of undersea explosions.

"Bridge, this is Sonar" sounded from the bridge speaker above his head. "We have multiple undersea detonations! They are shooting at one another down there!"

"I know that, sand rat," he snapped, but he spoke in Russian and the retort lost its sting. "Make full speed, brothers," he ordered, shifting to Arabic. "Now we're going to taste blood!"

\*     \*     \*

**Blue Hunter Squadron**
**May 10, 0733 hours**

At last the falling SFV shuddered, lurched, then started to pull up. With a grumbling whine, his MHD generators came to life. Water surged through the Barracuda's intakes, pressures building. The whine spooled higher, and he pulled back on the stick, urging the minisub to climb . . . *climb.* Then he *was* climbing, engine whining, the SFV's stubby jet shape rising out of the depths like a rocket slowly breaking free of Earth's clinging grip.

Higher and faster . . . higher and faster. The other Barracudas had restarted their engines as well and were following, but Gray was far in the lead, keening upward through the sea toward the top of the cliff. Then he was over the lip, flattening out into level flight less than ten feet above the rugged bottom, which rushed past his keel in a blur of blue-green motion.

*Teigei* was just ahead and three hundred feet above, her twin screws churning the sea to boiling froth in her wake.

"SUBVIEW, targeting!" he called, addressing the Barracuda's voice-command circuits. "Laser designation!"

He could have ordered acoustic homing, but he wanted to be sure. At close range, the laser designation option would let him guide the torpedo straight to where he wanted it. His central MFD replied, the words scrolling from the top.

TARGET LOCK. LASER DESIGNATION.

PASSIVE/ACTIVE?

"Active."

DESIGNATE TARGET.

Cross hairs winked on against his canopy. Holding the Barracuda steady on course with one hand, he used the other to thumb a small joystick set into the arm of his seat, and as he moved it, the cursor above his head moved with it dropping to center itself on *Teigei*'s tail.

"SUBVIEW!" he called. "Laser designation, lock *now*!"

His cockpit view dimmed, growing dark as his dorsal ULTRA-C laser disengaged from its steady, flickering sweep of the surrounding water and became a target designator for Gray's four Mark 62 torpedoes. He could still see *Teigei*, a gray ghost partly illuminated by his second ULTRA-C laser on his keel, and by the noise of her own props.

TARGET LOCK.

READY.

Gray squeezed the trigger on his control stick again. With a loud rush of sound, his first rocket torp slid free of the Barracuda's wing mount. Sensors in its nose read the intense point of laser light reflected from the enemy submarine's hull and fed course-correction data to its onboard computer.

"That's Fox two!" he yelled. Strictly speaking, the fighter pilot's term announced the launch of a heat-seeking missile. Since there was no such thing as heat-seeking guidance underwater, it seemed to fit well with the concept of a light-guided torpedo.

The target was so close that the torp closed the gap in seconds.

**Imperial Navy Submarine *Teigei***
**May 10, 0733 hours**

"Captain! This is Sonar! There's something coming up fast astern!"

Tanaka pivoted in his chair, looking aft across *Teigei*'s long deck. He saw nothing but the turbulence of the huge submarine's wake, the steady turning of her twin screws.

"What is it? I don't see—"

"We've got an acoustical track, Captain. Listen to this!"

He heard it then, the sound fed to his helmet by the sonar officer, a faint but steadily growing roar. It sounded something like tearing paper, but deeper-voiced . . . a rising, pulse-quickening thunder from the deep.

"Hard right rudder!" he yelled. "Quickly! Quickly! Launch decoys!"

*Teigei* shuddered as her helmsman threw her into a sharp turn. Tanaka knew what that sound was . . . the rapid approach of a rocket-powered torpedo screaming up *Teigei*'s baffles. The only reason Sonar had picked it up at all was that it was already close enough for the sub's external sonar pickups on her tail to hear it above the steady throb of *Teigei*'s engines.

A noisemaker dropped from the sub's flank . . . then another, broadcasting the sound of *Teigei*'s passage. As *Teigei* went into her turn, however, Tanaka glimpsed a blue-green flash astern and realized that the Japanese carrier sub was being painted by an American laser.

A laser-guided torpedo!

Then there was no more time for analysis. The American Mark 62 rocket torp slammed into *Teigei*'s stern just above her starboard screw. Tanaka saw the flash, felt the lurch as the blast clawed at the huge submarine.

Then his *siranui* imaging system failed, and he was plunged into blackness.

**Blue Hunter Squadron**
**May 10, 0733 hours**

Gray saw the flash, a ballooning, quicksilver sphere, as the thundering undersea shock wave was translated into light by his SUBVIEW display. His Barracuda hit the wave front head-on, lurching and bumping and riding it out.

Ahead, the stricken carrier sub materialized out of the fading blast cloud, her starboard screw gone, a gaping, oil-and-bubble-streaming hole torn into the fairing between the screw mount and her vertical stabilizer. Her rudder was jammed hard to the right, holding her in her right-hand turn, and she was starting to lose altitude as well, drifting closer and closer to the rugged bottom.

"Hunter Six. Nice shot, Commander!" sounded over the laser com.

"Thanks, Hernandez. You guys form on me."

"Hunter Two. I'm lining up for another shot at that bastard. He's not dead yet!"

"Negative, Monk, negative. He's out of it for the moment, and we've got to give *Leviathan* an assist."

He could almost hear the struggle in Young's mind as he weighed his hatred of the Japanese against Gray's order.

"Roger, Hunter One," Young said at last. "I'm with you."

*Teigei* was crippled. They would be able to finish her off or capture her at their leisure. But right now, every torpedo was needed in the melee now shaping up around the *Leviathan*.

# CHAPTER
## 23

**Blue Hunter Squadron**
**May 10, 0733 hours**

Gray held his Barracuda steady as it swept across the deck of the wounded Japanese carrier sub, passing closely enough that he could see the sound-absorbing, acoustical tiles covering her hull in a pattern that made her look as though she were constructed entirely of bricks. As he passed over the damaged sub's afterdeck he could hear a rapid-fire stutter transmitted through the water, a fluttering sound caused by the rush of the sea across the raggedly torn hole in her tail. Another such hit would destroy her, but he was satisfied that she was simply out of the fight.

"Hunter One to Hunters Two, Four, and Six," he called. "Go after that Tyogei. The rest of you, stay with me. I want those Jap fighters!"

"Hunter One, Hunter Two," Young replied. "We copy. Save some for us."

With a sharp bank to the right, Young, Dominico, and Hernandez broke clear of the Barracuda formation, angling northwest toward the big Japanese attack sub.

"Roger that," Gray replied. "Luck!"

Two miles directly ahead, the Japanese fighter sub formation had just disintegrated into chaos.

## Blue Hunter Squadron
## May 10, 0733 hours

Lieutenant j.g. Albert Dominico was breathing so hard he wondered if something was wrong with his SFV-4's environmental controls. Twice he checked the cockpit $CO_2$, verifying that it was at the proper setting, but his breath continued to come in short, hard gasps.

He was scared. He didn't want to admit it, but he was terrified, enough so that his hands would have been shaking if he'd taken them off the hand controllers for an instant. Flying Navy jets, even bringing them down on the rain-slick deck of a carrier at night, had never done this to him. Figuring he was running a pucker factor of at least nine-point-eight, he blinked his eyes, trying to clear the sweat that threatened to blind him, trying to focus on his MFDs and cockpit display discretes.

He wished now he'd never gone home on that damned medical leave. Ann was threatening to walk out on him now, and that last blowup had been a bitter one. She'd told him she couldn't take it anymore . . . the secrecy, the not knowing, the endless waiting for the dreaded telegram from the Department of Defense.

It was damned ironic when you thought about it. Seegar's old lady had been about to divorce him for the same reasons. Now those two were back together again, and with his feet the way they were, it looked like Cigar was on his way to a medical discharge. Hell, he'd probably end up as an insurance salesman or something, with a happy family and a house in the suburbs, while Dominico was here, flying this misbegotten cross between a sub and an airplane while Ann told him she couldn't take the strain anymore.

Well, the marriage had been getting shaky anyhow, or he wouldn't have let Seegar talk him into going to that whorehouse in Jerez. But he still didn't know why he'd insisted on coming back to Spain, or why he'd told Commander Gray that he wanted in on this damned op. He'd thought it was because he wanted to get even with the UIR bastards for what they'd done to him in Tangier, but now he wasn't so sure.

Maybe Ann was right. He didn't belong out here, always trying to prove himself. "Playing warrior," she'd said. He didn't need this. Ever since he'd accepted the transfer to fighter subs, the stress on both of them had been tremendous, like the crushing pressure of the water around him. The divorce rate for men in the submarine service was higher than for any other group in the Navy. Maybe that was why.

Ever since Tangier he'd been wondering if it was worth it anymore. He was beginning to think it wasn't.

He was surprised to find that his hands were steady now, his breathing controlled as the Japanese attack sub grew larger on his cockpit display.

## U.S.S. *Charlotte*
## May 10, 0733 hours

Commander Katkowski heard the thunder of the detonating torpedoes and for one brief instant thought the *Charlotte* had been hit . . . but then he reasoned that the explosion had occurred several miles off. The torps fired by the Alfa were still closing. He could see them in his SUBVIEW helmet, twin points of light coming in over his left shoulder.

"Torpedo impact in twenty seconds," the voice of the sonar operator called as the roar subsided, as if he wanted to be sure the captain knew that *Charlotte* was still in deadly peril.

Close enough. "Hard right rudder!" he yelled. "Blow main port ballast! Launch decoys!"

The Los Angeles sub rocked over to starboard, compressed air boiling from her left side vents as her rudder kicked over and she went into a sharply climbing turn. Crewmen standing on her decks were forced to grab stanchions or overhead piping to keep from falling. Her hull, strained to the limits of its engineering tolerances, groaned and creaked like a living thing, and somewhere, someone yelped in pain as he was hurled against an unyielding bulkhead.

Those UIR torpedoes were wire-guided, which meant the enemy sub's people were guiding them by listening to *Charlotte*'s acoustical signature and steering them toward the target.

By blowing ballast, Katkowski had both helped *Charlotte* bank into her turn and created a momentary wall of sound, a sizzling mass of bubbles and churning water that swallowed her in sound. Decoys dropped from her flanks, shrieking engine sounds as they sank. Katkowski held his breath as the lead torpedo passed a scant handful of yards astern of the *Charlotte*, passing starboard to port. The second torpedo, trailing the first by a hundred yards, seemed to hesitate . . . then dipped its nose, plunging after the decoys.

*Charlotte* was coming out of her turn.

"Flood port ballast," he ordered. "Weapons Officer, I have a target, bearing . . . mark!"

"Alfa-class submarine, bearing zero-one-eight, range three thousand. Target lock."

"Fire one!"

There was a hiss and a thump as the Mark 48 ADCAP lurched from *Charlotte*'s bows. "One fired, sir. Wire-guided, acoustical homing. Running time one-point-five minutes."

Katkowski had the same data in his SUBVIEW display. "Fire two."

"Two fired."

"Where's that other son of a bitch?"

"Contact Hotel at three-four-eight relative, range five-three-hundred."

"Target!"

"Alfa-class submarine, target lock."

"Fire three!"

"Torpedoes one and two have acquired."

"Cut them loose!" They could home in on the Alfa on their own, and he wanted *Charlotte* free to maneuver.

"Three has acquired."

"Cut her loose too! Maneuvering, come hard right!"

That first Islamic torpedo, after missing by a hairsbreadth, would be circling back soon for another try.

## *Kiku* Squadron
## May 10, 0734 hours

Larger submarines would have been twisted apart by the shock waves generated by the ADCAP torpedoes' three-hundred-kilo warheads detonating at close range, but ten of the eleven *Ei* fighter subs, each less than eight meters from bow to stern and very nearly as wide as it was long, rode through the blasts with little outward damage. One Stingray, Yamagura's, was by chance less than three meters from the detonation of one warhead, however, and the blast broke his vessel's keel, peeled back the hull plates from its dorsal surface, and sent the sea cascading into his cockpit with the force of a bursting dam.

Shioya had been stunned by the blast, but as he groped his way back from the fog of pain and darkness that had swallowed him, he realized that his submarine's systems were still functioning, his craft still intact. For a blurred moment, he imagined he'd been hurled from his cockpit into the sea, that he was sinking . . . and then he felt the reassuring pressure of his couch beneath his outstretched legs and body, the touch of the control sticks in his hands. He was still secure within his Stingray's coffin-sized cabin, and the water surrounding him was image only, displayed inside his *siranui* helmet.

A glance around showed that the other *Ei* fighter subs had survived . . . all save one which was fluttering like a falling leaf into the depths, trailing air and oil. But the others were scattered about everywhere, their orderly attack formation shattered. *Leviathan* was approaching with a heavy, ponderous grace, less than half a kilometer ahead.

"*Kiku* squadron!" he called, switching on his lasers. "*Kiku* squadron! This is *Kiku* Leader! Form up on me! We will attack the Yankee carrier. . . ."

"*Kiku* Leader, this is *Kiku* Five," a voice called, cracking in near panic. That was *Chu-i* Kokura. "Fighter subs! Enemy fighter subs! Coming in at zero-nine-four!"

From the *east!* Behind them! Shioya jerked his hand controllers over, swinging about in a tight, hard-driven turn away from the looming American carrier sub. There they were! Six of them, rocketing toward the center of the disorganized cloud of Japanese fighters like stooping hawks! How had the squadron managed to miss them?

"Forget the carrier!" he ordered. "Go for the fighters!"

In seconds, he was engulfed in a swirling, underwater dogfight.

## UIR Submarine *Muqarrar*
## May 10, 0735 hours

Nazer did not need the sonar operator's shrieked report. He could hear the American torpedoes approaching, the high-pitched chirring of their drives growing louder and louder as they homed on the Alfa's own engine noise.

"Come hard left!" he bellowed. Perhaps, if they could turn toward the Yankee torpedoes . . .

"Right! Come right!" The Russian adviser, Gromyko, was screaming in the helmsman's ear, his face purpling.

For one stunned, fear-charged instant, the helmsman held *Muqarrar* steady, as though unable to decide between the conflicting orders. The delay—less than two seconds before he decided that the glowering Captain Nazer held supreme authority even though the Russian was supposed to know submarine tactics—probably made no difference at all. The first ADCAP torpedo, homing on *Muqarrar*'s screws, struck the Alfa on her port side, the blast penetrating her sealed aft engine room and reactor compartment and all but severing her cruciform tail. Instants later, the second torpedo slammed into her amidships, just aft of her sail, punching through outer and inner hulls and sending a high-pressure blast of steam and molten metal through her communications room and the crew's aft berthing compartment. The shock hurled Nazer against the chart table, breaking both his legs. Clinging to the table's edge, he had time only to meet the fear-glazed eyes of his adviser before the control room's aft bulkhead gave way, and the boiling sea came howling in.

**Imperial Navy Attack Submarine** *Umiryu*
**May 10, 0735 hours**

*Chusa* Shigeru Oshida was waiting for the water turbulence ahead to clear. He'd had *Leviathan* in his sights, with an acoustic target lock, when the undersea explosions had torn through the fighter sub formation and drawn a silvery curtain across the middle of the battlefield.

There she was, still moving forward, a whale passing the school of minnows nipping at her flanks.

Oshida had already decided that the fighter subs were of no importance, toys with no place in modern undersea combat. He was aware of the American fighter subs behind him and to his left, but his only real concern was the carrier sub less than three kilometers dead ahead.

"Weapons!" he snapped. "Stand by!"

"We have a sonar lock, Captain. Bearing three-five-five relative, range three thousand . . ."

"Fire one!"

A Soviet Type C-1 wire-guided torpedo, with a three-hundred-kilogram high-explosive warhead, slid from the *Umiryu*'s number-one tube.

"One fired, Captain!"

"Fire two! Fire three!"

The spread of C-1s raced toward *Leviathan*.

## Blue Hunter Two
## May 10, 0735

"He's fired!" Hernandez cried. "God, no, he's fired!"

Young glanced at his MFD, already showing the glowing characters he'd been waiting for.

    TARGET LOCK.
    ACOUSTICAL HOMING: PATTERN SET.
    CONTACT DETONATION: COMMIT.
    READY.

He could fire now and send a torpedo squarely into the Jap sub's engine room, but he overrode the target commit and pushed his throttle to full forward. "You boys take this bastard!" he yelled. "I'll get the torps!"

Seconds later, Dominico, riding in on Young's port side and astern, loosed one of his torps, the spearing thrust of exhaust gas looking like the white contrail of an air-to-air missile leaping from beneath an interceptor's wing. Behind him, Hernandez held his approach a moment longer, then loosed one of his Mark 62s as well. The torpedoes swept below Young's Barracuda, their contrails converging on the bulk of the Japanese Tyogei as he swept low across her deck. . . .

## Imperial Navy Attack Submarine *Umiryu*
## May 10, 0735 hours

"Enemy torpedoes approaching from the stern," the sonar officer reported. "Impact in ten seconds!"

Oshida turned, using his helmet to look back over his shoulder. Fighter subs and their torpedoes were clearly visible, coming in from behind and to his right.

He froze, momentarily undecided. If he attempted to maneuver, the wires guiding his three torpedoes would be cut. The torpedoes had not yet acquired *Leviathan* on their own, and without guidance from the sub, they might pick up a different target entirely.

The rocket-powered torpedoes carried by fighter subs carried warheads a quarter the size of those mounted by a C-1 or an American Mark 48, powerful enough to damage *Umiryu*, perhaps, but not to destroy her without an extremely lucky hit.

"Release decoys!" he ordered. "Maintain course."

The enemy torpedoes were so close and so fast that he doubted he could maneuver clear of them in any case.

The first torpedo hit *Umiryu*'s afterdeck midway between sail and stern, ripping open her outer casing but causing no serious damage. The second torpedo swerved at the last possible second, angling to the right in pursuit of a shrieking, bubbling decoy.

Movement captured Oshida's eye and he looked to port just in time to see one of the American fighter subs hurtling past *Umiryu*'s sail, so close that the Japanese captain felt that he could reach out and touch the craft's starboard wing as it passed.

*     *     *

**Blue Hunter Two**
**May 10, 0735**

The explosion had shaken Young, but he was already in front of the shock wave, outracing the worst of the turbulence as he flashed past the vast, dark gray cliff of the Japanese Tyogei-class attack sub.

Seconds had passed since it had launched three torpedoes at *Leviathan*. With luck, they'd not acquired their target yet but were still being steered by the Tyogei's sonar crew.

There! Three white dots, vanishing toward the looming whale's shape of *Leviathan*. Their guidance wires, too thin to be seen with the naked eye, vibrated as they unreeled, disturbing the water enough for Young's SFV sonar to sense them, and for his micro-Cray to paint them in. Sweeping past the Tyogei's rounded bow, he brought his helm over, hard right. The fighter sub nearly rolled onto its back as it banked at high speed, shearing so close to the attack sub's bow that Young could look up and see nothing but bricks, the rectangular pattern of acoustical tiles covering her blunt snout.

There was the slightest of jars, a rippling shock that momentarily slowed the high-speed undersea fighter. For one nightmare second, Young thought the onrushing Tyogei was going to run him down, but then he was past, circling to the Japanese sub's starboard side. Torn fragments of guide wire trailed from his wings and stabilizers.

Then his SFV jolted as though it had struck something hard. Warning lights flashed on his console . . . and he could hear the keening whine of his engine changing pitch, feel a kind of fluttering through the hull.

*Damn!* Something, probably the torpedo guide-wire fragments, had caught in the compressor blades of his water intakes. His engine was overheating fast, and it was losing power. Already, his Barracuda was nosing over, plummeting into the depths.

Young bit off an acid curse. He wasn't going to get a kill, not today. He could already tell that the damage was nothing he could correct from inside his cockpit.

As he plunged toward the floor of the Strait, his hand closed around the ejection ring protruding from his seat between his feet.

Half a mile away, the three Japanese torpedoes, cut loose from their master, began running wild.

## Blue Hunter Squadron
## May 10, 0735 hours

It was the first time ever that fighter subs on opposing sides had fought one another in the depths, a dogfight of nerve-searing intensity. Aviators called such engagements "furballs," a fitting description of the tangled contrails left writhing across the sky, and the metaphor seemed even more apt here, five hundred feet beneath the surface of the sea. SUBVIEW painted the sonic wakes of each fighter sub as a white turbulence against the blue-green background. The biggest difference was that air-to-air combat takes place across ranges of several miles and at speeds close to that of sound; here, the combatants were crowded into a sphere half a kilometer across and their speeds were comparatively slow—sixty to eighty knots or less.

Eighty knots—ninety-two miles per hour—was more than fast enough, even for a man who'd once flown supersonic interceptors. Gray held his Barracuda in a hard, tight turn, banking past a Japanese fighter sub as it rose to meet him a scant twenty yards below. For a horrifying instant he thought they were going to collide, but then he was past, his SFV bumping as it collided with the other's wake. He found himself above and behind another Japanese minisub, on the other guy's "six," a favored firing position.

"Target!" he yelled, using the sub's voice command system. "Acoustic homing!"

TARGET LOCK.
ACOUSTICAL HOMING: PATTERN SET.
CONTACT DETONATION: COMMIT.
READY.

Gray squeezed the trigger on his pistol-grip joystick, sending a Mark 62 hissing toward the target. The Japanese sub turned sharply; Gray could see the control surfaces on the disk's trailing edge opening wide as it dumped speed, sliding sideways and down in a desperate attempt to sidestep the killer now screaming toward its dorsal surface.

*Hit!* Torpedo merged with fighter sub in a flash and a mushrooming roil of hot gas bubbling toward a distant sky, as jagged black fragments, streaming air, and shredded bits of debris plummeted toward the bottom.

A warning shrilled in Gray's headset. His Barracuda's computer had detected a threat, something approaching from *his* six at high speed. Without stopping to see what it was, he went to full

throttle, outpacing the enemy's warshot, then swept
into a hard port bank that carried him straight
through the cloud of bubbles rising from his kill.

*Kiku* **Squadron**
**May 10, 0734 hours**

Scant meters astern of the American fighter sub, the
Japanese torpedo lost the target when it slipped into
a wall of sizzling white noise. One hundred meters
behind that, Shioya hissed his frustration, then pulled
to the left, hoping to follow the escaping Barracuda
through the rapidly thinning cloud of bubbles.

The Mitsubishi *Ei* fighter subs still held a clear
advantage, both in numbers and in maneuverability,
but the American Barracudas had made up for that in
the sheer ferociousness of their attack. The
Americans were everywhere, and they were fighting as
a unit, while the scattered *Kiku* squadron fighters
were still recovering from their surprise.

Shioya flashed through the wall of bubbles, and his
Stingray jolted as it hurtled through the turbulent
water. Where was the American now? He looked left
and right, searching for some sign, a contrail, anything. . . .

**Blue Hunter Squadron**
**May 10, 0736 hours**

"Got you!"
An instant after flying through the bubble cloud,
Gray had brought his stick up and sent his Barracuda
into a sharp, vertical climb, rising a hundred feet

before allowing the SFV to stall, slip onto its back,
then nose over into a long dive straight down along
the path it had come. In an air-to-air dogfight, the
maneuver was called an Immelmann after the WWI
ace who'd invented it. As the pressure built in Gray's
intakes, he saw the Japanese sub that had fired at him
passing left to right, fifty yards below.

"Target! Acoustic homing!"

*Fire!*

But the angle was too sharp for the high-speed torpedo to correct its aim by more than a few degrees.
The Japanese fighter accelerated, then went into a
climb, and Gray's torpedo missed it by scant feet.
Seconds later, the two subs passed back-to-back, Gray
diving, the Japanese pilot rising. Had their cockpits
been transparent, they could have looked into one
anothers' eyes. . . .

# CHAPTER
## 24

**R**amsay had seen the Tyogei attack sub's launch and released countermeasures of his own, hoping to seduce the enemy torpedoes clear of *Leviathan*. When the three torpedoes went wild, their control wires cut, he ordered the Typhoon to full speed, rushing past the torpedoes before they could acquire him on their own.

Two of the torpedoes whined past *Leviathan* and into the darkness, but the third, more distant than the others, refused the siren's song of the decoys, recognizing instead the thrum of the American Typhoon's screws as it slipped into its first turn in its programmed search procedure. Continuing its turn, the Russian-built C-1 torpedo slid into *Leviathan*'s wake and accelerated, leaping ahead at forty-five knots.

**Blue Hunter Squadron**
**May 10, 0736 hours**

Dominico had swept past the damaged Tyogei attack sub seconds behind Young, had seen Young cut the guide wires to the three torpedoes. He was pushing his throttle full forward now, sending his Barracuda shrieking through the water toward *Leviathan*. If he could put one of his own torps among the enemy weapons before they dispersed, he might be able to take them out.

No, that was no good. His cockpit display showed that they'd already spread apart so far that he'd have to take out each one separately. Two, at least, had been successfully decoyed. The third . . .

Dominico was still well in front of *Leviathan* when he saw the third Japanese torpedo swinging into the Big Vi's wake. Had *Leviathan* picked it up? Possibly not. The thing was coming down the Typhoon's baffles, and Captain Ramsay was probably watching the battle unfolding among the fighter subs off his bow.

Damn, that torpedo was going to catch *Leviathan* right square in the ass!

Still holding the SFV at full throttle, he nudged his steering control, flashing down the Typhoon's starboard side at a range of less than thirty yards. At that distance, the huge ex-boomer was like a solid, dark gray cliff looming off to his left. Then he was past, and the oncoming torpedo was less than a hundred yards dead ahead.

Dominico's options were sharply limited. He doubted he could lock onto the torpedo with one of his own, not with a closure rate of something like 120 knots. Nor could he nudge the torp out of control, not without circling around behind it and matching course and speed with the thing. Even as he considered and discarded each option, the last couple of seconds ran out and the Japanese torpedo seemed to leap right out of his cockpit display and into his lap.

In that last instant, though, Albert Dominico *knew*

why he'd come back to Spain—not for revenge, and not to prove himself. He'd returned because of the bond he shared with the other men in the squadron, and aboard *Leviathan*.

The torpedo didn't hit him. Programmed to detonate when triggered by the magnetic field of its target, its sensors detected the twenty-ton SFV while it was still yards away. The explosion smashed Dominico's plane controls, killed his engine, knocked his electronics off-line, and cracked his cockpit dome in three places. In utter blackness, he struggled with his controls, trying to right the craft as it spun helplessly toward the bottom. Water blasted through the damaged hull in shrieking jets, ice-cold and as hard as razor-edged daggers. He could feel his craft breaking up around him, understood that he had only seconds to live. Ejecting would do no good if his cockpit shell had already been breached.

His last thoughts were of Ann, of how good it would be to see her just once more. . . .

**U.S.S.** *Leviathan*
**May 10, 0737 hours**

Ramsay heard the torpedo explosion astern but could spare it none of his attention. The Japanese attack sub was huge in his view forward, a fat, gray whale turning away to Ramsay's left.

"Weapons!" he called. "I have a target."

The computer automatically fed range and bearing data both to Ramsay and to the weapons officer, standing unseen a few feet away on the control deck.

"Target lock. Range twenty-one-hundred, bearing zero-zero-one, relative."

"I want two fish, acoustic homing. Magnetic-contact detonation."

"Acoustic homer, mag-contact det, aye aye. Set and ready, tubes five and six."

"Fire five! Fire six!"

## Imperial Navy Attack Submarine *Umiryu*
## May 10, 0737 hours

Shigeru Oshida saw *Leviathan*'s second launch, heard the hum of approaching torpedoes. He had only seconds to act, but he was a fighter and he was determined to go down fighting.

"Blow all ballast!" he yelled. "Emergency surface!"

The deck shuddered beneath him as the big submarine lurched heavily to port, then starboard, then began rising within a cloud of her own bubbles.

"Fire countermeasures! Now!"

The enemy torpedoes were closer now, much closer, but the *Umiryu* yet might make it. If she could rise above their flight path before they could react, or if the decoy seduced them away . . . .

But the damage to his dorsal hull, inflicted earlier by an American rocket torpedo, while not serious enough to disable the Tyogei-class sub, was enough to slow it down. Pumps had been damaged, and the portside ballast tanks emptied only partially. *Umiryu* rose slowly, heavily, her sail tipping drunkenly to port.

The first torpedo struck her sail, low and on the starboard side, the Mark 48 ADCAP's sub-killer warhead ripping a hole through the periscope housing and smashing through the deck to the control room in a blast of steam and molten metal, killing Oshida and the officers with him instantly. The second torpedo passed five meters beneath *Umiryu*'s keel, sensed her presence magnetically, and exploded with a second, volcanic roar that lit up the sea around her and all but tore her in half.

**U.S.S. *Leviathan***
**May 10, 0737 hours**

Someone on the bridge raised a cheer, but Ramsay bellowed a curt, "Belay that! As you were!"

The crew fell instantly silent, attending their consoles and screens with a concentration superhuman in its intensity.

Grimly, Ramsay tried to pierce the boiling column of water that marked the Japanese attack sub's undersea funeral pyre, masking a broad stretch of the sea like a dense fog. *Teigei* was still out there somewhere, wounded but still deadly. Where the hell was she?

**UIR ASW Frigate *Zauba'a***
**May 10, 0737 hours**

"Damn you, sand rat, I want a target!"

Lyko was furious, screaming into the bridge microphone. He was losing his chance to participate in the battle!

The frigate had slowed to quarter speed as it entered the center of the undersea battle area. For the past several minutes, explosions had continued to boom and thunder on all sides, but the sonar targets were fleeting and fragmentary, the contacts broken each time another detonation disturbed the sea.

"I . . . I may have a damaged submarine," the sonar operator said at last. "Bearing one-eight-nine, range . . . range three thousand."

"Which side, damn you? Theirs or ours?"

He realized as soon as he spoke how stupid the question sounded. How, after all, could one tell from its sound which side a submarine was on?

"Sir, the target is moving west to east. It's a very large target . . . but moving under a single screw. I can hear a . . . a flushing sound, sir. They may be blowing their ballast tanks."

"Put it on speaker."

Lyko closed his eyes as he listened. His training in ASW warfare with the Red Banner Fleet had been thorough and complete. As soon as he heard the rushing, burbling noise issuing from the speaker, he knew that it was not the sound of ballast tanks being blown, but of water pouring through a gaping hole in a submarine's hull.

West to east . . . an American sub, without doubt. And from the sound of it, it was big, like one of the Soviet Navy's monster Typhoons.

His anger faded, and he smiled. "That is our target," he announced. "Fire RBU!"

Seconds later, the twelve-barrel antisubmarine weapon on the forward deck began its throaty, two-by-two detonations.

**Imperial Navy Submarine** *Teigei*
**May 10, 0737 hours**

With a grumbling, lurching crunch, *Teigei* settled to the bottom in 250 meters of water. Still blind inside his dead helmet, Tanaka listened stoically as the damage reports came in: the starboard screw was gone, the rudder jammed hard right. The starboard shaft compartment was flooded, and seals had burst in the reactor and aft engineering spaces; at least twenty men were trapped in the aft engine room and would be dead in minutes. The reactor had gone off-line, and power throughout the boat was being maintained now only by batteries. The *siranui* imaging system, obviously, had shorted and gone down, leaving him literally in the dark as to what was going on around him, but electricians were already tracing the problem and would restore the network soon.

Damage, fortunately, was not too bad, overall. The flooding was being brought under control, and if they could use air under high pressure to pump out the engineering spaces, they would soon be under way once more.

Still, it was annoying. A single midget torpedo from one of the American fighter subs had crippled his command at a critical moment. He wondered how Shioya was doing, now that he finally had his chance to face the Americans.

What he could not see, with his underwater imaging system out, was *Teigei*'s position, grounded at the very edge of and almost parallel to a sheer drop, the rugged cliff line that once had been the falls of Gibraltar.

"Captain, this is Sonar. I'm picking up surface splashes."

Tanaka fumbled with the straps holding the heavy helmet to his head and lifted the apparatus from his shoulders. His back and neck ached from the hours he'd worn the thing, and the darkness that had enclosed him when the *siranui* system failed was claustrophobic.

Suddenly, he realized how very much he hated the dark . . . and how much he hated this black, enclosed combat in the depths.

He felt afraid.

"Splashes?" he said. "What kind of—"

The spread of twelve RBU warheads had been fired dead on target, but the watery bull's-eye was so large that it was still sheer chance that one of them, sinking rapidly through the water, should pass within meters of *Teigei*'s bow. It missed, dropping past, but the sensors registered the big submarine's magnetic signature, noted that the range was now increasing, and detonated.

By itself, the RBU round was not enough to destroy a submarine the size of *Teigei*, but the shock wave pushed her bow up . . . up . . . then released it as the turbulence dispersed. The bow came down hard, and the damaged sub lost its precarious balance on the edge of the cliff.

With a low, moaning groan, *Teigei* began canting to starboard, her sail tilting farther and farther over the abyss yawning beneath her bow. She dragged forward, meter after meter, the groan rising to a trembling wail as her keel scraped across the rocks. Then her tortured stern, sluggish and weighted down with hundreds of tons of seawater, caught on a boulder. Momentum kept the rest of the sub moving forward, faster now . . . and still faster. With the bellow of some huge, dying, marine dinosaur, *Teigei*'s hull tore open. Her back broken now, her bow sliding far out over the chasm, the tail section tore free in a swirl of sky-reaching bubbles and floating debris.

On her control deck, Tanaka clung to an overhead brace, his feet swinging out into empty space as the compartment rolled wildly, the lights failed, and the officers and crew with him screamed with sudden, panic-crazed terror, drowning the death shriek of the dying submarine.

Long before *Teigei* reached the base of the cliff, the sea smashed through bulkhead after weakened bulkhead, a wall of water slamming through interior partitions like a steel fist, pulping every man aboard.

## Blue Hunter Squadron
## May 10, 0738 hours

Gray twisted his Barracuda in a tight, left-handed corkscrew, bringing the fighter sub level as he tried to sort through a disjointed jumble of impressions. Four hundred yards away, the Japanese fighter he'd tried to kill and missed had pulled an Immelmann of its own and was dropping smoothly onto Wilder's six.

"I've got one on my tail!" Wilder called over the ULTRA-C link. "Get him off! Get him off!"

"I'm on him," Koch's voice snapped, and the furball became tighter, harder as fighter subs on both sides pushed their envelopes, closing for a killing shot.

Gray dropped into Koch's wake a second before the other pilot loosed his last torpedo at the Japanese fighter sub. A second Jap fighter angled in from ahead and above, its saucer form like some alien invader from an SF movie. Koch's torpedo missed, skimming past the Stingray, the range too close for acoustic homing to get a solid lock.

"Break right, Bob!" Gray told Koch. "Clear so I can fire!"

"Rog!" Koch's Barracuda rolled to starboard, and Gray's targeting discretes closed on the Stingray a hundred yards beyond. He squeezed the trigger, loosing his last Mark 62, but an instant later a slender lance speared from the belly of his target, streaking toward Wilder's craft.

"Wildman!" Koch yelled. "You've got a missile tracking you! Take her down! Hard!"

Wilder's Barracuda flipped onto its back and plunged into the depths, the torpedo rolling into a dive in pursuit. If Wilder could build up speed faster than the Jap torpedo, he might be able to get clear. The fighter pilot's refrain beat in Gray's head: Speed is life.

Another Japanese torpedo whined in out of nowhere, hitting young Mackey's Barracuda from below. The explosion gutted the SFV's engine outlet and shredded wings and stabilizer. The nose, tearing free in a cloud of bubbles, tumbled end over end, dropping deeper and deeper on a stream of escaping air. Gray found himself willing Mackey to yank his ejection ring, to blow his life-support pod free and make it to the surface.

But the escaping air was proof enough that Mackey would not be able to eject. Moments later, the broken SFV dropped past the edge of the cliff and fell into night.

The Japanese fighter Gray had targeted, meanwhile, had pulled up, trying to double back past Gray's rocket torp, but the maneuver twisted in exactly the wrong direction. Gray tried to shout warning, but the Japanese saucer closed bow-on with Koch's Barracuda, which was angling for a second shot. Gray shouted a warning . . . but too late. The fighter subs scraped past one another and there was a confused flutter of whirling debris. The Mitsubishi Stingray, solidly built and compact, appeared undamaged, but one of the Barracuda's stubby wings had been sheared off close to the hull.

For a moment, it looked as though the saucer was going to escape, but then Gray's rocket torp closed the gap, detonating at the tip of the Japanese sub's port lifting surface, the flash magnesium bright.

Seconds passed as the sea saucer plowed ahead, port side down and streaming black oil. There was a small explosion . . . then another. The two "wings" of the saucer, each with intakes, engine, fuel tanks, and exhaust nozzle, split free of the central core of the craft, which now, freed of the weight of the two side pieces, rocketed to the surface.

He'd not seen one of the Japanese fighter escape pods before, but he knew at once what it was.

Almost, Gray wanted to pursue it, wanted to strike back for what the pilot had just done to one of his men. But he was surprised at the realization that he did not hate that other pilot. In fact, he found he could muster no emotion at all save a dull, aching exhaustion that threatened to penetrate and sap every fiber of his being.

### At the surface
### May 10, 0740 hours

Battle is always ruled by chance. Throughout history, more often than not, it has been the *unluckiest* side that loses, rather than the most skillful—or luckiest— side that wins. Often, too, the side that loses is simply the one that makes the most mistakes.

One of *Umiryu*'s torpedoes, cut free of its guide wire, had been circling aimlessly for several minutes, its thumb-sized, Sony-manufactured brain searching for a new target.

It found one, the seductive *chug-chug-chug* of heavy screws, somewhere in the sea ahead. It locked on, and the torpedo's circling stopped.

At fifty-five knots it sprinted through the water.

Aboard the frigate *Zauba'a*, officers and crew alike were cheering and slapping one another on the back, celebrating the hit scored by one of their RBU sub killers. So intent was the sonar operator on describing the sound of a large submarine breaking up as it sank that he completely missed the telltale scream of high-speed screws approaching from a different direction until it was too late.

The Soviet Type C-1 torpedo passed beneath *Zauba'a* just abaft of her bridge, moving from starboard aft to port forward. As it passed the frigate's keel, magnetic sensors detonated the warhead's three hundred kilos of high explosives.

Water fountained into the sky, lifting the ship bodily from the water, snapping her spine, and dropping the pieces in a cascade of foam and spray like a giant child wantonly discarding a broken toy.

An hour later, the British Type 42C guided-missile destroyer *Nottingham*, probing south out of Gibraltar, spotted two feebly waving men clinging to a piece of wreckage. The debris, it turned out, was the central core of one of the new Japanese fighter subs; the men, oil-blackened and exhausted, were Captain Victor Yegorovich Lyko and Lieutenant Takeo Shioya. Both of Lyko's arms were broken, and the Japanese fighter sub pilot had kept him afloat, holding him with one hand while clinging to the escape pod with the other.

## Blue Hunter Squadron
## May 10, 0850 hours

The battle was clearly over, if for no other reason than that the combatants were so widely scattered now that continuing the fight was impossible. Seven Japanese fighter subs had fled toward the south after their carrier sub had died, along with the two Islamic attack subs that had been circling to the south of the American formation. The Barracudas had pursued them, nailing at least one more Stingray before they'd had to break off, their torpedoes spent, their power cells growing weak.

Now they were rallying, as *Leviathan* prepared to take them back aboard. Gray felt numb as he tallied the American losses. Dominico, killed taking out the torpedo that had been about to mark down *Leviathan*. Wilder, last seen plunging toward the bottom, a Japanese torpedo on his tail. Koch, his Barracuda damaged by the collision with an enemy fighter, also last seen heading for the bottom. Mackey, dead. Young, missing after he'd broken the guide wires on a spread of enemy torpedoes.

God . . . five out of nine of his people dead or missing, for a casualty rate of fifty-five percent! That six of the twelve Japanese fighter subs had been downed in the fight, as well as at least two attack subs and the *Teigei* herself, was no consolation at all.

Gray was still having trouble with the bane of all combat commanders, the knowledge that his plan, his orders, had guaranteed the deaths of his men. There was nothing that could be done about it, of course, except be damned certain that the orders he gave were the best that he could possibly give . . . and take comfort in the fact that he'd been there to share their outcome.

But oh, Lord, how was he going to explain it all when he wrote the letters to the wives and mothers?

Wearily, Gray opened a communications channel with *Leviathan*, and prepared to take his fighter sub aboard.

# EPILOGUE

U.S.S. *Leviathan*
Tangier Harbor
May 12, 2050 hours

It was well past sunset, two days after the battle in the Gibraltar Strait. Tangier was in flames, with ruddy tongues flickering at a sky heavy with smoke and soot, and sparks swirling skyward like dancing stars.

From the open cockpit of the U.S.S. *Leviathan*, T. Morgan Gray could look out across the harbor as the huge submarine maneuvered carefully just outside the harbor mole. Off the starboard bow, the wreckage of the Krivak torpedoed by members of his squadron eighteen days ago still listed sullenly against a crumpled pier. Beyond, the government offices and headquarters of the UIR occupation forces were burning furiously after an attack by Marine Cobras and the awesome firepower of an AC-130 gunship strike.

Offshore, a mile away, *Oceanside* and *Charlotte* both were surfaced, riding the gentle swells of the Atlantic. They'd added their firepower to the attack on Tangier as well, loosing twenty Tomahawk missiles apiece at the UIR facilities ashore.

Gray raised his binoculars to his eyes, scanning the waterfront. Across a stretch of fire-tinged water, he could make out a huddled mass of civilians clustered in the imaginary shelter of a broken, whitewashed wall. Several U.S. Marines stood nearby, watchful, their assault rifles at the ready. Many of the refugees were kids, ragged and dirty and hungry.

War, with all its attendant horrors, had come once again to this ancient, North African crossroads of empires.

Ramsay leaned against the cockpit windscreen, staring into the flame-shot darkness. "War is a damned awful thing," he said, almost too low to be heard. He nodded toward the distant civilians, invisible without the aid of binoculars. "*They* aren't our enemies. It's those bastards in Cairo."

Somewhere in the distance, a dull rumble sounded in the night, echoing from mountains and shattered walls. The UIR forces were lodged in the hills southeast of Tangier, and they'd been dropping mortar rounds on the city all evening.

The U.S. Marines had stormed ashore early that morning, coming in aboard hovercraft off the U.S.S. *Nassau.* The MEU, backed by air and artillery ferried in the day before from Stateside, had grabbed beaches from Cape Spartel to Cape Malabata. Elements of the Spanish Foreign Legion and the British SAS had landed at Ceuta and Mellita, taking back those ancient bastions of Spanish power in Morocco just hours after UIR forces had seized them.

The landing was a temporary one only; no one in London, Madrid, or Washington seriously expected the allied forces to hold the hostile shore and port for long, but as a raid it had already been highly successful. Some five hundred landing boats, small craft, and barges had been seized and destroyed, and the arms and ammunition stores of the UIR general who called himself Tariq had been blown up in a savage detonation that had been heard that evening clear across the channel in Gibraltar.

The planned UIR invasion of southern Spain had been dealt a decisive setback . . . possibly even a fatal blow. The Mahdi was unlikely to bother himself with Spain now that the United States and Great Britain both were firmly in the alliance against him.

"You know," Ramsay said when Gray didn't answer him immediately, "I spent most of my adult life in submarines, trying to see to it that World War III never got started. It looks like I failed. *We* failed."

The captain's grim mood roused Gray. "I wouldn't say that, Captain. You won the Cold War. Preserved the peace with the Soviets until the Soviets were gone."

"Yeah, but that was a long time ago. Times change. *Enemies* change. Who'd have thought, back fifteen, twenty years ago, that today we'd be stumbling into World War III with the UIR?"

"Hell, there was no UIR back then. If history's taught us anything, it's that there's always another war after the last one. The war to end all wars was a dream. . . ."

"God, Morgan, the whole world's coming apart around us."

Ramsay turned away to give orders to *Leviathan*'s helm through the cockpit's intercom. Slowly, the great submarine drifted to a near stop, adrift just outside the harbor. Elsewhere, Marine boats and landing craft scuttled along the shore and the broken pier sides. Another rocket or mortar round fell somewhere beyond the walls of Tangier's old city, which loomed above the harbor like some gaunt, white necropolis.

Gray wondered at Ramsay's mood. The battle had been an undeniable American victory. Both Japanese subs and one Alfa sunk, along with at least six of the Japanese fighter subs and a UIR frigate. A second Alfa had been hit and was listed as a probable kill.

And in exchange, the Americans had lost just five fighter subs, a spectacular victory that had swept the area clear of UIR submarine forces and made the Tangier raid possible.

Gray thought he understood Ramsay's feelings, though. Modern warfare tended to be fast, *fast* . . . with a battle ending scant minutes after it began. Had things been only a little different—if Joe Young had missed snaring those torpedo guide wires, for instance, or if Dominico hadn't intercepted that one rogue torpedo—*Leviathan* would be lying on the bottom now, a broken, flooded tomb for over one hundred men. It was a common postbattle emotion: the feeling that one had merely survived by some quirk of luck. *Victory* had very little to do with it at all.

A boat flying a large American flag was passing through the harbor entrance now, approaching *Leviathan*'s starboard side. On the sub's huge forward deck, sailors had gathered with lines, ready to bring the visitors aboard.

Gray raised his binoculars again, studying the faces of the men aboard, and as they were illuminated by the light of the burning city, his heart gave a small, glad leap. He could easily pick out the two familiar faces from the rest in the boat. Wildman Wilder. Monk Young. Wilder, he'd already learned, had nearly died when the torpedo following him had hit the bottom and exploded, crippling Wilder's SFV and sending it helplessly out of control past the cliff edge and into the abyss toward *Teigei*'s grave. Battered, nearly unconscious, the young sub driver had managed to eject before reaching the bottom. Both Wilder and Young had reached the surface safely, but currents and the prevailing winds had carried them south, toward the Moroccan coast, where they'd been picked up by U.S. Special Forces units operating behind enemy lines. After two days of hiding, now they were being returned to their sub.

Lieutenant Robert Koch, apparently, had been unable to eject when his SFV was damaged. He was still listed as missing, presumed dead.

Like Dominico and Mackey. Gray still wasn't sure whether to weep for joy at the survival of the other two, or with sadness at the loss of the three.

Ramsay put the microphone down and folded his hands, watching the approaching boat. "We lucked out the other day, Morgan, you know that? They had better technology and bigger numbers and, God help me, we shouldn't have won at all. Sometimes I wonder if it's all worth it."

"Oh, it's worth it, Captain," Gray said. "I wondered about what we were doing out here myself, but now, seeing this . . ." He gestured at the burning city. "I don't know about you, but I'm fighting to keep this kind of hell just as far away from Wendy, John, and Heather as I can. That would be worth just about anything, wouldn't it?"

"Uh. You're right, of course. But how much longer can we keep on going, just being lucky."

Gray was watching Young and the others climbing aboard. He was remembering how determined Young

had been to get a kill . . . and how he'd given it up
without even thinking to save *Leviathan*. And how
Dominico had died to accomplish the same thing.

"You know, Captain, maybe it's not luck or technology that wins battles after all," he said. "Maybe it's
the *men*."

**BILL KEITH**, a former U.S. Navy Hospital Corpsman, laboratory technician, and illustrator, lives with his wife and daughter in the hills of western Pennsylvania. For the past seven years he has been a full-time writer, specializing in science fiction and in military technothrillers.